SONG

OF THE

Shaman

A FIVE DIRECTIONS PRESS BOOK

SONG
OF THE
Shaman

A NOVEL

C. P. LESLEY

SONGS OF STEPPE & FOREST 2

ISBN-13: 978-1947044258

Published in the United States of America.

A Five Directions Press book

Cover images: Konstantin Makovsky, *Christmas Divinations* (oil on canvas, c. 1905), public domain via Wikimedia Commons; autumnal field under dark thunderstorm sky © Oleksiy Fedorov/Shutterstock. Map adapted from "Map of the Volga River System," © Karl Musser (reused under Creative Commons Attribution-Share Alike 2.5 Generic license).

Book and cover design by Five Directions Press
Five Directions Press logo designed by Colleen Kelley

FIVE DIRECTIONS PRESS

'Tis distance lends enchantment to the view,
And robes the mountain in its azure hue.
                              —Thomas Campbell

CONTENTS

Map labels: Volga, Moscow, Kolomna, Oka, Kasimov, Ryazan, Kazan, Kama, Sura, Winter camp, Ural, Summer camp, Volga, Azamat's camp, Don, Nogai Tatars, Crimean steppe, Nogai Tatars, Nogai Tatars, Crimea, Astrakhan

RUSSIA AND THE STEPPE, 1540S

Cast of Characters

(in alphabetical order by first name)

FICTIONAL CHARACTERS

Aibanu Khanim: The youngest child of Ogodai and Firuza; sister to Irek, Altan-Alia, and Sibai. The Tatar title *khanim* (ha-NIM) refers to a daughter or daughter-in-law of a khan; the Russian equivalent is *tsarevna.*

Akbars: a warrior in Ogodai's horde who guards Anfim during his captivity.

Alexei Sultan: Half-brother of Ogodai and Nasan; married to Maria; father of her two children and of Timur by a premarital relationship with Guzel. In Tatar usage, *sultan* (sool-TAN) means "son of a khan," not "supreme ruler," as among the Ottomans; the Russian equivalent is *tsarevich.*

Altan-Alia Khanim: One of Ogodai and Firuza's children; twin sister of Irek and older sister of Sibai and Aibanu.

Anfim Fadeyev: Russian captive transferred to Ogodai's control after a raid; potential love interest of Grusha, although his main goal appears to be winning his freedom and returning to Russia.

Borya: Oldest son of Nasan and Daniil; Stepan's close friend.

Daniil Nikolaevich Kolychev: Ogodai's brother-in-law, sworn brother, and commander of military operations, in conjunction with Ruslan Sultan; former head of a Russian noble lineage; husband of Nasan and father of her three children.

Dina: Wife of Ruslan Sultan; mother of Mergen and a daughter who dies of diphtheria early in the story; a close friend of Grusha.

Firuza Khatun: Ogodai's chief wife and the mother of his four children—Irek, Altan-Alia, Sibai, and Aibanu. *Khatun* (ha-TUN) is the title for the wife of a khan.

Grusha: Heroine of *Song of the Shaman*; former slave of the Kolychev clan; once lover of Daniil, then Stenka; mother of Stenka's son, Stepan; shaman of Ogodai's horde.

Guzel: Alexei's former lover and Timur's mother; a good friend of Grusha's who often looks after Stepan while Grusha is shamanizing.

Haji Rahman: the Sufi imam of Ogodai's horde; widower and father of three sons and a daughter.

Irek Sultan: Ogodai and Firuza's oldest son; twin brother of Altan-Alia and older brother of Sibai Sultan and Aibanu; Stepan's closest friend.

Kiraz: Rasima's daughter.

Mansur: Tatar warrior in service to Alexei Sultan.

Nasan Khanim: Ogodai's younger sister and Alexei's half-sister; Daniil's wife and mother of his three children—Boris (Borya), Natalia (Tasha), and Nikolai (Kolya); known for her medical skills and learning.

Ogodai Khan: Ruler of the horde where Grusha lives and practices as a shaman; Firuza's husband and father of her four children; full brother of Nasan and half-brother of Alexei.

Rasima: Nasan's cook.

Ruslan Sultan: Alexei's sworn brother and ally; Ogodai's military commander in conjunction with Daniil; husband of Dina, by whom he has a son, Mergen, and a daughter who dies early in the story; fictional half-brother to Sahib-Girei Khan of Crimea.

Sibai Sultan: Ogodai and Firuza's third child; brother to Irek, Altan-Alia, and Aibanu.

Stenka: Grusha's former common law husband; Stepan's father; dead before the story opens.

Stepan: Grusha's six-year-old son and Stenka's namesake (Stenka is one of several nicknames for Stepan).

Suzukei: Grusha's beloved teacher in the shamanic arts and predecessor as the horde's shaman.

Timur: Alexei's son by a premarital relationship with Guzel. As the son of a sultan, Timur bears the Tatar title of "prince" (*mirza*).

HISTORICAL CHARACTERS

As often happens with medieval and early modern people, we have limited information about Russians and Tatars, even royalty, who lived in the sixteenth century. To the extent possible, I have ensured that details about real people included in my novels match the historical record, but often these details do not extend much beyond dates of marriages, deaths, and sometimes births. Therefore, these characters' appearance, personalities, words, and motivations are just as much my invention as those of their fictional counterparts.

Ivan IV Vasilyevich: Grand Prince of Russia (1530–1584, r. 1533–1584); crowned tsar 1547.

Sahib-Girei Khan: Ruler of Crimea, 1532–1551; an enemy of Shah-Ali Khan and his family, including Alexei and Ogodai. The Girei dynasty ruled Crimea for centuries; the name is often spelled Giray.

Shah-Ali Khan (1505–1566): Russian appointee in charge of the subordinate principality of Kasimov for most of the period between 1516 and his death in 1566; appointed as khan of Kazan three times (1519–1521, 1546, 1551–1552); uncle of the fictional Alexei, Nasan, and Ogodai. His name takes varying forms, including Shahghali, Shigalei, and Shah Ghaly—versions that reflect the Tatar pronunciation but not the derivation of the name.

Sheikh-Mamai Bey: The ruler of one group of Nogai Tatars. Although two Crimean Tatar princes did organize a large raid on Russia in the summer of 1542 and often secured Nogai support for their attacks, the inclusion of Sheikh-Mamai and his followers in this campaign is entirely my invention, as is their prior defeat by Ogodai, detailed in *The Shattered Drum*.

Chapter One

SMOKE—STINGING, ACRID, REDOLENT WITH SAGE AND THE heavy odor of dried dung—filled my nostrils. Flakes of ash floated before my eyes, and I coughed as I reached for my drum. All around me, the tent rocked with the pounding rhythm of an instrument not my own, held in hands more experienced than mine, summoning me to the dance. Suzukei—the shaman of this camp, my teacher— whispered to the spirits of the hearth fire, the ancestors of the horde.

Squinting, I settled the plaits over my face to remind the snake spirits, guardians of wisdom, that they had chosen me, too, to serve them as a journeyer among the realms above and below. When I'd hidden my features, I lifted the rimmed circle, large enough to conceal my torso from waist to shoulder. The familiar heft of the drum, the smooth wood clapper in my other hand, the steady *bam-bam-bam-bam* as I beat the tanned hide—these things drew me out of myself despite the blistering smoke. The rhythm of my strokes, regular as the beat of my own heart, worked its way into my body, resonating in my chest and pulling me away from the present, into the places that lie beyond the middle lands of earth and water.

Against the crackle of the fire, each upward leap of the flames releasing another swarm of ash flakes, I heard the steady croon of Suzukei's voice. Moving to the outer rim of the tent, I joined her song, matching her tone as best I could, adding the stamp of my own felt-clad feet. Strings of beads and shells, interspersed with metal shapes etched with sacred symbols, hung from the drum's rim, adding sounds soft and sharp. I imagined them whispering my name to the listening spirits—*Gru-sha, Gru-sha, Gru-sha*. I loved the shushing of those beads and shells.

As Suzukei and I danced around each other, I watched her for clues. I couldn't see her face, because like me she had concealed it behind several dozen plaits—black tinged with gray in her case, light brown in mine. Although half a head shorter than I, she appeared taller, the result of the red felt circle stitched with beaded eyes, nose, and mouth tied around her head and extended by a set of plumes as long as my forearm. Her leather robe, which fell loose from her shoulders, added to the sense of her being larger than life.

"O ancestors," she called to the spirits of the hearth fire. "O grandmothers, save this child."

"O grandmothers," I echoed. "Return his soul to his body. Make him well." *Bam-bam-bam-bam, bam-bam-bam-bam*—I punctuated each word with a drumbeat. Suzukei nodded her approval.

In response to a second nod, I redirected my dance in an inward spiral, aiming for a spot closer to the fire, beating my drum with every step and adding my prayers to Suzukei's. She had charged me with monitoring the condition of our patient, the three-year-old Sibai Sultan—second son of Ogodai Khan, ruler of our horde. The child lay sick unto death on a pile of felts next to the rough stones that contained the fire, motionless except for the occasional sobbing breath and croaking cough. As I moved in, she spiraled out, as if we were two puppets pulled by the same set of strings.

"Grandmothers—*bam*—come to us—*bam*—see the child—*bam-bam*—your own descendant—*bam-bam*—save his life—*bam-bam-bam*—so that he can grow strong—*bam-bam*—and one day sire children to continue your line." *Bam-bam-bam-bam.* I spoke to the drum as much as the ancestors, and the drum spoke to me, a wordless conversation.

Suzukei circled the outer trellis, drumming and chanting, as I moved toward Sibai. Her voice rose and fell with the unchanging monotony of waves against a shore, yet beneath it all an otherworldly hum spoke of the realms beyond this one—her destination. I had to take care not to follow her there—to balance my drumming, my chants, and my songs in such a way that I eased her passage without sweeping myself up in the rhythm as well. With the khan's own son at risk, we had agreed that Suzukei's greater experience made her the best person to attempt his healing. My skills at soul retrieval still needed work—my throat singing, too.

As I approached the fire, the inside of my nose itched, portending a sneeze to come, and my throat felt raw. A sharp gasp, a hollow groan, stripped these concerns from my mind, and I whirled to look at my teacher. I saw her press her hand against her stomach. She winced, staggered my way. I caught her before she could tumble into the fire and lowered her to a pile of felts. She groaned once more, touched her forehead, then lay quiet, her chant stilled.

The trance, so fast? Or has the demon plaguing Sibai attacked her too?

I reached for her, only to stop midway. Her body lay relaxed against the coverings, although she groaned from time to time. Perhaps the mushroom potion she took—and I did not—had worked more swiftly than usual. Or she had ridden her urgent desire to help the khan's son into the worlds beyond. If so, my touch would distract her, robbing our patient of her full attention. I must let her finish, then aid her if need be.

Indeed, I must *help* her finish. If I stopped my singing and drumming, she might fall out of the other world before she could complete her task. I blinked hard and knelt beside the child, softening my chant to a lullaby, like the ones I sang to my six-year-old Stepan each evening. An image of my son's sweet face, his wild blond curls untamable by any comb, his gray eyes and sturdy frame—so like his dead father's—tugged at me.

Why am I here, when I should be caring for my own child?

But Stepan was with my friend Guzel, who would keep him safe. And if I left, who would care for *this* child? Or for Suzukei, using all her strength to aid him?

Sibai's forehead burned under my palm. Three days, and his fever raged as fiercely as ever. His breath became more strained and gasping with each dawn. Neither his aunt Nasan, who derived her medical knowledge from books, nor Suzukei and I with our herbs and spells had succeeded in cooling him or easing his pain. Each time he awoke, his breath rasped as if a man clasped him by the throat.

A spirit was stealing the air as it entered his lungs. That much was clear, the three of us agreed. A vengeful spirit, determined to smother a child who should be laughing and playing, not lying as if pierced by an arrow.

Sibai was not rasping now. Lit by flickering flames and scattered sunbeams filtered by the smoke hole, he lay so still I feared he'd already departed this earth. His soft black fringe pressed damp against my tentative hand. His eyelids, squeezed shut against the smoke, didn't part when I lifted him, intending to slip a few drops of apple juice into his mouth.

The press of the spoon against his lips produced no response. I wouldn't improve his chances by choking him, so I returned him to his pile of felts. I drank the fruit juice myself, then stood and picked up my drum once more, determined to support Suzukei on her journey. *Bam-bam-bam-bam.*

I spiraled outward until I again reached the trellised frame of the tent. My feet danced the helpful spirits into motion. "Look at him, Great Ones. See how he suffers, bereft of his soul. Find it, Great Ones, and persuade it to return!"

Sensing no response, I shifted my attention to the spirits painted on my drum: horses and turtles, birds and wolves, tigers and lynxes, strange beasts with long multi-pronged horns—reindeer, Suzukei called them.

Here I enjoyed greater success. As the power filled me, the beasts of the lower world flocked to my call. They swirled around me, sweeping past my face like wisps of the smoke that clogged the fetid atmosphere of the tent. I rejoiced at their embrace. They bore me up, as if I were riding a winged horse through the clouds—I who had never sat unattended on a real one. As I danced, I circled once more toward the hearth.

Through my inner eye, I searched the other realms for Suzukei, for Sibai. I didn't see them. I begged the animal spirits for aid, but caught up in the drumming, the dancing, the chanting, they answered only with songs of their own. Their unearthly sighs and squawks, whinnies and barks, growls and roars surrounded me like morning fog in the northern woods where I was born.

A chill wind swept over me, as if sent from that wintry land. I saw Sibai, his throat gripped by a demon. And my Stepan, gurgling and rasping like the khan's son, clutched in the demon's other hand. As I watched, helpless and horrified, the demon opened his enormous maw, bared his pointed fangs, sank them into Sibai, and devoured him. Then he turned red, glaring eyes toward my son.

I tumbled into darkness.

The drum fell from my hand as my fingers went limp. Bells and beads cried a protest. I fell forward onto the layers of felt mat that protected those inside the tent from the damp feather grass beneath. My palm hit one of the large rocks surrounding the hearth fire, and I swore in my native Russian as I glanced at my hand and saw it red with blood. I dropped back onto my heels, dragging one of the scarves that dangled from my leather robe loose and wrapping it around my cut palm.

What happened?

I had no answer to the question, only the certainty that I'd never experienced anything like that in my five years training to become a shaman. Drumming and dancing had put me into a trance—that I understood. It was their purpose, after all. But what threw me out of the trance so hard and so fast?

I turned my head toward my teacher, but Suzukei lay unmoving as before. Even the groans had stopped. I dared not interrupt her journey. If I did, both she and our patient might become lost between worlds.

The memory of that dreadful vision caused my limbs to tremble, forced me to blink back tears. I wrapped my arms around my middle and keened.

I couldn't lose Stepan, I couldn't. Every bone in his body was precious to me. I had been his sole support since the moment of his birth. And with his father gone, I had no one else—and could not expect another child, since I had no man in my life. I refused to let any spirit, no matter how vicious, rob me of my son.

I took deep, slow breaths to steady myself, counting each in-out on my fingers until I completed one full cycle. Only then did I feel strong enough to push myself to my feet and circle the fire, resuming my seat next to Sibai Sultan. As I reached him, the child gave a long, gasping breath—almost a cry—that ended in a gurgle more ominous than any he had uttered yet. The gurgle faded into silence.

Complete silence. The flickering light made it difficult to tell, but squinting against the smoke, thicker and fouler than before I picked up my drum, I couldn't see his chest rise or fall.

I placed my undamaged hand above his heart. No motion pressed his ribs against my palm. No release of air drew them back. And in the instant between that gasping breath and now, Sibai's stillness already seemed less natural: the lines of his body stiffer, the air surrounding him eerier in its hush.

No. He was teasing his big brother a few days ago. He can't be dead!

I touched the boy's throat, where the blood vessels should pulse. Nothing.

I clasped his wrist—fragile, fine-boned, like the legs of a quail. Nothing.

My stomach tensing, I pressed my palm against his forehead. Perhaps the fever had broken, and the sultan's breath, freed of whatever evil spirit had shown its wickedness through its rasping presence, gave only the appearance of having stopped.

Either way, I must summon Suzukei to return. The evil one, robbed of its victim, would seek another. It might have attacked her already. I hadn't forgotten those groans.

I clasped her wrist, speaking softly, calmly. To wrench her out of a trance could leave her third soul trapped in a distant realm. "Suzukei," I said, "come back. Your efforts ..." I couldn't finish the sentence.

The stillness in the tent became menacing. From outside I heard scraps of chatter—anxious, reassuring, unconcerned. Children's cries, children's laughter—like the sounds that ought to be pouring from Sibai's mouth. The lowing of cattle, the neighs from the horse herds.

Inside, the quiet bore down on me like a mighty weight. Against the crackle of the fire I heard my own breathing, Suzukei's, but not the child's. I searched for enveloping spirits, animal helpers, a divine presence, but the solitude within flowed out beyond the trellises and filled the vastness of space. I released my grip and pressed my hands together lest I shake Suzukei too soon into an awareness of time passing, things changing. I turned my pleas into song in hopes of meeting her in that other world. I called on the grandmothers to find and protect her, to keep me safe as I sought her, to release Sibai's soul to rejoin his suffering body.

But as I glimpsed my mentor in the distance, a great force again thrust me back into the realm of everyday life. In my mind I again saw my son gasping for breath, his throat gripped in the demon's clawed hand. The demon who had taken the life of Sibai Sultan.

I pulled the beaded headdress from my tightly braided hair and buried my face in my tanned leather skirts. Devils danced around my bent head, as ugly as those in the icons I'd glimpsed in those long-ago days when I attended church, their infernal shrieks of glee and stamping feet banishing the very concept of light and warmth. They shouted at me in Russian, calling me a sorceress and a fake, yelling that even my parents had no use for me, that they loved my brothers best, that God had abandoned me. I would lose my son as I had once lost his father and my family, everyone I loved.

The familiar croak of Suzukei reawakening from her trance interrupted the cackling demons. "Grusha," she said. "What's wrong?"

Slowly, almost reluctantly, I dragged myself into the present, found a cup and the jug of koumiss she preferred, poured a small amount into the cup, and handed it to her. I fetched a second cup, filled it with juice, ignoring the flecks of ash that turned it bitter, and drank it down, but the devils continued to prance around the edges of my sight. I would have confessed my vision about the demon and my son, but my fears as a mother shrank into nothingness against the greater disaster we faced.

When Suzukei held out her cup, I took it, then pointed to the unmoving boy wrapped in the felts. "He's stopped breathing," I told her.

She exclaimed. "Are you sure?"

"No, but I think so." Through the haze of smoke from the hearth fire, I watched her reach for the khan's son and touch his chest, his face, his throat, his wrist—each movement more frantic than the last. But the dancing, gloating devils and the demon's maw had already shown me what she would find.

Suzukei, too, pulled off her feathered headdress, tossed back the narrow braids that concealed her face. For an instant she looked at me, her dark eyes wide, the pupils enormous, horror visible on her face. "But I found him," she said. "The spirits promised to heal him. How could this happen?"

I had no answer. I had yet to settle on so much as a consoling word when she emitted a loud cry, grabbed the section of her robe closest to her heart as her face convulsed in agony, and collapsed.

People came running at the sound, harsh as the call of an eagle in flight. Ogodai and his chief wife, Firuza—the anxious parents of the sick child—arrived first, but the tent soon swayed on its frame as more members of the horde shoved their way in. The khan's sister Nasan and her husband, Daniil—once my lover. Ruslan Sultan, who aided Daniil in directing military operations, and his young wife, Dina. My friend Guzel and her fourteen-year-old son, Prince Timur. A host of other children whom I did my best to shoo away, to little effect.

I stood before the prone bodies of Sibai Sultan and Suzukei, thought myself into ceremonial mode, and addressed the crowd in the loudest voice I could produce. "Get the children out of here!"

Shocked questions and protests swirled around me like mist. "Now!" I added in the same authoritative tone. "Then I will answer those who remain."

Older children ushered younger ones from the room, Timur chivvying his juniors ahead of him. A responsible lad, a natural leader, it made sense that he would be the one to step forward.

"Mama!" Stepan broke out of the pack, and I waved him back, but heedless, he pushed his way toward me.

Timur grabbed my son by the shoulder. "Come along, imp," he said in Tatar. "Your mama told us to leave. You'll see her later." I sent him a silent prayer of thanks.

"Do as Timur says," I told Stepan. Although I usually spoke to my son in Russian because I wanted him to learn both languages, this time I used Tatar so that the entire camp would understand. "Stay with him until I come for you." I raised my voice again. "All the children should stay with him."

At that, the mothers less closely related to Sibai Sultan—realizing, I assumed, that Timur couldn't ride herd on so large a group by himself—came to their senses and followed him and the other youngsters out. The tent frame rocked again as they pushed through the door, and the wind created by the rocking doused the hearth fire. The stench of dung and herbs lingered, and the acrid smoke continued to sting the eyes, but as the air cleared and the ash settled, it did become easier to see.

I surveyed the group that remained: Ogodai and Firuza, Nasan and Daniil, Ruslan, Dina, Guzel. A lump formed in my throat, and I blinked back tears. I didn't want to share what I knew with them, but I had to. My teacher had fallen, perhaps died, in pursuit of Sibai Sultan's soul—a failed quest, it seemed, whatever the spirits promised. I couldn't keep what had happened a secret; nor could I handle the situation alone.

"There has been a tragedy." I worked to keep my voice steady. "Perhaps a double tragedy. I haven't had time to find out." I stepped aside, showing them the two motionless bodies.

Firuza dropped to her knees next to her son. She cupped his still face in both hands and gasped. "Nasan, look!"

Nasan knelt beside her, felt for a pulse, listened for a heartbeat. I knew she wouldn't find them; I had checked, and so had Suzukei. "I need light," she said.

I fetched a lantern from the corner and placed it near the extinguished hearth fire. "Suzukei said she retrieved his soul," I told them. "That the spirits promised to heal him. She told me just before she fainted. But it's not true, is it?"

Daniil raised the lantern by its brass handle. "Where do you want it, love?" he asked his wife, then lifted and lowered the light at her direction.

I moved to the other side of the fire and crouched next to my teacher. I had few doubts that Sibai Sultan had gone beyond human aid, but Suzukei might yet cling to life. Although the spirits hadn't kept their promise to her, she had exerted great effort to save the child. It behooved me now to plead with the ancestors to restore her to health.

If I still had a way to contact them. A shudder ran through me as I remembered the outrush of spirit, the dancing demons, and the loss of those I loved.

I thrust the thought away. I must try. I didn't myself wield the power to heal; I only provided a channel for those who did. Surely the gods to whose service my teacher had devoted her life still had a use for her here in the middle world.

Suzukei lay still. With some difficulty, I pushed her onto her back. In the flickering lantern light, her skin appeared pale, her eyes sunken in their sockets. The pulse under my fingers fluttered like a bird in a cage—irregular, weak. Her heart pounded too fast; her breath came in shallow pants, off-rhythm. She lived, but I feared that might not long continue.

I pulled the nearest felt mat over her, hoping the warmth would steady her. In truth, I had no idea what had gone wrong. Before the ceremony, I would have sworn she enjoyed her usual health. I'd heard her voice strong, seen her face calm, sensed her confidence that she could discover the child's soul and persuade it to return.

Ogodai Khan roared in anguish. Firuza's wails flew beyond the tent and assailed the heavens. I looked up to see her raking her cheeks with her nails, drawing blood. Tears poured down her ravaged face, the two streams— red and clear—mingling, then pooling at the edge of her high-collared robe. Nasan, her head bowed, wept silently next to her sister-in-law. Daniil placed the lantern next to the hearth fire, his mouth set in a grim line, then bent his head, as if praying. Ruslan placed a comforting hand on Ogodai's shoulder, and Guzel, sobbing, knelt and wrapped both arms around Firuza. Dina sat next to them, her hand on Firuza's knee.

"Alert the imam," Ogodai said, and Ruslan bowed and withdrew from the tent.

For a few moments, I allowed myself to mourn with them. But I still had duties, the most pressing being the need to shepherd the third soul of Sibai Sultan toward the eternal hunting grounds. I closed my eyes and forced my grief into a locked chest within my mind. Then I stood, untangled my beads and shells, picked up my drum, and began to beat it, to dance, and to chant. I couldn't smudge the tent with purifying sage because the fire had gone out; that would come later. But I commended the child to the ancestral spirits of the horde, urging them to watch over and protect the young soul, to guide it as it traveled to join them, to assist it in letting go of life, to keep it from drowning in resentment at having its time on earth cut short—before it could grow to adulthood, find a wife, raise children of its own. So many pleasures this poor child would never experience.

I hoped the chants helped the grieving parents, the others present, the larger community that would hear what went on in the tent. I hoped they reached Suzukei in her unresponsive state, that the spirits would send her back to us and not seize her, too, for their own. I altered the chants to include that plea, but I sensed no response, no presence that could be Suzukei herself.

Desperation drove me back to the religion of my younger days. I redirected my prayers to the Christian Lord and his Most Merciful, Most Pure Mother, patroness of children and childbirth. Prayers for Sibai, of course, and for Suzukei, although nothing I'd learned from the priests suggested that Jesus and Mary would exert themselves on behalf of a woman who embraced pagan traditions passed down since time immemorial. Perhaps they'd help Sibai, because Muslims honored Jesus and Mary as a prophet and his mother.

After a while, I shifted my attention, praying for my Stepan without saying his name aloud. For all the children in the camp, and for their parents. Where one child falls ill and dies, it too often happens that others sicken as well.

A man's voice joined mine, praying in Arabic, and I knew the imam had arrived. Out of respect for him and his religion, I quieted my chants, stilled my dance, and let him take the lead. Ogodai, Firuza, Ruslan, Dina, and Guzel, all Muslims—as well as Nasan, who'd grown up in the faith—participated as needed. Daniil joined me in silent observance.

Keening surrounded me, wave after wave of pain and grief. Sorrow for Ogodai and Firuza, who had welcomed me and my son into their lives with grace and compassion, threatened my unspoken attempts to help their child reach his home among the grandmothers.

Every sobbing breath resounded in my heart. How could I go on if that were Stepan? If I knew I'd seen his tousled curls and quicksilver movements, heard his rapid-fire speech in two languages intermingled as one, touched his petal-soft skin and snub nose, returned his hug for the last time?

Yes, Ogodai and Firuza had other children, and Stepan was my one and only, but is not each soul unique?

I lost track of whom my prayers addressed—the Christ, his Holy Mother, the grandmothers, Allah. Is there not, in the end, only one God behind the many divine faces? I even begged my long-lost almost-husband to look down on us and guard his son as he had once guarded me.

But however passionate my pleas, Suzukei and Sibai remained out of reach.

Chapter Two

WRAPPED FOR BURIAL, HELD IN HIS FATHER'S ARMS, SIBAI looked like a swaddled baby. The sight tore at my heart—at the hearts of everyone present, I guessed, because sighs rose and fell among the crowd like gusts of wind.

My head ached, and my eyes itched as if I walked amid a hailstorm of grit. Yesterday evening, after Sibai's family carried his body away to prepare it for this funeral at first light, I stayed in the tent with Suzukei. Only as the skies turned from black to gray did I give up, if only temporarily, my attempts to reach her elusive spirit. By then, knowing the service would soon begin, I saw no point in trying to sleep. Instead, I went to fetch Stepan from Guzel's tent, where he'd spent the night.

The vision of my son in the demon's grip still tugged at me. Since Stepan stood at my side, healthy and sturdy as ever, whatever curse or warning the vision portended must have to do with the future, not the present. Yet I couldn't overcome my fear of what might happen to my child.

Unlike yesterday's ceremony, this one fell entirely within the sphere of the imam. A cheerful middle-aged man with a ready tongue, intelligent dark eyes, and an appealing roundness despite his embrace of asceticism,

Haji Rahman combined a deep understanding of human frailty with a rich appreciation of the spiritual world and a fabulous array of stories and poems that kept every child in the camp, especially mine, enthralled. He spoke often of divine love and practiced it through laughter and dance as well as the five daily prayer services and the month of fasting, and although we approached God and His heavens from different starting points, we worked well together. I had great respect for Haji Rahman and believed he felt the same for me. He ran a school for the boys in the camp, and soon I would send Stepan to study with him. It would do my son good to learn from such a man.

Today, of course, Haji Rahman focused his energies on consoling the grieving family through ritual and prayer. The ceremony must have a special meaning for him, as he'd lost his wife right after the spring migration. Their three grown sons stood in the front row facing their father, a daughter in the back with us women. I could imagine how difficult this funeral must be for them, too, and sent them sympathy on wings of spirit.

The pale sunshine turned Firuza's tears to diamonds as the service began. On either side of her stood her twins, a year older than Stepan, looking as perplexed as any small girl and boy would under such circumstances. The children's nurse carried their baby sister, a one-year-old who sucked her thumb and stared round-eyed at the crowd, making no sound. In later years, would she even remember the brother she'd lost? It seemed unlikely.

I noticed that the few remaining Russian soldiers who had come south with Daniil and Nasan four years ago had chosen to attend the service. Once there had been fifty or so of them among a larger group of Tatars, but more than three-quarters of those had either found their way home or moved to the Russian-speaking lands held by Poland-Lithuania in the west, where they could expect most people to share their religion and understand their language. Of those who stayed, almost all had converted to Islam, since Christian priests rarely visited the steppe.

I stood in the back, among the women, using their words and gestures as guidance. After a while, Stepan tugged at my hand, reminding me that he'd rather be with the other boys. Although I suspected he grasped the meaning of the prayers no better than I did, he could repeat them verbatim and knew exactly what to do at each moment in the service. He'd learned by mimicking the older children. I allowed it, even though it widened the gulf—already vast—between the land of his birth and his present home. A child could only benefit from divine protection.

When I didn't release Stepan's hand, he tugged harder. "You can't stand with your friends today," I told him. "We're saying goodbye to Sibai Sultan, and I need you here."

"But where's he going?" The childish whisper, loud enough to turn heads, made me wince. "May I go too?"

"Pray God you don't." I hugged him until he squirmed away. "He's gone to live with his ancestors."

"The grandmothers," he said. He nodded as if he understood what that meant, but I knew he didn't. "They sound like fun. They let you play as much as you want. You can hunt and ride and shoot." These were sore spots: he had as yet no pony of his own, although Ogodai and Daniil were teaching him to ride, and the men insisted he was too young to go out with them when they hunted.

"Hush." I knelt so that our eyes were level. "You have your own ancestors, so you wouldn't see him there. We'll talk about it later. Right now it's time to pray."

I held his gaze until he nodded a second time, then, clutching his hand, directed my pleas heavenward until the service ended.

The funeral feast followed, but I had no plans to attend. My teacher needed me. To show my respect, however, first I dragged my protesting son with me toward the pair of great bonfires that blazed at the western approach to the camp, purifying the ground and those who pitched their tents on it from the contamination of death. The old beliefs remained strong in the horde despite its adherence to Islam, and neither Ogodai Khan nor Haji Rahman objected to the ceremonial flames.

After Stepan and I had passed between the fires and returned, I fulfilled my second obligation—stopping by to express my sorrow to Ogodai and Firuza, Nasan and Daniil. Then, after exacting a promise from Stepan to behave, I again left him in Guzel's care.

"If you need me, you'll find me in Suzukei's tent," I told her. "I'm worried about her. It's a full day since she collapsed, and I see no signs of recovery. She breathes, her heart pumps, if not strongly, but otherwise she might as well be a stone."

"Perhaps Nasan Khanim should examine her." Guzel glanced in the direction of the tightly clustered family. Nasan was not visible, although her brother's and her husband's heads showed above the crowd. "She seems to have a gift for these things, and what can you do for Suzukei today that you didn't do yesterday? Think of Stepan. You can't care for him properly if you're exhausted. Take this time to rest."

I flinched. My gritty eyes told me she was right. At the same time, I refused to abandon my mentor as those I loved had abandoned me.

"I shouldn't ask Nasan to look at Suzukei today," I said in the most reasonable tone I could manage. "Her sister-in-law needs her more. It's bad enough that we couldn't convince the spirits to release Sibai Sultan. I won't also demand that his family cut short the celebration of his life to help us."

"I suppose." Guzel frowned, not at me but at the pack of boys, Stepan among them, who had again gathered around Prince Timur. "I'd better go rescue my son. He ought to stand with his family."

"Of course," I said, remembering. I tended to think of Timur as Guzel's son, but his father, Alexei, was Ogodai's and Nasan's half-brother. These days Alexei lived in Moscow with his wife, but he'd sent Timur here to establish the boy's place on the steppe. "Thanks for watching Stepan. I don't plan to enter a trance, just to keep an eye on Suzukei and make her more comfortable if possible. Dull work for a small boy. But send for me if he misbehaves or you get tired."

"I will. Promise you'll ask Nasan tomorrow to check on Suzukei if she hasn't recovered by then? Don't try to handle it by yourself. And get some rest."

"I'll ask her," I said, although tomorrow still seemed too soon to make such a request of a grieving aunt. But why waste time arguing about a good suggestion that I might never need to adopt? Instead I thanked Guzel once more, then walked as quickly as I could toward the shaman's tent.

When I entered, I found Suzukei propped on one elbow. I released a long, relieved breath and pressed a hand to my aching head. I had despaired too soon. My efforts had borne fruit after all.

Saints be praised, I can sleep.

"You're better," I said. "I'm glad."

In fact, she looked not much better, although she no longer resembled a corpse. Her skin had a yellowish hue—perhaps an effect of the dim light. The whites of her eyes, when she gazed blearily at me, also appeared yellowed.

I could tell that she'd vomited since my last visit, right before the short funeral service. The smell imparted a sickly sweet odor to the tent. I searched for a bowl and a cloth. Before I could find them, she lay back on her pile of mats once more. From the way she rubbed her forehead I guessed she too had a headache or felt dizzy, maybe both. I wondered if she could speak.

When I'd cleaned her and the floor and placed a second bowl nearby in case the sickness returned, I sat next to her and clasped her hand in mine. "What else do you need?" I asked in my gentlest voice. "Do you have any idea what happened?"

I'd almost lost my battle with exhaustion before she opened her eyes again. "I'm not sure," she said. Her voice sounded harsh, as if she spoke from a dry throat, so I forced my drooping eyelids apart, poured a cup of boiled river water, and supported her while she drank. Three sips later, she added, "It may have been the mushrooms."

"The mushrooms?" I frowned, my fatigue forgotten. I hated that mushroom potion of hers, whatever she said about it easing a shaman's flight to other worlds. But she'd taken it many times without ill effect. "Weren't they the same as before?"

She gave a quick shake of her head. "The same merchant, but a new combination."

I stared at her, uncertain how to respond. I'd watched her drink the potion yesterday. She'd offered it to me, as she always did. As usual, I reminded her I'd sworn never to touch mushrooms. Still, I'd had no reason to suspect the potion itself. But a new combination? What had the merchant put in it?

When I asked her, she shrugged, indicating ignorance. "Mottlegills, he called them. I hadn't seen them before, but they worked as he said."

I wanted to shake her. How could she trust a peddler who aimed, first and foremost, to make a sale? And about mushrooms that might be poisonous, at that!

Still, it could have been worse. I'd seen enough mottlegills to know that although some of them would give you divine visions, they'd not do much harm. I was surprised Suzukei didn't use them already: they liked grasslands and horse dung; you'd think she'd have an easier time finding them than the toadstools she preferred. But if she took only mottlegills, or even a mixture, what caused her collapse?

Suppose the merchant got it wrong.

Unlike Suzukei, a lifelong resident of the steppe, I grew up in the Russian forest. There I learned early that one mushroom looks very like another, and even the most skilled forager doesn't always guess right.

"Where are the mushrooms?" I asked. "Do you have any left?"

She jerked her chin toward a bag hanging from the trellis near the lefthand side of the door. "Over there."

I scrambled to my feet, grabbed the bag with one hand, and ran outside to examine the contents. Once I'd passed through the door, I closed it behind me, then untied the leather thong that kept the bag closed and rolled back the top, reluctant even to reach inside until I got a good look at what Suzukei had purchased.

A handful of dried fungi lay within. Many had the classic reddish tops and white stalks of fly agaric—*mukhomor*, we Russians call it, the fly killer—deadly to insects if usually not to people. But intermixed with these toadstools were others, similar in shape but a dull greenish-white.

Mottlegills are brown.

My stomach clenched. I remembered that greenish-white. My mother pointed the mushrooms out to me once, told me not to touch them and never, ever, to eat them. If I didn't listen, she said, I'd end up like my cousin Pavel, dead before I had a chance to grow up. I recalled that afternoon as if it were yesterday. I could still see how she took a stick and poked the little ones that grew nearby, pure white orbs on fat stalks. "Those too," she said. "They look like puffballs, but they're not. If you see the green ones nearby, stay well away from the whole patch."

Surely no one would pick them, dry them, and market them just to make a sale. I stared once more into the bag.

I couldn't be certain. The slicing and drying had altered the shape and darkened the color, destroying the features so crucial in distinguishing edible mushrooms from their poisonous relatives. And even when fungi were new and whole, as I said before, anyone could make a mistake.

They *could* be mottlegills, but they didn't look like mottlegills to me. Not with that greenish tinge. The gills should be dark, too, and these were closer to beige, like those of the fly agaric.

The invisible hand that twisted my stomach told me I was grasping at straws. If the young toadstools could be mistaken for puffballs, that was not true once the tops turned green. Then they resembled nothing else that I'd seen. Especially fly agaric, with its scarlet caps flecked with white.

If I was right, Suzukei would be taking no more journeys. Because that greenish-white toadstool had a common name: Death Cap. It didn't kill right away, but it produced all the symptoms she was experiencing, and there was no antidote.

She'd be lucky to survive the week.

Suzukei didn't ask me what I'd found, and I didn't tell her. I retied the bag and returned it to its place, determined to show it to Nasan at the first opportunity, then set about trying to make my mentor's last days as painless as possible. Solid food wouldn't stay down, but a light broth moistened her dry throat and a tea steeped from valerian helped her sleep.

I stayed ready to assist her if she again felt nauseous, but after a while I concluded that stage had passed. It probably helped that she had eaten little before the soul retrieval ceremony, although that would only have increased the toadstools' lethal power. Death Caps were dreadful things, no less poisonous when dried or cooked than when picked fresh. I still couldn't imagine what idiot would add them to a preparation for a shaman, but it seemed useless to wake a woman on the brink of death to discuss the point. What good could it do to tell her that any relief she experienced would, most likely, last no more than a few days?

With nothing left to keep me awake, I constructed a new bed of felts that neither Sibai Sultan nor Suzukei had used and settled down for a much-needed nap. When Guzel stopped by toward evening, I met her at the door and walked her out of earshot before speaking. I asked about Stepan and learned that he'd gone off to the khan's tent with the twins, Irek and Altan-Alia.

"They'll keep him for the night if you like," Guzel said. "I think they'd be delighted if you let them, in fact. It's hard for such young children to understand why Sibai's not in the tent with them, never mind what makes their parents so sad. A friend to distract them keeps the twins from pestering the khan and khatun with questions they'd rather not have to answer right now."

"It would be a big help. Please thank them for me." Then I told her what I'd found in the bag, what I expected would happen to Suzukei over the next week. "Her jaundice troubles me. It suggests the poison worked swiftly. That may cut the number of days she has left."

"And she took this deadly mushroom for the first time? She must have, I suppose, or she would have sickened before."

I explained about the merchant and his new combination. "She took fly agaric often. Urged it on me, but I refused." I stopped, thinking about the effects of fly agaric. "It's poisonous too, just not as much. But if she ate the two toadstools together—as it seems she did—they would be more deadly than one by itself."

"And you're sure that's what it was? Of what will happen to her?"

"I'm not completely sure that's what she took. But I can recognize Death Caps by sight, and I'm almost positive that's what I saw in the bag." I told her about my mother's warning. "I had a cousin who died from eating them by mistake. So I also know what the dying looks like. I vowed then never to put a wild mushroom in my mouth."

Guzel tapped her fingers against her chin, as if considering something. After a pause, she said, "You don't think you should share your suspicions with Suzukei? Suppose you're wrong?"

I wrinkled my nose, thinking back to the bag and its contents. As much as I wished I'd seen something harmless, I didn't believe it. "I could, but I hate the idea of telling someone she's eaten something deadly, and there's no cure. It seems cruel."

"You don't have to mention that part," Guzel pointed out.

"True. I don't trust myself to keep the secret, but if I can think of a way to tell her that the mushrooms made her sick without giving away the rest, I will." I caught Guzel by the arm. "Which reminds me. If you see Nasan Khanim, especially if she's by herself or with only her husband, could you ask her to visit me in Suzukei's tent as soon as she can? Give her a hint of what I discovered? I doubt she knows of a remedy, but her books may contain ideas about ways we can relieve the symptoms."

"I'll ask her," Guzel promised. "If not today, then tomorrow morning. Will you stay throughout the night?"

"I must," I said. "Suzukei is like a mother to me—more than my own."

Guzel nodded her understanding. I'd told her my story when she first offered me her friendship. How my parents sold me into slavery in the Kolychev household as I approached womanhood—not the worst fate in the world, for the Kolychevs were kindly people and took better care of me than my own poverty-stricken family could have.

Their son Daniil even loved me for a while, until marriage turned his gaze toward Nasan. I'd long ago accepted that he was not for me.

I bade Guzel goodnight and went into the shaman's tent.

At first I saw nothing wrong—by which I mean nothing more wrong than the likelihood that my teacher would soon die thanks to her own insistence on drinking the mushroom potion and the act of a careless merchant. Suzukei lay curled on her sleeping mat, eyes closed, her breathing ragged and shallow. She had tucked one hand under her cheek; the other clasped a flask of koumiss. She must have fetched it while I walked outside, and while I didn't think she should be drinking alcohol and removed the flask as soon as I saw it, I reassured myself with the thought that she would have had to sit up and move, if only at a crawl, around a quarter-circle of the hearth fire to reach it.

I'd intended to stand watch until morning, but I was too tired. I helped myself to a chunk of bread and some sheep's milk cheese from Suzukei's stores, washed it down with more apple juice, and returned to my makeshift bed. Sending another blessing to Firuza and Ogodai for taking Stepan into their tent, I settled amid the felt and promised Suzukei that she need only whisper and I would be at her side.

A low moan woke me. I rolled onto my hands and knees, shedding my covering with difficulty and blinking. The tent looked much like my own, and I shook my head, panicked for a moment about not finding my son until the sight of the leather bag and the koumiss flask reminded me that the moan had to come from Suzukei, not Stepan.

She sat across from me, her head in her hands, what I could see of her face ashen in hue. As I reached to comfort her, she lurched to her feet, gasped, and clutched the loose tanned skins of her robe, just as she had the night before. Another moan, a great shudder, and she fell back, still gripping the leather with one hand while the other twisted in the tight braids I hadn't had a chance to undo. The long false sleeve of her robe fell onto the hearth.

I struggled to my feet, grabbed the jug of river water, and doused the fire. With a stick, I pushed the smoldering sleeve onto the stone circle and pounded it until no trace of flame remained. Only then could I kneel beside my teacher and touch her throat.

I felt nothing. No pulse, no breathing, no heartbeat.

In a flash, I relived the moment when I saw Sibai Sultan die. Terror strangled my soul, stripped my brain of thought. First a child, and now my teacher, my guide, my spiritual protector. Was I cursed, that I must endure two such deaths in as many days?

When I understood at last that it was true—Suzukei would not need Nasan Khanim's ministrations, because Suzukei had died—I howled my grief to the four winds. My cries again brought the horde running, but I heard only a flood of meaningless sound.

I had lost my mother—first the one who bore me and now this teacher who had meant so much to me. I had lost my man. Although surrounded by people, I was wholly alone. Except for the child who depended on me.

Chapter Three

"ANOTHER CHILD?" I STARED AT NASAN, MORE RESIGNED than surprised. "That makes five, in not much more than a fortnight. And we still have no idea what it is."

"Oh, I do." She pulled a dark blue book from the leather pouch draped over her right shoulder. "Alas, it's not good news. The khan's twins are recovering, *mashallah*, but I fear for their baby sister as well as my own three. Even though mine aren't sick yet, they often played with Sibai, and Borya follows Irek and your Stepan as a duckling trails its mother."

"But what do you think it is?" I left that last comment unanswered, because we both knew that Stepan was also at risk, for the same reason as Nasan's three. "We ruled out that version of the plague that kills by stealing the breath, because none of the adults have been stricken—either Tatar or Russian. Nor have the older children fallen ill."

She beckoned, and I followed her to the tent next to Guzel's, the home of Ruslan Sultan and Dina. They had a three-year-old son, Mergen, another playmate of Sibai Sultan's. Their infant girl had succumbed to the mysterious disease a few days after Sibai. I had still been arranging the tools I would need to contact the spirits when word came of the baby's death.

How dreadful if Ruslan and Dina lost both their little ones! So far, neither Nasan nor I had enjoyed much success against this fast-moving illness.

Inside, Mergen thrashed against his covers in a sight that had become distressingly familiar. I moved to the child's left side, leaving the right for Nasan, and bent to touch the little boy's forehead. As expected, he had a fever. I heard the rale caused by the evil spirit and, out of habit, made the sign of the cross over the child, then myself. Dina flinched at the sight, and I muttered an apology.

I looked at Nasan. "It's the same," I said. "I'll start my preparations."

"Wait." She caught my hand. "There's something I want to show you." She flipped open her book, and I saw she'd marked a page with a strip of leather. The letters would have meant nothing to me if written in Russian, and this script was Arabic, but I guessed she sought only to refresh her memory. She knew I couldn't read.

Nasan returned the book to its pouch and reached for Mergen's chin. "Come around here," she said to me, so I moved to kneel at her side. She caught my hand and pressed it against the child's swollen throat. As my eyes met hers, I had a flash of memory—another cousin, not the one who ate the Death Caps but much younger, no more than four.

Could it be?

He'd survived, that little cousin, but it had been touch and go, and not every child in the village had been so fortunate. I bit my tongue, again hoping I was wrong—that seemed to have become my natural state these last two weeks—and waited to see what else Nasan had discovered.

She released my hand and gently pried open Mergen's mouth. An ivory spoon, sized for a child, lay nearby, and she used it to hold down his tongue. That's when I saw it: a grayish membrane covered his tonsils, extending up the back of his throat. No wonder the poor child struggled to breathe.

"Damnation," I said in Russian. "Diphtheria." God had turned away from us for sure. Every child born since the last outbreak was at risk, whether they'd played with Sibai Sultan or not, and I had no idea how long ago that last outbreak had been. More than six years—I knew that for a fact.

"There's no remedy. Other than an appeal to the spirits." I spoke to Nasan, still using Russian to avoid alarming Dina, who hovered nearby. "At least, I've never heard of one. Have you?"

Slowly, sadly, Nasan shook her head.

The imam had his work cut out for him. It would take a miracle to ensure that the poor man didn't end up burying half the horde's children.

I took my time walking to the tent I shared with Stepan, planning what I would need for the ceremony to come. I must perform it as soon as possible, because I could tell from Mergen's wan appearance and difficulty in breathing that one of his souls had fled. The longer I waited to retrieve it, the greater the risk that it might never return.

But which soul? All of us have at least three. The animating force seldom strays far and is easily convinced to return. The second soul hides in a tree or a rock or some other element of the natural world, but it could not be the culprit or Mergen would already have died. The third soul is the most difficult to work with: at times it lingers in our middle realm after death, haunting the living and causing mischief; at other times it travels to the lower world too soon and can be retrieved only through a long and difficult shamanic journey—one I was not sure I had the power to complete.

As I walked, the vision of the red-eyed monster that had tormented me on the day when Sibai Sultan perished hung like a mist before my eyes. How could I tackle such a demon, never mind prevail against it?

I did my best to talk myself into a better state of mind. *I know the rites, I trained for this moment, Suzukei trusted me. I can do what needs to be done.*

The reassurances rang hollow. A simple healing ceremony had cured the khan's twins, together with herbal preparations to reduce their fever and ease their discomfort. Dina's infant died before I could attempt to save her. But today I must retrieve a soul, a task I'd not had to handle alone before. I wasn't sure I could handle it now.

Should I drink Suzukei's mushroom potion, even though I'd vowed never to take it? It might ease my journey, but the act of breaking my vow would put me at odds with the heavens. Not a good choice, that.

I could substitute koumiss, although I seldom drank it, so it might just slur my speech and cause me to stagger. Worse, it might put me to sleep, and I'd do no good at all.

I'd reached my home. As I crossed the threshold, I half-expected to catch a glimpse of my son's tousled head. But of course, I had sent him to Guzel's tent, and he would be playing with his friends. I had plenty of time for the ceremony.

No mushrooms, I decided, and no koumiss. The problems they could cause outweighed any benefits.

What other tools did I possess? Drumming and dancing, the fumes of juniper and thyme. Throat singing would help too, because of the regular hum it produced. I had yet to master the sound enough to trust it under such dangerous circumstances as these, but Suzukei had shown me an alternative. I rummaged through the chest where I kept my shaman's robe and tools until I found a flute shaped like a hollow stick compressed at both ends. I tested it, and it produced the steady buzz I remembered. I'd give it to Ruslan Sultan and ask him to play it, because I needed both hands for my drumming. He might like having a part in the ceremony. It would give him something to do besides pacing and imagining the worst that could happen.

Having made my choices, it was time to prepare myself for the journey to come. I took a deep breath, closed my eyes and released it, then repeated the pattern of breathing in-out, in-out in a slow but steady rhythm. I turned my face—lids still shut—toward the open smoke hole. I would do this. I *could* do this. I could find Mergen's missing soul and convince the otherworldly powers to return it to his body. My hands opened, palms upward, in silent prayer to the helper spirits. No more doubts, no more fears.

If it is meant to be, it will happen.

Once calm, I collected the things I would need: juniper and thyme, burners to hold them, the flute for Ruslan, a bowl for milk and a spoon to toss it to the four directions, the fist-sized stone that held my personal helper spirit. I placed each object in my leather bag and said a prayer over it as I dropped it in. When I'd found everything, I took out the pieces of my costume and laid them on the chest.

I twisted my hair into the several dozen tiny braids designed to harness the spiritual power of the snake. I begged the snake to lend its wisdom to my words, to guide my steps, especially if I needed to visit the lower world. I asked it to prevent flashes of light that might pull me away from my task. Then I donned my shaman's robe, taking slow steady breaths as the leather settled onto my shoulders, raising and lowering my arms to hear the shushing beads and sense the swishing back and forth of the scarves that dangled from hooks sewn into the robe.

I kissed my magic mirror before hanging it around my neck, imagining how it would catch and reflect the firelight as I danced. I took a few steps, forming a circle before the unlit fire, traveling in the direction followed by the sun throughout the day. In this way I honored the spirits of life and readied myself for the journey.

I picked up the flat red disk that formed the center of my headdress—the same one that had once adorned Suzukei's brow. I had adopted it both to honor her memory and to invoke her aid. She, after all, already moved in the worlds I must visit in my quest.

With reverence I pushed the five long eagle feathers into their holders on the back of the mask, pulled the braids until they obscured my features, and arranged the headdress in such a way that the spirit face replaced my own. Then, my preparations complete, I picked up my drum and my bag and left for Ruslan Sultan's tent.

The heavy aroma of juniper, the lighter fragrance of thyme, the underlying stink of dung from the fire—smoke swirls around my face. I hear drumming, a whisper of skirts, a whistling flute.

I relax, letting powers greater than myself direct my feet in the dance. As those eternal forces sway my shoulders, raise and lower my arms, hit the clapper in a steady beat, I open the inner eye. One breath: juniper. Another: thyme. The fumes separate my third soul from my body. I command the life force and the second soul to stay. On wings of scented smoke I rise, passing through the wooden circle at the top of the tent.

I turn in a sun-wise circle, searching for Mergen's animating spirit. I see the camp, white tents everywhere, spirit banners blowing in the breeze, some with souls sitting cross-legged on the copper circles that constrain the dangling horsehair. These are dead ancestors visiting from the realms beyond. I bow to honor them, welcoming their presence and showing them respect so they will not attack the living, then rise higher in the sky, borne on the back of a winged horse. We circle the surrounding steppe, alight at every nearby shrine and pray to the spirit revered there for assistance. After three rounds I know I must travel farther, to the lower world ruled by Erlik Khan. As I suspected from the beginning, Mergen's third soul has deserted him.

I search for a way down to that lower world, but I see only a mighty river, filled with rapids. At a touch my winged horse responds, and we fly north, toward the river's mouth, the place where, according to legend, the entrance to the lower world lies.

We fly and fly, as if we will never stop. The dry steppe gives way to trees and water, rapids and pools. In the far distance I see mountains, snow-capped even in midsummer. Beneath me the occasional grassy clearing stands out amid the forest. I cry out at the sight of a great eagle, swooping down on my winged horse and me. The horse vanishes, and I fall, tumbling toward the rock-strewn river, my hands flailing as I reach for help and clutch at nothing but air.

Wings form beneath me, outstretched to break my fall, and bear me up once more—up and up, pushing through one gauze curtain after another until we emerge in a brilliant magenta sky filled with tufted light-blue clouds.

Only then do I recognize my eagle as Suzukei. Her feathered head presses soft against my hands, and the wing bones and their powerful muscles rise and fall against my knees. "I'm so glad to see you!" I say. "I thought you lost to me."

"Silly child." Laughter fills her voice. "How can you lose me? You will find me here whenever you need me. Let's retrieve Prince Mergen's soul. Is that not why you came?"

"Yes," I say, and on the word she dives. I shriek, grabbing her neck with both arms as we plummet earthward, dropping through a round tunnel into a realm as dark as the upper world was bright, a place of endless twilight. Father Moon lights our way, his silver the only gleam against the gray.

Suzukei flies straight as an arrow, undeterred by the dim glow. After a while I see a massive tent hung with golden silk, its frame as pure and delicate as ivory. Somewhere within I sense Mergen's third soul hiding. Another presence—grim, foreboding—hangs like a thick fog between us. The roiling cloud presses against my chest like a physical barrier.

My feet hit the ground with a thump in front of a red-painted door. I bounce as my spirit self strives to rise again into the air. Symbols intertwine around the door frame, but I don't stop to read them. Where is Suzukei?

I twist to one side, searching. She is there, to my right, an eagle larger than I am with Suzukei's wise gaze visible in its golden eyes. "Remember," she says, "you are stronger than you think. Call on your protectors. All your protectors, from every stage of your life. And whistle when you're ready to return. I'll hear you, wherever I am."

I don't know what she means, but I don't ask. The force on the other side of the door demands my attention. It is not evil, *exactly, but it radiates strength—anger, vengeance, menace. I flinch at the thought of confronting such power, but I can't abandon Mergen so deep into my journey, leaving him in the grip of that threat.*

I comfort myself with the thought that I am alone yet not alone, a shaman in search of a child. The spirits of life will flock to my call. They will not stand by while the Lord of the Underworld takes a three-year-old for his own. Or so I hope.

I thank Suzukei, then watch her fly away. So short a time we've spent together. More than I'd expected, yet far from enough. Will I really see her again?

I face the door. Painted and carved, its solidity repels thoughts of entry. But as I approach, it opens of its own accord. I step into a corridor. To either side sheets of netting mark a series of rooms, the kind one might see in the grandest khans' dwellings. In contrast to the world outside, light suffuses the structure, although I see no hearth fire and no windows. Instead the draperies themselves glow like candles, illuminating everything within. The beauty of it leaves me gaping.

Beauty, light—and silence. Where are the spirits? I search one room after another, praying to my guardians and animal helpers for aid. I draw closer to the child that I can sense but not see. I have only the impression of a small, questioning being, uncertain and afraid.

Thick smoke hides Mergen's soul from me, as if spewed out by an ill-tended hearth fire hidden in a distant chamber. The smoke carries the scent of death. The more I push forward, the thicker the smoke becomes, the vaster the distance between myself and the child I came to save, the stronger the sensation of menace.

I enter a room with scarlet hangings. A handsome young man sprawls on an embroidered divan. He has light brown hair and dark eyes, a short but neatly trimmed beard. He is husky and broad-shouldered, like a warrior, and he reminds me of the lover I lost years ago. "Stenka," I cry as I rush toward him, my arms outstretched in anticipation of his embrace.

Halfway across the room, I skid to a halt. I grab for the arm of the divan as my heels slide against the richly patterned carpet with its oriental designs. Memory pricks me. Stenka's eyes were gray, like his son's, not dark brown like these. And if this young man is a warrior, he doesn't dress like one. He has no armor, and he carries no weapons. He wears trousers tucked into fine leather boots and layers of elegant robes with long, flowing false sleeves—like a nobleman or rich merchant. This cannot be my child's father.

The smoke that has plagued me since I entered the tent puffs and swirls from an iron brazier in the center of the room. Its stinging, pungent odor half-chokes me. My stomach tightens, and my hands clench. I straighten and pull back, searching for the source of the danger I smell.

A light melody sounds from the opposite side of the chamber. I look for musicians and find neither them nor their instruments. I frown at the young man.

Is this Mergen? Surely not!

No, he can't be. I still sense Mergen hiding, almost close enough to touch but not here in this room.

The young man rises smoothly to his feet and strolls toward me, his hand outstretched as if he intends to caress my cheek.

A warning bell rings in my mind, and I jump away from him, raising my arms in self-defense although I have no idea what to do if he attacks me. As I retreat, the pungent odor strengthens; the lilting melody acquires a jarring note. Fangs grow in the man's mouth, his skin reddens, his nose rounds into a pig snout. The demon who devoured Sibai stands before me, ugly and brutal. This time I recognize him.

Erlik Khan, Lord of the Underworld.

Who will decide Mergen's fate. I should be glad to have run into him so soon.

But I am not glad. I recall how he swallowed Sibai Sultan, how he threatened my Stepan. The image is burned into my brain: Erlik Khan with a child in each paw, mouth open and fangs bared. I cannot reason with a demon. Only shamanic power will spare me long enough to save Mergen.

Erlik Khan towers over me, his hands reaching for my shoulders. I can't move. I can't speak. When I open my mouth, the only sound I produce is a terrified squeak. Some shaman I am!

I try again, and this time I manage to state my purpose in coming here. "I ask to talk with Prince Mergen. To persuade him to return to his parents. It's too soon for him to join you."

Erlik Khan laughs. "And you can judge these things?"

I must not let him see my fear. "Yes," *I say in the firmest voice I can manage.* "He is three years old. He has not yet lived, so how can it be his time to die?"

"You must fight me for the right to approach him." *His fangs give every word a sinister twist.* "Win, and I will give you a chance to convince the soul. Lose, and you are mine for eternity."

Fight him. It is the answer I dread most. How can a human, even a shaman, defeat the Lord of the Underworld?

Suzukei's advice sounds in my head. "Call on your protectors. All your protectors, from every stage of your life."

I shudder, thinking. I will need protectors. She spoke the truth there. Erlik could not have made the stakes clearer. Lose this battle, and I will become his slave in the lower world for eternity.

Win, though, and I will have a chance to persuade Mergen to return. Fear twists my feet one way, hope the other. For better or worse, I will reach the end of my journey soon. I gather my strength for the contest.

Erlik comes closer. I shut my eyes, blocking out his demonic shape. I gather my mental energy into a single burning flame and direct it to flow around me like a cloak. I call on my spirit guides, my animal protectors, the Virgin Mother, every saint I can name. Only when I sense them circling me do I dare raise my lids once more.

The demon has doubled in size. He waves a saber in great strokes above my head. The flame barrier and the ring of guardian helpers keep him at bay. He can't touch me.

But neither can I touch him. A standoff.

I need a counterforce, strong enough to turn the tide in my favor. Suzukei? I purse my lips to whistle, but no sound emerges.

Not Suzukei, then. Not yet. But if not Suzukei, who?

Summon all my protectors, she told me, from every stage of my life. And I have. So why can't I defeat Erlik Khan?

Again the image of Stenka fills my head. The real one, not the imposter dressed like a prince I saw when I first entered this room. The man I loved, who swore he'd care for me always. The one protector I haven't summoned, because in the end he didn't keep his vow. He went off to steal for his wicked lord and died the same day, leaving me and Stepan to fend for ourselves.

And just like that, I am angry. No, furious. Furious with Stenka, whose death left me reeling for more years than I care to count. I can't breathe, I'm so consumed with a rage I have never let myself feel.

Anger is a weapon.

I harness the anger. Inside me it glows like a hearth fire, but as I allow it to flow free through my fingers it burns the tips before billowing into an enormous column of spitting flame. The smoke surrounding Erlik Khan is nothing next to the power of my rage.

I aim a long spear of fire at my enemy, engulfing him. I shout at him, "Return Mergen's soul!" I scream, "How could you send diphtheria to kill our children? What kind of devil are you?" I curse Stenka for deserting me, for being dead when Stepan and I need him.

Erlik eats up the hostile energy as if I have prepared a delicious feast just for him. He grows stronger, larger, more vicious.

Watching him swell into something even more monstrous than before, I understand that I've taken the wrong path. Suzukei is right. I must do as she says. Otherwise I will be lost— and so will Mergen.

"Stenka," I cry in the loudest voice I can muster. "I need you!"

And in the blink of an eye, my man is there, towering over Erlik Khan. Stenka's pointed steel helmet and mail shirt gleam in the brilliant light, and he wields a broadsword as deadly as the demon's saber in his hands.

One swish, and the pig-faced demon's head separates from his body. A flash of red light, and he vanishes. Stenka disappears at the same time, and with him goes my entire group of protectors. My cloak of flame swirls into nothingness. The scarlet hangings fade to the same pale gold I've seen in the other chambers; the smoke dissipates, leaving a whiff of brimstone; the jarring music ceases mid-note. Everything is calm once more, and I am alone.

Stunned by the suddenness of Erlik Khan's defeat, I stand blinking at the peaceful scene. Every muscle in my body trembles. I can barely stand. I hear a pitiful whining. Myself.

I release a long breath. I've passed the first test, but my journey isn't over. I must still find Mergen's third soul and persuade it to return.

I put one foot in front of the other—again and again until I reach the far side of the chamber and pass through the veil, not knowing what to expect.

Another demon? Can I really have defeated Erlik Khan with one blow, and that from a sword not even wielded by me?

But when I reach the chamber beyond, I sense only the hidden child, its hold on life weakening. I break into a run.

Three rooms later, I at last find a spirit. A lion cub. One glimpse, and I know I'm looking at Mergen's soul. It's something in the eyes—an openness, a quiet courage. I can't say exactly what, but I recognize him.

I slow my pace as I walk toward the cub. I don't want to take the slightest risk of scaring him off. Mergen doesn't back away or bare his teeth and growl, although he hunches into himself like a frightened animal. I emit a stream of soothing, meaningless phrases and take one step at a time, stopping whenever the cub moves. When I reach him, somewhat to my surprise he allows me to stroke his soft furry ears.

"Greetings, Mergen mirza,*" I say, using the Tatar word for "prince." "Your parents have sent me to bring you back to them. They fear for your life. Will you come with me? We can ride on an eagle."*

He looks at the glowing hall, the distant door at the end of what is again a single straight corridor with rooms opening to either side, then at me once more. "You're an owl. Why do you ride an eagle?"

An owl? When did I become an owl? I rode here. I didn't fly here!

I look at the hand that stroked his ears and see only feathers. I glance down. More feathers, and when I bend forward, taloned feet press against the tiles. I turn my head and discover I can look over my own shoulder. I twist my neck the other way, and the

SONG OF THE SHAMAN

same thing happens. Mergen has told the truth. In the short time since I defeated Erlik Khan, I have become an owl.

I let the thought go. Mysteries and miracles, shapeshifting and flashes into and out of existence fill the other realms. What else makes them other?

But I don't know the answer to Mergen's question. Right now I am an owl, and he's right: I can fly myself home. But he is a lion, not a bird. He needs help. I doubt I'm strong enough to carry him on my back. If the prospect of riding an eagle doesn't lure him, what will convince him to return?

The answer appears in my mind as if summoned. "I'm a young owl," I tell him. "As you are a young lion. We're still finding our way in the spirit world, but I know a powerful eagle who has agreed to help us. She will bring you back to the horde if I ask her. You'll have centuries to spend here, but little enough time on earth. Won't you let me call for her? Your parents want so much to see you. What is there for you here, compared to their love?"

He doesn't speak for a long time. I search my head for more arguments.

"Don't you want to grow up?" I ask. "Become a husband and father, live a full life?"

Behind the lion hangs a curtain of crimson velvet. At one corner I see two more spirits: a roly-poly wolf cub and a miniature dog, graceful and slim, with long legs, a narrow head, and the loveliest brown eyes I've ever seen. I recognize them too.

"Sibai Sultan and your sister," I say. "They can't return. Their bodies have died, but yours hasn't yet. They'll be playmates here, and the grandmothers will care for them until you and your parents can join them. Don't leave your mother and father bereft in the middle lands. They love you both very much. They grieve for her. They asked me to search for her as well, but she left before I could reach her. So they've sent me to bring you back instead."

Another long pause. I wait, counting each breath. In the distance I hear the slow, steady beat of the drum. A woman's whisper. The voice calls me home. The urge to obey its summons tugs at me.

I stand there, clinging to my last shreds of hope. If he doesn't make up his mind soon, I'll have to leave without him. To fail. I don't want to fail. I don't want to see his parents' eyes when I tell them that I saw Mergen but couldn't persuade him. That he didn't love them enough to live.

While I stare at him, wretched, the lion cub stands and, without a word, strolls toward the door. Spreading my wings, I take to the air and fly after him, emitting a screech never heard from any Russian owl.

Suzukei is waiting when we reach the door.

The familiar aroma of burning thyme signaled my return from the upper world. I opened my eyes and stared at the frame of a tent far less glorious than the one I'd left, filled with the usual crush of furnishings ringed by off-white felt. Dense smoke and dim, flickering light replaced the glowing golden silk of my vision.

I pushed myself to a sitting position and looked around. My drum was propped at my side, at an angle against the mats as if recently dropped. The flute I'd asked Ruslan to play lay next to it. Off to one side, I saw Ruslan and Dina huddled over the bed where their son lay. I heard no weeping, but no laughter either. Had Mergen's soul reentered his body or not?

Did the spirits mislead me as they did Suzukei? Could they not bear to release such a sweet child after all?

Nasan placed a clay cup in my hands, as I used to do with my teacher, and I sipped a fragrant rose-hip tisane that seldom came my way.

"Mergen?" I croaked once the tea went down. I held out the cup, and Nasan refilled it. "Thank you."

"It's we who thank you." She stepped back, and Ruslan moved far enough away from his wife and son that I could see the child. Although not sitting up, he too had his eyes open. His breathing sounded easier, and his color seemed more natural—a pale brown flushed with pink at the cheekbones, neither fiery red nor ashen. The young lion looked at me through the boy's dark eyes.

And I was an owl—a magical bird, filled with ancient wisdom. A sorcerer, the Russians said. I shivered, recalling the fairytales of my childhood.

Then chided myself for foolishness. Thanks to the spirits and Suzukei, I'd brought Mergen back from death. And I'd seen the other worlds. Except for Erlik Khan, defeated by my protectors, I'd witnessed nothing in those magical realms but beauty. How could anything so lovely be evil? Even the Lord of the Underworld was not truly wicked. He too had a position to fill, assigned by the spiritual forces that set the course of the interlocked spheres above, here, and below.

Dina, who'd been clinging to her son as if she couldn't believe she had him safe at her side, rushed to hug me. She poured her thanks over my head, in chorus with her husband. I expressed my gratitude for their trust, smiled at Mergen, and told him how glad I was that he'd agreed to return to this world for his parents' sake. I shared the story of our journey, described how the spirits and Suzukei and

Stepan's father had helped us, and mentioned that I'd seen their precious baby girl and Sibai Sultan, together in the lower world. The whole tale astonished them.

Then, exhausted but happy, I left to rejoin my son. I'd had a very good day.

Unfortunately, it proved to be the last good day for a month. One after another, every young child in the horde contracted the disease. Nasan and I worked nonstop—often together, although at times we split our forces to look after as many children as possible. I became more and more comfortable on my healing journeys, although not every negotiation succeeded. Haji Rahman presided over far too many heartbreaking ceremonies for either his peace of mind or ours. Nasan, too, got mixed results from her medicines.

That last saved me, I think. As the two of us walked from tent to tent, our limbs heavy with fatigue and our shoulders drooping because one more patient had slipped from our grasp, I sometimes heard the other parents muttering against me. I wasn't as strong as Suzukei—no matter that she had died while striving in vain to save poor Sibai. I'd come from elsewhere and lacked the necessary ties to the ancestors of the horde. I favored my own child at the expense of others: why else did he remain healthy in the midst of so much sickness?

Nasan defended me, bless her. No one dared mutter against the khan's sister. And I understood that stricken families who lost their children to a force beyond their control might yearn for someone—anyone—to blame.

Yet when I staggered into Guzel's tent each evening to gather up my son and bring him home, when I collapsed onto my felt mats too tired to eat, when I lay listening to the sunset call to prayer as it echoed throughout the camp, I thought of those whispering voices and wondered how I'd ended up in a place that held it against me that while I pleaded to save every child I could, whatever it cost me, my own son remained well.

Until he didn't.

Chapter Four

"MAMA, I DON'T FEEL GOOD." STEPAN STOOD IN FRONT OF me, his face scrunched in pain. He pressed his left hand against his temple, and his right clutched his throat, the way Erlik Khan had gripped him in the vision I'd had the day we lost our first patient to the disease. Tears ran down my son's cheeks, and I could see the reddening of fever there. Sure enough, as I bent to touch his forehead, I felt the heat even before my hand made contact. Beads of sweat dampened his curls.

"Let's get you to bed," I said in my most reassuring voice. "I'll give you some of the willow-bark medicine Nasan Khanim makes, and you'll feel better in no time."

Instead he collapsed in my arms. I picked him up and carried him to his pile of covers, where I untied his shoes and pulled off his outer clothes, then wrapped him up well. He already had the absent look I'd learned to recognize and to fear, and I wondered how long his throat had hurt and he hadn't mentioned it, eager to avoid my doses and my hovering. For a six-year-old, my son at times displayed an extraordinary ability to hide his aches and pains.

Once I'd done as much as I could for him, I left the tent long enough to grab the first lad I saw and sent him in search of Nasan. Without waiting for her to arrive, I found my drum and donned my ceremonial outfit—everything except the headdress. I twisted my hair into plaits, to have them ready, then tied them back from my face. It's hard to converse with a person whose expression you can't see.

Nasan ran in, Guzel at her heels. "Borya's sick as well," Nasan said as she plopped down cross-legged next to me. "Can you work with them both, or is that too much to ask?"

"I think not at the same time," I told her. "I have to give the spirits one clear message, or they become confused and don't know how to help. How sick is Borya?"

"I can see the glaze of fever in his eyes, but he's awake and sitting up. Not like this little one." She patted Stepan's cheek, then touched his swollen throat. He didn't awaken, although he curled himself tighter into a ball, whimpering. His breath had the rattling sound caused by the illness.

My stomach tightened as I watched him, and my own throat ached in sympathy. Fear of losing him held me rigid, until I wondered yet again if this time I shouldn't take Suzukei's mushroom potion, despite my vow. Not the dreadful stuff she'd bought from the merchant; we'd destroyed that after her death. But someone else in the camp might have fly agaric or mottlegills that I could use.

I hated the thought. And if I killed myself with mushrooms, I'd be no use to Stepan. But in my terrified imaginings, the false allure of the potion tugged at me. What kind of mother wouldn't risk her life to save her child's?

My own.

49

The thought came unbidden. I brushed it aside. It wasn't true. My parents had sold me because they were dying of hunger. They'd sent me to a richer house, a better life. You'd think me younger than Stepan, the way I was behaving. If the money they got for me kept them and my brothers alive, how could I begrudge them that boon? I'd done well enough since then.

Nasan's voice called me back from panic and harsh memories. "You'd better search for him first. He's yours, after all. I'll leave Guzel to work with you while I keep an eye on Borya."

I thanked her in a voice that shook. "I'll come to your tent as soon as I can," I said. She nodded and left.

Potion? No potion?

I slapped my forehead. Fear had muddled my brain. I hadn't time to hunt down mushrooms, test them for safety and potency, then turn them into that devil's brew Suzukei favored. My son's soul had fled while I watched, and I must go after it before his body followed.

"What do you need from me?" Guzel asked.

"Look after Stepan." I handed her a bowl of warm water and a soft cloth, then placed a cup and a clay jug on her far side. "Wipe his face from time to time, and if he awakens, try to get him to take some apple juice. He may not be able to swallow, though, so don't insist. If he has trouble breathing, raise him up and hold him as long as you can. I'll be in a trance, but I'll probably come out of it if something terrible happens." As a result of the many healing journeys I'd undertaken this past month and a half, I'd come to realize that it was my unspoken sense that Sibai Sultan neared his end that had dragged me out of my trance the day he died.

"And if I need to wake you?" Guzel dipped the cloth in the bowl, wrung it out, then placed it on Stepan's hot forehead.

"Speak quietly. Touch my shoulder. Tell me it's time to return." I recalled the day I'd tried to wake Suzukei and shivered. My little boy, my sole comfort.

Can I do this?

I must. No one else knows how to save him.

"Just nothing sudden," I added.

"I understand," she said, and I smiled to show her I trusted her. Then I untied the plaits and pulled them to cover my face, tied the mask around my head, lit the burners of juniper and thyme, picked up the drum, and moved into the dance.

I am chosen by the spirits. Come to me, sacred ancestors. Save my child.

This time my owl wings take me to a primeval forest. Birds carol from the treetops, and the shush of wings draws my attention upward. The scent of wildflowers mingles with the rich aroma of soil never dried by the sun that glimmers through a canopy of fresh green leaves. Among the roots of a nearby tree I see a cluster of puffballs mixed with pale green adult Death Caps. Farther off, classic red tops flecked with white mark a group of fly agaric.

I am home. Not in the upper world, not in the lower world, but home. A place I haven't lived since I was twelve years old.

Where is my mother? My father? My brothers?

Turning my head this way and that, I see no sign of them. I can't tell whether I should. I don't know whether they're dead or alive. Only the dead would meet me here, so perhaps it's good that I can't find them.

Tamping down a flicker of disappointment, I rejoice as I stand amid the familiar sights of the clearing. Looking around, I understand for the first time in years how much I miss my home. The steppe is beautiful—grasslands vast as the northern sea, extending to the horizon under a cobalt sky filled with billowing clouds and winged horses, clean-smelling and ever-changing— but it's not me. It's not who I am, the person I was born to be.

Or is it?

The question surprises and confuses me. I set it aside for later.

At the center of a clearing stands a wooden cottage. A single room, I discover as I enter—on my own spirit feet, I see when I glance down; no owl's talons here—with an entryway and a separate area to house animals, although I hear no livestock within.

I walk into the room, where a clay stove with a flat top exudes a soft gray steam and the familiar scent of burning pine branches. Benches line the other three walls, and a heavy wooden table fills most of the center.

At the table sits my child's father. This time, Stenka looks as I remember him, without the armor or the sword. His dress is that of a bandit—a padded vest, linen shirt, and homespun trousers—the same clothes he wore the day he rode off to die. Only his leather boots hint at the more honorable past he enjoyed as a man-at-arms.

My yearning for that lost childhood home has betrayed me, I see. This is not the cabin where I grew up but the one Stenka and I shared for more than a year before he got me with child and, desperate to secure a steadier source of income, sought out his former master. The decision that led to Stenka's death. I should have recognized where I was right away. Peasant huts look much alike, but this one has received better care than my parents could afford. Stenka may have failed as a farmer, but he was good at carpentry.

In the far corner Stepan crouches, his arms around his knees. The fear visible on his face turns to joy at the sight of me, and he hurls himself against me. I see no signs of illness in him. I pick him up—in this spirit realm he has no more weight than a kitten—and carry him to the table, where I take the bench opposite his father.

"This is your papa," I tell Stepan. I settle him on my lap and hold out a hand to Stenka. "I miss you," I say, and it's true. That battle with Erlik Khan consumed my anger, opening a space for softer feelings. "I'm glad to see you."

He nods, as if a supernatural visit means no more than passing someone a bowl of soup. I open my mouth to coax my child's soul to return to his body, then stop, uncertain.

Where are their spirit animals? Why a hut and not the golden tent? Are my guardians and assistants near enough to hear my pleas for help?

I pelt Stenka with questions. "Are you alone? Have you been here since you died? What went wrong that day?"

Stenka stares at his clasped hands, his face solemn. "It was supposed to be a simple raid on a group of pilgrims. Go in, grab their goods, ride off. I wouldn't have agreed to take part in it otherwise. Not with you so close to giving birth. But our lord miscalculated. He sent us to attack a Tatar escort—with a khan's daughter at the center of it! We took them by surprise and killed a few, but they rallied fast. As the bandits' captain I was in the lead, so I got it in the neck." He touches his throat, where the pulse once beat right under his jaw. "One stray arrow, and I found myself here." He looks around, as if his surroundings puzzle him.

At the edge of his neck, where his beard meets the rounded collar of his linen shirt, I see a red line. A mark left by the arrow that killed him. My anger surges once more. I still nurse that old rage, then. I sigh.

"Your lord was a fool," I tell Stenka. I hear the bitterness in my voice. And I speak the truth: his lord was a fool, a dangerous fool who robbed me of everything I valued except my son. "And you a bigger fool to do his bidding. I hate that we lost you because of his mad schemes."

The warmth I love returns to Stenka's face, and he laughs. "So we were, a pair of fools. But you say 'was.' Is he no more, like me?" His voice, which until then sounded rusty, as if from disuse, warms as well.

"You don't know?" I frown. The twists and turns of the other worlds never fail to perplex me. "But yes, he's dead. Consigned to Hell, I hope. He earned it."

"I don't believe you're my papa." Stepan, who's remained unnaturally silent as we talk, wriggles off my lap and interrupts whatever his father might have said in reply. Our son's chin juts out, as if he expects an argument. "I know about papas. Irek has one. Borya has one. They live in their tents with them and their mamas. But you don't live with me and Mama. So what kind of papa are you?"

"A fine lad, this one," Stenka says to me. "Is he really ours?"

"Born not three weeks after you died," I tell him.

Stenka nods. Sadness fills his eyes as he lowers his gaze to meet Stepan's glare. "I don't live with you," my man says. "That's so. I'd like to, but I can't. I died before you were born. I am your papa, though, and I love you and your mama."

Our son's upper lip trembles as he looks at the wooden cottage, unlike any house he knows. "Can we live here, then? The three of us, together?"

I pat his back. "No, sweetheart. Your papa died, as he said, but we're alive. He has to stay here while you come home with me. So you can play with your friends again and get to be a big boy."

I glance at Stenka, wondering how he will take the news. "He's very sick in the everyday world," I say. "He has diphtheria. I came to beg the spirits to release his soul, to send him home with me. It's something I've learned how to do, but I didn't expect to find you here. I'd love to bring you back with us, but without your body ..."

I leave the phrase unfinished. Without a body, his third soul would wander as an aimless ghost among the spheres, becoming ever more restless, vengeful, and lost. One of those spirits who steal the breath of children and cause havoc among the living. If I encountered him, I would have to banish him once more to the lower realm. Here he has—well, in truth I don't know what he has, only what I learned from Suzukei, but I hope eternity offers occupation, companionship, bliss. Even though I see no evidence of those things.

A hard lump forms in my throat as the permanence of our separation hits me anew. Is my man lonely? Will he fight to keep his son with him?

"I miss you," I repeat. "But I need to take our boy back, so he can live a normal life. Grow up, fall in love, become a father—as you did."

"If I don't go with Mama," Stepan asks, "will you be my papa then?" For the first time since he ran to me, I see him reach for his father. The hope in his voice forces me to blink back tears.

What will Stenka do? This is his only son, begging for time with him. If I were here, and my husband still in the middle lands, would I have the strength to urge our son to go? I hope so, but I don't wholly trust myself to do the right thing.

Stenka leans across the table and clasps our son's hand. The longing in his eyes reflects the pleading in Stepan's voice, and I ache for them both. "No matter where you live, I'll always be your papa." His voice, rough-edged, shows me what the next words cost him. "One day you'll join me here and we'll have fun. I have things to teach you, but I can't share your tent because, as Mama says, I don't have a body anymore. And you can't stay here because you do. Whatever happens, remember I'm watching over you, even if you can't see me. I'll help you as much as I can."

Our son's face crumples, and tears run down his cheeks. Stenka pulls a cloth from his belt and pats at Stepan's face. "For now, you need to go home with Mama and get well." His voice is gentle but firm. "If you stay here with me, Mama will be alone in the middle lands. We can't do that to her. As men, we have to be brave and protect our families even when it's easier to run away."

Our son sniffles. I hug him, and after a while his blond curls wave as he nods. "I'll go," he says. "But I wish you could come too. I do need a papa."

"Yes, you do." Stenka stands, bends forward, and brushes his lips across mine. I lean closer, yearning to deepen the kiss after so many years without the comfort and the passion of our love. Stepan bumps against my side, and startled, I draw back.

"The boy's right, my sunshine," Stenka says, his voice husky. "Find another man to look after you both. You've mourned this fool of yours long enough."

"But where will I find another man like you?"

I get no response. Just as before, he disappears in a puff of smoke, and the cottage and the forest dissolve around him. In the sudden silence I hear Guzel calling me. Stepan tumbles into my arms. Glancing at him, I see a fluffy white eaglet with a black beak.

A golden eagle. Is his father also an eagle, then?

Another question that has no answer. Meanwhile, my child's life dangles by a thread blown in the wind. "Come with Mama," I say, then sweep him onto my owl self's back and fly him home.

It wasn't easy to leave Stepan in my tent and go at once to rescue Borya, but I'd promised Nasan I would visit her as soon as possible. And as tempting as I found the prospect of curling up next to my darling son, now relaxed amid his covers with one hand under his cheek, and joining him in sleep, I couldn't imagine willfully depriving another mother of that pleasure. Especially Nasan, who'd done so much to help me keep this dreadful disease at bay. So I removed my headdress, tied back my plaits again, and checked Stepan's head, neck, and throat as thoroughly as I could without waking him.

Once convinced that he seemed to be recovering and had no sign of the gray membrane that had restricted Mergen's breathing, I gave Guzel a brief description of what I'd seen while grabbing a bite to eat and as much liquid as I could down.

"Why do you think it was so different?" she asked as I reached the end. Before I could answer, she reached out and brushed Stepan's curls away from his forehead. "A golden eagle. I should have guessed. He's brave and strong, despite his youth."

"I should have guessed, too. I wonder each time: will this child be a lion or a wolf, an antelope or a dove. I expected to find a stallion and his colt, or a stag and a fawn— something strong and protective but not a predator. The whole thing surprised me. As for why, I don't know what made this time different, except that my man was Russian and I am Russian, so Stepan's ancestors are Russian. I didn't expect the other worlds to differ depending on how people lived on this earth, but it seems they do." I bent to kiss my son's cheek. "Sleep tight, dearest. Mama will be back soon. I have to make sure Borya is getting well. Guzel will look after you."

"Absolutely." Guzel smiled and patted my arm. "We'll have him running and playing in no time. Off with you."

"How would I manage without you?" I hugged her, then gathered up the rest of my shaman's gear and went to visit my next patient.

Daniil stopped me at the door of the tent he and Nasan shared. "It's good of you to come and visit us," he said. "I think Borya's doing better, though, and you look exhausted. Did you manage to save Stepan?"

"Yes." He was right: I struggled to keep my eyes open. But a promise is a promise. "The spirits took pity on us and let him go. And I swore to your wife I would check on Borya as soon as I returned." I hadn't the energy to tell him about meeting my child's father—and besides, Daniil and I were no longer that close. I'd share the story with Nasan instead.

"Good." He touched my elbow. "Borya's improving, as I said. Go home and rest. It won't do to have you falling ill as well."

"I had diphtheria as a child," I told him.

He stopped arguing then. Closer to the fire, Nasan knelt beside their son. I caught no glimpse of their daughter, Tasha, or baby Kolya, both of whom would normally be playing or crawling nearby, as befit their ages, under the watchful eye of their nurse.

"Since I'm already here, may I see him for myself?" I asked Daniil. "And where are your other children?"

"With their aunt," Nasan said. "All their cousins have had the sickness already, so they're safer there than here." She waved me in. "Yes, come and take a quick look. Then you can safely rest, I think. I'll call for you if Borya gets worse, but so far the willow bark and the honey mixture I gave him for his throat seem to be working."

Daniil stepped aside with a quick dip of his head and left the tent. I called after him, expressing my thanks for his concern, and received a wave in reply before I joined his wife at the hearth. "If only these tents weren't so dark," I said as I knelt beside her. Daniil had left the door open, which helped, but I still couldn't see much more than a shape under a pile of covers.

"I know." Nasan reached for a lantern and held it up. "Even those murky Russian windows let in more sunshine than this. But you can see that he's not sweating and his breathing sounds almost normal. I think it's the honey. I should have remembered ages ago that it heals wounds. Usually you spread it on, as thickly as possible, but I decided to see if it would work if I diluted it in warm water and added some of the healing herbs. Sage and thyme, especially."

I pressed my palm against Borya's cheek. It was warmer than usual but not burning as Stepan's had been this morning. "You're right. What a find. Who would imagine such simple ingredients could work so well?"

Nasan shrugged. "I don't know that it will work for every child, but I'm glad to have another medicine we can use." She laughed. "And with luck, you'll be spared a few healing journeys. My husband may be tactless, but he's right: you do look exhausted. You've been positively heroic, whatever those idiots in the outer tents say."

I laughed too, with relief as much as gratitude. "Thank you," I told her. "I suppose they'll have to stop complaining now that Stepan has caught the sickness as well. But do send for me at once if Borya worsens. Meanwhile, I'm going to my tent to sleep."

Nasan's honey treatment proved a powerful weapon indeed. It didn't cure every incidence of diphtheria by any means, but between that and my spiritual journeys and the number of victims we'd already saved or lost, we gradually made headway against the disease. Over the next two weeks new cases became rarer, until it seemed at last that every child who could contract the sickness had done so. The spirits had indeed relented.

We soon discovered, however, that trouble had not yet decided to leave us to our own devices and move on to spread its miseries in someone else's camp. Hardly a day after Nasan and I pronounced the last child cured, we were walking together toward the khan's tent. The sun hovered right above our heads, and the noon prayers had just ended, so the midday meal would soon take place. I spared a moment to run a list of supplies through my head. As shaman, I could claim part of the dinner prepared for the khan and his family, but I had saved mutton and bread from yesterday. It would do for Stepan and me, together with the cheese curds the other women and I always had on hand. I wished for carrots and cabbage, cucumbers and cherries, but the nomadic life didn't often allow for such items. So odd to live in a world where meat was a food for every day and vegetables a rare and appealing luxury.

"What's that?" Nasan pointed to a cloud of dust on the horizon. "Quick, sound the alarm!" She spoke that last not to me but to a warrior passing by, whose arm she grabbed without ceremony.

"Yes, Khanim." He clanged his sword against his shield, and people came running from the four directions in response. Nasan raced to her tent, returning with a bow in her right hand and a full quiver slung over her left shoulder. Men buckled on their swords, then grabbed bows and quivers from their women, not a few of whom carried weapons of their own. The approaching cloud needn't indicate an enemy, but raiders appeared without warning, and every horde member learned what to do before he or she was old enough to ride.

Tempted to run back to my tent and check on my son, I saw him dart out the doorway. Raising my voice to pierce the clamor, I yelled at him, "Come here at once!" When that had no effect, I waved my arms. Scuffing his boots against the grass, Stepan joined me. His sulky expression faded when I lifted him onto the fence that contained the horses at night and let him balance against my shoulder.

Ogodai, clad in chain mail and helmet, strode the length of the walkway and stopped at the edge of the camp, not far from Stepan and me. His nephew Timur took up a position at the khan's side, Daniil on the boy's right and Ruslan at Ogodai's left. The other men arrayed themselves behind their leaders. But as the cloud came close enough to distinguish the riders, they abandoned their aggressive stance, thrust their bows back in their cases, and howled a welcome. That was when I saw the scarlet winged horse embroidered on a gold-rimmed white silk background, flying proud and free above the foremost rider's head.

"*Ata!*" Timur broke rank, about to run, but his uncle caught his arm.

"I don't think so," Ogodai said. "Look, Timur, there are a dozen riders at most. Couriers from your father, I'd guess, but not Alexei himself."

Timur stopped, his expression somewhere between disappointed and shamefaced. By my count, he'd seen little of his father in the last year. He must miss Alexei, although past experience made me pretty certain that Alexei missed him too. I thought of Stepan and Stenka, together in the Russian cottage—how wistful they seemed at that moment just before their parting. I grieved for the four of them, although the reunion of Timur and Alexei would, I hoped, take place before my son reunited with *his* father.

With all the nursing and journeying, I'd had not one spare moment to think about what Stenka had done for me: relieved my mourning, freed me to find another man—a husband for myself and a guardian for our son. Not a moment to consider whether that was what *I* wanted or what our little boy needed—never mind how to answer the question I'd posed that day in the hut. If I did decide to look for another man to share my life, where could I find one as generous and openhearted as the one I'd lost?

Chapter Five

OGODAI KHAN WAS RIGHT: THE NEW ARRIVALS BORE messages from his half-brother Alexei Sultan, stationed in Kolomna and charged with coordinating the Russian defense against various Tatar forces—a never-ending mission. If the nomads didn't ride up in droves from the south, they launched raids from the east. Often they did both. The khans required a steady stream of plunder to keep their warriors happy, and no agreement could satisfy them for long.

"Why are you smiling?" Nasan, standing next to me with Firuza on her right, frowned at the arriving couriers. "Look how they're tumbling off their horses and shoving those scrolls at my brother. I bet they carry a warning. Why else would Alexei send them?"

"I agree," I said. "That's not why I'm smiling. It amused me for a moment to think that your brother, a Tatar, is protecting Russians from other Tatars. Forgive me."

"It's common." Nasan shrugged. "The Russians recognize that Alexei is loyal and competent, and he's spent enough time in Crimea to guess which way the khan will jump."

"I know," I said, eager to drop the awkward subject. I hadn't expected my private flash of humor to provoke a response—especially dismay or affront, both of which I heard in Nasan's reaction, whether she felt those things or not.

Ogodai stripped off the red ribbon that kept the scrolls confined in a tight cylinder and scanned the innermost document before sending the couriers to rest. Then he muttered words I couldn't hear to Daniil and Ruslan, and the three of them spun on their heels and stalked toward the khan's tent, trailed by Timur.

When Ogodai reached the place where Nasan and I stood, he stopped in front of us. "Grusha, join us, please. Stop and get your robe, if you like, but I'd prefer not to wait for you to don your entire costume." The frown still creased his brow, but I could tell from his distracted air and the courtesy of his greeting that he was preoccupied rather than angry. He glanced at Nasan and Firuza. "The two of you are welcome as well."

I ran for my tent, but behind me I heard Nasan speaking to her brother. "Thank you. Information from Moscow, from our brother? Naturally we want to be there." Firuza echoed her.

"Come along then," Ogodai said. A glance over my shoulder as I ducked through my door revealed that he'd resumed his rapid stride, not checking to see whether his wife and sister followed. Ruslan, Daniil, and Timur had already passed from my line of sight.

Once inside my home, I dug through the chest where I kept my shaman's things, pulled the robe out, wrapped it about me, and draped the mirror around my neck. Eager to hear the khan's news, I didn't bother with the headdress, the multiple ribbons, or the many tiny plaits, instead sending brief prayers to the snake spirits to beg for their understanding. I saw no reason why I'd need the drum, and its size made it cumbersome to manage, so I left it behind and went to join the others.

As I hurried toward the tent set aside for such meetings, I muttered assurances to myself that I could handle this new responsibility. In the furor over Suzukei's death and the weeks spent nursing sick children and retrieving their souls, I'd not had time to consider that the loss of my teacher advanced me to a position in the horde not much lower than that of the khan. I had become the camp's chief spokesperson on behalf of those who held to the old faith, the guardian of their relations with the spirits above and below just as Ogodai led and defended the Muslim community with assistance from the imam. They had ten times my level of experience, of course, as Suzukei had also had in her time. I couldn't claim that I felt up to the task, but since I was better prepared for it than anyone else here, I shoved my worries aside and moved as quickly as my bulky leather robe allowed.

By the time I entered the meeting tent, the others had already arranged themselves around the circle of stones that girded the unlit hearth fire. Usually Ogodai sat apart on a raised platform, but today, with only family members and myself present, he occupied the central space in the circle, his back to the north and Timur to his right. As I came in and circled the tent sun-wise searching for an empty place in the circle, Ogodai gestured to the spot on his left. I sat there, with Firuza at my left elbow and Nasan beyond her, next to Daniil. Ruslan filled the space between Daniil and Timur. Haji Rahman, a Sufi mystic, avoided any meeting dedicated to political or military matters, so he was not present.

Usually Tatars chatted for ages before getting down to business, but I soon realized that this time we could avoid the prolonged exchange of courtesies—one advantage of an impromptu family gathering. As I settled into place, Ogodai unrolled the cylinder of scrolls once more, paged through the documents, and selected one.

"I hope everyone's safe and sound." Daniil voiced the wish going through my head as well.

"Last Alexei heard, yes. He's been in Kolomna since mid-June." Ogodai glanced at Timur. "Your stepmother, her children, and her sister Lyuba send their love from Moscow. They miss you. Your *ata* too." He held out a second scroll to Timur, who took it but didn't open it. "That letter's for you."

Timur nodded. "I miss them," he said, his voice more subdued than usual. I sent him a glance of sympathy. Unlike my Stepan, Timur had a father who cared for him, supervised his education, and took an interest in him and his future. But Alexei and Guzel had parted ways when their son was Stepan's age. Timur loved both his parents and spent time with each of them, but rarely together. And since they lived far apart and Alexei had since married, wherever Timur stayed, in effect he had no contact with his other parent for months, even years, except by letter. Much as I wished that Stepan might enjoy the benefits of having a father to look after him, I was glad I hadn't created such wrenching split loyalties for *my* child.

"What's going on, then?" Ruslan, a gifted warrior in his mid-thirties and sworn brother of the missing Alexei, asked the question we all wanted answered.

"Alexei warns us to expect an attack from the southeast." Ogodai nodded at Ruslan. "Two of your half-brother Sahib-Girei's princes have launched a massive raid on Russia from Crimea."

Ruslan cursed, and I recalled that he and his half-brother, the khan of Crimea, did not see eye to eye—and had not for many years. "Damn him," Ruslan said. "I thought Sahib swore eternal friendship to Moscow earlier this summer."

"Oh, he did." Ogodai waved the scroll, as if in confirmation. "He insists he has no control over these renegade princes."

"Of course not." Ruslan produced a sarcastic laugh. "How could he? He only leads the khanate. What he means is that he will accept no responsibility for their actions. Clever. I bet he'll demand they pay him off when they get back, though."

"Right," Ogodai said. "They take the risk and gather the plunder, and Sahib-Girei sits in safety until he has a chance to collect his share. The Russians can protest—and they will, because according to this letter the renegades have captured a group of Russian envoys and are holding them to ransom—but they can't prove that Sahib-Girei ordered the attack."

"Well, that's a mess," Daniil said. "In itself, though, it doesn't endanger us. Crimea lies to the southwest of here, not the southeast, and there's a whacking great river between us and them. Why does Alexei warn us to expect an attack?"

Ogodai nodded, acknowledging this point. "The renegade princes have sent out a call for support to every nomadic camp in the Nogai Federation—and many of the camps have responded to the summons, including those south of us. That means we can expect raiders from the Volga river basin to ride past our grazing lands on their way to join the Crimeans, and even if we start the fall migration early, they'll reach us before we can get to a safe location. Alexei advises us to strengthen our defenses and prepare to repel invaders. If nothing else, we can expect the advancing Nogai to steal our animals for food."

Nasan leaned forward, elbows balanced on her knees and an intent expression on her face. Firuza mirrored her pose. "But that's terrible!" I said. "Praise be to God that Alexei Sultan's message reached us in time. Otherwise the raiders could have fallen on us before we even knew to guard against them." I raised my palms skyward and thanked those otherworldly forces who had chosen to act on our behalf. The others murmured their agreement.

Daniil stabbed a harmless chunk of bread with his eating knife, then stared at it as if it had offended him in some way. "So Sahib pledges friendship," he said after a moment. "Then he sends his princes to attack the Russians while their suspicions are lulled, knowing he can pretend his minions acted without his authorization. He's desolated, betrayed, furious, and so on. You say it's a big force heading for the southern border, but that's a long line. Which trail are they following?"

I shuddered as the implications of Daniil's words struck me. He spoke, not casually—I could see his anger and concern—but in such a military way, as if the question involved only troop movements and defenses, not human lives and health. Yet no one—man, woman, or child—grew up in Russia without hearing horror stories about the Tatars razing towns and hauling captives off by the thousands to slavery in Crimea, Kazan, or Istanbul.

I hesitated, then reminded myself that I attended this gathering by invitation. I took a deep breath for courage and spoke. "And how can we keep our own people safe?"

"Let's consider that." Ogodai addressed me first, then glanced around the circle. "We need to develop a plan that will protect our homes and our families. Everyone here can contribute, including you. I'll tell you later what I have in mind, after I have a chance to think it through."

When I nodded—glad that he'd heard my real concern, to preserve life—he turned to Ruslan and Daniil. "From what Alexei has heard, it's a huge force. The leaders *could* be renegades, I suppose, but I doubt it. Not with so many men at their command. The bulk of the army is heading for Serpukhov and Kolomna, and if it breaks through there, the princes will go on to Moscow unless Alexei and his fellow generals can stop them."

"Farther west, then," Daniil said. "However large a force, they won't cross the river Don to get to us."

Ogodai tapped the scroll against the side of the rug. "No, *they* won't. But anyone coming up from the Volga basin will take the Nogai Road to Ryazan and Kasimov. They're the ones who'll get too close for comfort."

"Nogai Road?" Nasan asked. If she hadn't, I would have. The steppe contained no roads that I knew of.

"It's a trail," Daniil said. "Not a real road but a route through the grasslands that the Nogai have taken so often it might as well be a road. Lets the horses avoid the more challenging river crossings and such." He looked at us women as he spoke, most likely because the men already knew that.

"A big army needs lots of pasturage," Ruslan noted. "If the raiders come anywhere near us, we have to assume they'll take over our grazing lands as well as steal our flocks for meat."

"I see," I said. "Then what can we do to protect our camp?"

"Yes, what can we do?" Nasan and Firuza echoed.

"The first step is to establish whether raiders are on the way." Ogodai waved the scroll for emphasis. "If they are, we should move the camp to a more sheltered location as soon as possible."

"You'll send out scouts then?" Daniil asked.

Ogodai indicated agreement with a tip of his head. "Right away. One group south, to check for raiding parties, and the other group west to discover whether the Crimeans will keep their distance or approach closer than we might like."

"It may be useful to find out where the princes are holding the captured Russian envoys," I said, thinking out loud. "If you can free them, you'll have an additional source of information. If they met the princes or got a good look at their forces, they might confirm what Alexei Sultan has heard. Or, better yet, know more than his scouts."

The three men sent me glances of startled admiration, and I suppressed a flicker of pleasure. Perhaps I could succeed in my new position after all.

"Good point." Ogodai held out his arm, palm up, toward Nasan. "Meanwhile, alert the women. Organize a defense among them, just in case. But don't act unless I give the word. If our enemies don't scruple to steal flocks or capture envoys in service to a foreign government, they won't hesitate to kidnap you and the other wives. And chances are they'll not bother to hold women for ransom. Instead we can expect them to divide you among themselves and use you as concubines until we manage to free you. Understand me?"

He scowled in a way that would intimidate most people, and Daniil glared at his wife as well. Knowing them, I guessed they sought to underline the gravity of the situation.

"I won't go off on my own," Nasan said, as if she'd never think of defying her husband and brother. "Do you take me for an idiot?"

"Make sure you don't," Ogodai said, visibly unimpressed by this declaration.

"I won't," she repeated. "I promise."

I hoped she meant what she said. The more time I spent with Nasan, the more I liked her. The last thing I wanted was to learn that she'd been injured, captured, or killed.

But I'd seen her in action, and I didn't for a moment believe she'd hold back if she thought that by going on the attack she could save the people of the horde—whether her actions endangered her or not.

From the looks on her brother's and husband's faces, I suspected they didn't believe it either.

The first group of scouts, those sent to spy on the Crimeans, galloped into the camp a few days later, howling and waving their banners with their usual high spirits. Once more, people ran out of the tents, their natural fears at the unexpected arrival of a troop of armed men dissolving into welcome as soon as they recognized the riders.

When the men appeared, I was again outside, a heavy bucket of water hauled from the nearby river in each hand.

Stepan pulled off the half-dozen leather-covered flasks I'd slung around his neck—I knew better than to trust him with open containers, because any bucket he carried shed half its load between river and tent—and dropped them at my feet as soon as he caught a good glimpse of the advancing horsemen. He set off at a run for the edge of the camp, but I called him back and insisted that he take the flasks home before releasing him to join his friends.

Most of the incoming warriors had dismounted by then to greet their families, so I thought it unlikely that Stepan could get himself trampled in the milling throng. But I placed my buckets to one side until I could be sure he was safe. After a short while, I saw Ruslan Sultan, a mail shirt over his robes, a sword belted around his waist, and his steel-tipped helmet already stashed under one arm. He marched into the center of the crowd, which opened to let him through, then closed behind him.

The eight or so riders who had not dismounted formed a tight circle. As they walked their horses past me, heading toward the big tent at the end of the row, I saw a stranger in their midst, a man who from his coloring and build could only be Russian.

Broad-shouldered and compact, with a square jaw, light brown hair that seemed long for a fighting man, and a beard grown somewhat straggly, this ninth rider reminded me of my man Stenka. Only in terms of his coloring and build, though: his blue eyes had a spark of intelligence I'd never noticed in Stenka, who'd been loving and steady but not quick in word or thought, however swift in defense or attack. The mobility of this man's face, his rapid changes of expression, supported that first impression.

The newcomer wore clothes typical of a junior servitor, better in quality than anything Stenka once possessed—a light wool coat in a color close to turquoise, with green brocade strips around the sleeves and hem and bright brass buttons holding the coat tight against his chest. It must be hot in the August sunshine, yet he showed no signs of discomfort. Tanned leather trousers in a pale brown contrasted with his dark blue leggings and leather boots. A pouch, also leather, hung from his belt.

At first I thought he might be a man-at-arms, like Stenka but of higher social standing. I saw no sign of armor or weapons, though, not so much as an eating knife. From the way the Tatar warriors circled him, I guessed he must be a captive.

One of the missing envoys?

I picked up my pair of buckets and walked as fast as I could without splashing. Once I had them safely deposited in my tent—a good distance from the door lest Stepan kick them by accident on entry—I donned my shaman's robe. This time I didn't wait for an invitation. I headed straight for the meeting tent.

As I'd half expected, I found Nasan already there. Firuza sat on her right as before, her older daughter on her lap. A pretty, rosy-cheeked, happy little girl of seven, with dark hair as curly and unruly as Stepan's blond mop, Altan-Alia wriggled in her mother's hold. One of the first to catch diphtheria, she'd also been one of the first to recover, and I still rejoiced whenever I saw her that her parents had not suffered a double—or quadruple—tragedy.

I turned my attention to the men. Ogodai stood in the center of the tent, Daniil at his right. Timur watched from a corner of the khan's platform. The Russian whose unexpected arrival had brought me here in search of news faced Ogodai and Daniil, with a Tatar warrior gripping each of his arms. Definitely a captive.

As one, leaders and guards dipped their heads toward me as I entered. Because I could see that they'd already begun their meeting, I decided to interrupt them as little as possible. I circled the tent once in the direction the sun takes throughout the day, chanting softly. To clear the air and discourage evil spirits, I waved the burner I carried, creating puffs of smoke redolent with sage. When I reached the women, I allowed Nasan to grab my hand and pull me down next to her, then placed the burner in front of my crossed legs, where it continued to emit whiffs of sage.

As I took my seat, I saw the Russian swivel his head in my direction. He studied me, his eyes wide and his brows contracted. Was he confused by the sight of my ritual dress, which must appear strange to him? By my pink skin, light brown hair, and blue eyes? Either way, he looked straight at me, and when I returned his gaze, his lips curved into a smile.

What was this? I couldn't remember the last time a man looked at me in that assessing way, as if he found me attractive. Men called me pretty once upon a time, but only Stenka had said that since my pregnancy began to show so many years ago. The steppe warriors saw me as bland, my fair coloring as washed out. The Russians thought me too old at twenty-six. And both groups feared entanglement with someone who had access to other worlds. But this captive regarded me differently. A flicker of interest warmed my chest, and I glanced away, sure that a flush stained my cheeks.

"Pay attention," Ogodai said in a harsh voice. He spoke Tatar, and shocked at this sudden change of tone, I snapped my head to face him. Was he talking to me?

No. He'd fixed his intense gaze on the Russian, who stared back with equal intensity.

At least the captive was no longer looking at me. I blew a soft, silent breath through my lips. Next to me, Nasan wrinkled her nose like a hound picking up a scent, and when I glanced her way she gave me a conspiratorial smile. I guessed she'd witnessed the Russian's reaction and drawn conclusions similar to my own, but it wasn't the right time to ask her what she made of the whole exchange.

In front of the group that held the captive, a man I recognized as the head of the scouting expedition was in mid-report. "The Crimeans are coming by the thousands, Khan," the scout said in Tatar. "Perhaps the tens of thousands. They are spread out across the steppe."

Thousands, even tens of thousands. I tried to stretch my mind to imagine the grasslands covered with warriors, to think how it must feel to look down from town walls and see them racing toward you, howling and waving their weapons—to know they wanted nothing more than your capture and death.

I shuddered. We didn't even have walls to stand in their way. The Crimeans could slash through our tents with their swords, run us through or haul us off before we had a chance to resist. Who could stand against tens of thousands of warriors?

The scout was still talking. "Everywhere we looked we saw horses, most with men sleeping next to them. A few tents for the leaders. One of those had a larger-than-usual guard but wasn't fancy like the tent of a khan or sultan, even a bey or prince. We kept an eye on it for a while, and no one went in or out. So we raided it not long after sunset and found two men, tied up." He indicated the Russian with a jerk of his head, and the Russian flinched, as if he hadn't understood the scout's words.

That surprised me a little: wouldn't an envoy to the Tatars have learned the language?

"I see only one," Ogodai said. "What happened to the other?"

"His captors killed him. We took this man and fled. They chased us, but we lost them in the dark. Once we were sure they couldn't see us, we swam the horses across the Don and hid in the hills that line the bank on this side." The head scout looked apprehensive, although I couldn't imagine why. Was he expecting a rebuke for losing the second envoy?

That seemed unlikely. On the whole, Ogodai impressed me with his cool head; even his occasional performance as the powerful, raging ruler was deliberate. Only on the day Sibai died had I seen the khan lose control, and then he'd reestablished it by the next morning.

"Good work," Ogodai told the scout, and the man relaxed. "Leave these two guards here. I release the rest of you to spend time with your families. But first ask Ruslan Sultan to join us and to bring four warriors who didn't ride with the scouts. And have the women prepare a tent where your prisoner can remain under guard until we decide what to do with him. He'll need food, water, bedding, the usual."

As soon as the head scout and his comrades left, Ogodai addressed the prisoner. "Do you speak Tatar?" he asked in that language, his tone uncharacteristically harsh.

"Not so well as I'd thought," the man said. He seemed faintly embarrassed by his admission, his smile rueful. His Russian accent made the words hard to decipher, even for me—never mind that only a few years ago I'd found myself in the same position. "If you speak slowly, I will understand some. And talking is difficult."

Ogodai nodded in response and gestured to Daniil, who came forward and addressed the captive in his native tongue. "What's your name?"

Hmm. I wrinkled my brows. Ogodai had used nothing but Tatar this morning, but I knew he didn't need an interpreter. Like the rest of his family, he spoke Russian as if born to it. Not around the camp so much, but I'd watched him switch languages mid-sentence often enough to swear to his comfort in both. So why hide his fluency here?

"Well?" Daniil said when the Russian didn't answer. "Did the Crimeans take your tongue?"

"Sorry, Lord." The man managed a sketchy bow, despite the hands that gripped his arms. "They call me Anfim Fadeyev. I serve the grand prince as a junior clerk in the Foreign Office. The man the Crimeans killed was my superior. We were traveling south to deliver the grand prince's message of friendship to Sahib-Girei Khan when those bandits surrounded us." He sounded bitter, and I didn't blame him for that, although his use of the word "bandit" made me wince.

"And your companions?" Daniil asked. "What happened to them?" He relaxed his pose, which had been threatening in the extreme, and gave an encouraging nod.

"They split us up, Lord," Fadeyev said. "I don't know where they took the others. The Tatars said they'd send the whole lot of us down to Crimea, and the khan would negotiate our ransom from there. If our relatives didn't pay, they'd sell us as slaves."

More stories I'd heard as a girl. I experienced a certain sympathy for Anfim Fadeyev, with his outward resemblance to my Stenka. Could the grandmothers have sent him in response to my plea for a man as gentle and reliable as the one I'd lost?

An absurd question. I had no reason to believe this Anfim had any redeeming qualities. He might be a philanderer, a drunkard, a gambler, or any combination thereof.

If nothing else, he was almost certainly married. Fadeyev must be thirty or close to it, from the looks of him—old enough to have wed several times by now. Unless he'd already outlived the three spouses the Church allowed, he must have a wife in Russia.

At moments he struck me as quite appealing—ready to acknowledge a weakness or a fault as few men did. I sensed anxiety too, and that was easy to understand, but he controlled it well.

And he'd noticed me. My presence there surprised him, yet he smiled. That flicker of interest warmed my insides once more.

Fadeyev hesitated, then squared his shoulders, still looking at Daniil. "Might I learn your name, Lord, and what you're doing here among the barbarians?"

So much for controlling his anxiety—or perhaps distaste was a better word.

Nasan hissed in response. I hissed myself, and again Fadeyev twisted his neck to stare at me. I wondered what he'd conclude from Ogodai's and Daniil's matching scowls, which made them look like twins—one dark, the other fair.

So much for the pretense that Ogodai couldn't understand Russian. By the time Fadeyev turned back to them, though, Ogodai's shuttered face revealed no hint of anger.

"Daniil Nikolaevich Kolychev," Daniil said, snapping off each element of the three-part name that proclaimed his noble status. "My reasons for living here don't concern you. But if I were you, I'd show greater courtesy to my hosts. We aren't the ones who captured you, but we'll decide whether to let you go. And when."

"Apologies, Lord." Fadeyev repeated his sketchy bow. "I remember the boyar your father from his time as tutor to the grand prince—and earlier, during his service in the west. I've heard your name, too, although we never met."

Daniil acknowledged this with a curt nod. Anger still flashed in his brown eyes. "This is Ogodai Khan." He gestured at the khan, who stared unmoving at Fadeyev, then indicated Timur and us women. "His nephew Prince Timur; his chief wife, Firuza Khatun; his sister and my wife, Nasan Khanim; and our spiritual mother, Grusha."

"Spiritual mother?" Fadeyev jerked his head in my direction once more. "If she's an abbess, where's her cowl?"

No one answered his question. Certainly not me. By then I'd realized Ogodai and Daniil must have concocted some plan to keep their prisoner on edge while they figured out what to make of him. If they wanted him to know what they meant by "spiritual mother," they'd tell him.

But no one spoke. While Fadeyev stared at me through narrowed eyes, as if he could untangle his confusion by the power of his gaze, Ruslan came through the door. All heads turned in his direction.

Without missing a beat, Daniil continued his introductions. "Ruslan Sultan. Half-brother to Sahib-Girei

Khan of Crimea. And every last one of them has had a better education than you have, so mind your manners and watch whom you call a barbarian. I can assure you, you'll have a much better time here if you do."

Fadeyev tipped his head and murmured another apology. Daniil turned his attention to Ruslan. "Are your men ready for him?" he asked in Tatar.

Ruslan raised his brows at the switch of language, since his fluency in Russian matched Ogodai's, but he answered in the same tongue. "Yes, I have a watch set up. It's the tent next to the shaman's." He bowed in my direction. "Apologies, but that's the location least disruptive to the other families. Tell your son to keep his distance, please."

"Absolutely," I said, pondering how best to impress on Stepan the necessity for obedience, although past experience warned me that he was less likely to break the rules than to forget them.

"I'll warn Irek." Firuza sent me a sympathetic glance, as did Nasan.

"And I'll remind Borya," Daniil said, still speaking Tatar and looking straight at his wife. "Can you arrange some kind of oversight with the other mothers, love?" He was a realist, Daniil. "There are too many boys humming with energy in this camp."

Altan-Alia squirmed in Firuza's hold, and Daniil's stern expression relaxed into a grin. "Not to mention the girls," he added. "Better safe than sorry."

"We'll figure something out," Nasan promised. "The three of us, Guzel, Dina, the other wives and mothers, the older daughters—we've a small army to deploy. So let's deploy it."

Ogodai laughed, and Daniil, Ruslan, we women—even Timur—joined in. Only Anfim Fadeyev stared blankly at one laughing face after another until his wandering gaze reached me, where it stopped.

Again I saw that spark of attraction in his eyes, as well as something else I couldn't quite identify. Curiosity, perhaps, or calculation.

Without knowing why, I shivered. Why calculation? He didn't know me, anymore than I knew him, so what could he want from me?

I gave myself a mental shake. It must be curiosity. Him still trying to figure out what made me a spiritual mother, perhaps. Or more general wondering about my place in this horde. I was the only Russian woman present, and since the khan had introduced me as an equal, Fadeyev could probably guess that I was neither a slave, a captive, nor a concubine. I should get a grip on myself and stop making up stories about a man I had yet to exchange two sentences with.

Ruslan beckoned to the two men who gripped Fadeyev's arms, and together they strode toward the door, prodding their captive forward. They passed through, and I heard the voices of other warriors on the far side, no doubt surrounding Fadeyev and escorting him to the tent they'd designated as his prison.

Which stood right next to mine. Thinking of that odd, assessing gaze, I shivered once more.

What does he see when he looks at me? And more important, what do I want him to see?

Chapter Six

THE CAPTIVE ANFIM FADEYEV HAD NOT SPENT ONE WHOLE night among the horde before the second group of scouts came tearing into the camp, making a huge ruckus that woke me. So much noise, in fact, that you'd think the pig-snouted Erlik Khan himself chewed at their heels. The first call to prayer had yet to sound when I staggered out of the tent to see what caused the noise.

As I blinked in the cool gray light of dawn, Stepan joined me, rubbing his eyes with one hand and clinging to my skirts with the other. On every side, other members of the horde stood half-dressed and looking as befuddled as I felt. Nasan with Kolya in her arms; Daniil holding their daughter while keeping a firm hand on Borya's shoulder. Firuza and Ogodai, each gripping a twin; their baby held fast by the nurse. Ruslan with Mergen riding piggyback, Dina at their side. Guzel and Timur, the boy wearing a helmet that appeared out of place in combination with his crumpled linen shirt and loose trousers.

The tent next to mine at first showed no signs that anyone might be awake in there. As my head cleared, I stared at it, puzzled. Surely the prisoner couldn't have escaped overnight, or even during the furor caused by the returning scouts, who now clustered around the khan, all talking at once.

A tousled mop of hair poked out the door, and I recognized one of the guards assigned to watch Fadeyev yesterday. He ducked his head when he saw me. "Honored Shaman," he said. "What has happened?"

"The scouts sent to check on the Nogai returned." I grabbed Stepan, who'd recovered from being jerked out of sleep enough to make a dash for his friends, by the elbow. "I don't know what news they brought. Your captive is still inside?"

"Yes, Honored Shaman." The guard emerged from the tent, and I saw he was wearing full armor. I guessed he'd stayed awake throughout the night.

"You'd better go back then," I said. "I'll find out what's happened and let you know. They seem very excited, so something must have. Come, Stepan." I didn't wait for the guard's response, because Stepan was already tugging at my hand, but as I turned away, I saw the man duck under the door frame.

By the time I reached Dina, Nasan stood next to her while Ruslan went off, Mergen still clinging to his shoulders, to join the men. "Don't go far," I told Stepan as I released his hand. "Stay with Borya and Irek and their papas."

"Yes, Mama." He wriggled through the dispersing crowd.

Nasan's nurse arrived and took the baby from his mother's arms. "Good," Nasan said. "Now we can ask what's going on."

We pushed through the throng and found Firuza standing not far from the circle of men. She stopped us as we approached. "Get ready to move," she said. "Some of the Nogai camps the scouts checked contained only women and children, with a token force to protect them. We can assume the men are already heading north. Our scouts tracked a few raiding parties—nothing big, but they were coming this way, so my husband wants to take no chances. We'll move the tents southwest onto Azamat Bey's land, as close as we can get to the river. Once we're sure the Nogai have passed by and won't return for a while, we can start heading east, toward the fall pasturage, but it's not safe at the moment. We'd risk running into them as we cross the steppe. So pack up."

"How long do we have?" I ran through lists of household items in my head.

"A few hours," Firuza said. "The sooner we leave, the better. By noon, at the latest."

"I'll be ready." During migration it was good not to own much of value, and although I often received gifts in return for the rituals I performed, I kept only what Stepan and I needed to live on, plus a small reserve. I shared a herdsman with Guzel, and he would drive my sheep and goats to their new pastures.

I spared a moment of regret for the heavy buckets of water I'd carried and would have to empty unused. I'd need to roll and tie the bedding, check that my robes and shaman's tools were tucked away in their chest, pack our food, and look for clothing Stepan had tossed aside, but otherwise everything could go onto the cart without much work. The horde would take down the tents one by one, and as soon as they finished, we'd go.

I called to Stepan, who came running. "We're moving camp," I told him. "Come and collect your things."

He jumped up and down, clapping his hands. He loved the excitement of migration. "May I ride a pony, Mama? Please? Do say yes. I can manage. Promise!"

Azamat Bey's summer grazing lands adjoined our own. Getting to our destination wouldn't take two hours. And a cooperative Stepan was much more fun to deal with than a reluctant one.

But I'd learned the hard way not to promise a reward too soon. "Collect your things, my dove. Don't forget to pick up your clothes and drape them over Mama's chest. Then we'll ask Daniil if you can ride one of his ponies."

"Thank you, Mama. I'll be good as gold!" He dashed ahead, and I followed him, laughing at his eagerness. How adorable he was at this age: old enough to look after himself some of the time, but still loving and easy to direct. If I could, I'd keep him in this magical state forever.

Alas, I couldn't. He would grow up far too soon and move away from me into the world of men. He'd become a warrior, knowing nothing of his Russian heritage and caring less. As I reached the tent we shared and stripped it with the ease of six years' practice, I asked myself why I regretted that. What, in the end, had Russia done for me?

Yet I did regret it. Russia was part of me: the place where I'd grown up, where I'd loved and lost and loved again, then lost once more; the place of Stepan's birth and thus of my greatest joy. If my son knew nothing of it, could he ever understand me? Would he even want to?

Not until the men arrived to take apart my tent did I recall that I'd promised to tell the guards next door what to expect.

I knocked on the door, and after a pause, the same guard opened it. I'd forgotten his name and didn't want to ask—goodness knew I'd lived in the horde long enough to have no excuse for forgetting. I'd question Stepan later, but for the moment I gave the man the gist of what I'd learned from Firuza.

"What are our orders, Honored Shaman?" The guard pushed the door fully open, adding daylight to the lantern-lit interior. The gleam of a helmet drew my attention to the far side of the tent, where a second warrior sat next to a bound Anfim Fadeyev. Across the tent, his eyes met mine, and I again had that strange sensation of attraction mixed with wariness.

"We're migrating," I told the guard in Tatar. "To the southwest to escape the notice of any marauding Nogai raiders. The khan wants you to transport the prisoner, I assume, but why not run and ask?"

"Will you send someone to pack the felts, then? There's not much else: a few dishes, some bedding." The guard fidgeted, staring not at me but past me to where Ogodai and Ruslan stood, surrounded by a group of warriors. Most of the women and children had vanished from sight. I could already hear the snap of tent supports releasing from their smoke rings, the hubbub of camels objecting to loads, the clang of horse tack.

"I'll find someone," I said. "Go and talk with the khan first, so you know for sure what he wants from you. Just wait a minute while I fetch my son."

When he nodded, I ducked into my home, where Stepan was having a lovely time falling over the descending tent poles and jumping back and forth across the lattice frame. I called him. "Come here, Mischief. We're going next door."

He landed with a thud, and I groaned as a tent pole snapped under his feet. "Next door? Where the prisoner is?" He rushed toward me.

I caught him as he passed. "Yes, but you stay with me. This is important, and Ogodai Khan will be very angry if something you do leads to the prisoner escaping." With his hand in mine, I thanked the men working on my house and left. I couldn't help noticing the relief on their faces.

Back at the next-door tent, I didn't even have to knock. "Greetings, Akbars," Stepan said in Tatar as the guard appeared.

The name I hadn't remembered. It meant "white tiger." *Thank you, son*, I thought, imagining the guard as one of the tigers on my drum so I wouldn't forget again. "Hurry back," I told Akbars.

"As fast as possible, Honored Shaman," the guard said. "Meanwhile, could you explain to the prisoner what's happening, since you speak his alien tongue?"

That tinge of regret flicked at me again. My parents' tongue was not alien to me.

I wasted no time in arguing. Stepan was already pushing past me, eager to see the mysterious prisoner. I agreed to explain, then bent my head and followed my son inside.

A brief exchange with the other guard, and I turned to greet Anfim Fadeyev. Although I again saw the flicker of curiosity in his eyes, his face showed no change of expression when I greeted him in Russian. Stepan stood stock still and silent, his gray eyes wide as he stared at the prisoner.

I didn't have time to ponder this odd behavior before Fadeyev spoke.

"Our spiritual mother, Grusha," he said in a cool voice that only hinted at the bristling anger I saw in the tight set of his shoulders, the grip of his clasped hands. "A pleasure to make your acquaintance. And how, pray tell, does a good Russian girl become spiritual mother to the heathens?"

Not liking his tone, I chose not to answer the question. "That's a long story, and we don't have time for it at the moment. This camp is moving. Your guard asked me to explain to you what will happen. We'll pack up the goods. The guards will get you onto a horse while other members of the horde take down the tent and secure it for the journey. Your hands will remain tied, and the guards will take charge of your reins. They mean you no harm, so don't fight them. We'll reach our destination before suppertime."

"No harm!" He raised his bound wrists to chest height and shook them at me. "Then why don't they free me? Is your khan holding me for ransom too?"

"Don't be absurd. They're worried you'll try to run and endanger us as well as yourself." I didn't know this for a fact, but it seemed as good an explanation as any, and one that might calm him. "An unknown number of Nogai raiders are heading north, and we're getting out of their direct line of advance. To protect our people, our grazing lands, our flocks—and you. Even after we move, the camp will be on a war footing until the raiders pass by. So I expect the khan will confine you for a while, but if he does free you, you'd be mad to try to leave."

In my annoyance, I'd stopped paying attention to my son, but as I crossed my arms over my chest and glared at the uncooperative prisoner, Stepan pushed forward to stand at my side. "Are you my papa?" he demanded in Russian. "Because I won't have a papa who's mean to my mama. You were nice to her before!"

Fadeyev blinked, and now it was my turn to stare. Did Stepan recall that day in the otherworldly cabin? Had he seen the similarity between his father and Fadeyev? Or was this a guess based on the man's Russian appearance and speech?

"He's not your papa," I told Stepan when I could speak. Like him, I used Russian so that Fadeyev would understand that we kept no secrets from him. "You know Ogodai Khan wouldn't tie up your papa. This is Anfim Fadeyev, and he's angry because he doesn't like being cooped up anymore than you do."

I stared hard at the prisoner, warning him not to contradict me. He didn't. Instead, he looked at Stepan, then at me, and his stony expression relaxed into something closer to pleasant. I saw his lips twitch, as if being compared to a bored six-year-old amused him.

"Yes," he said. "Your mama's right. I'd rather be free than stay tied up." He glanced my way. "I'm sorry I took it out on you. I understand you're trying to help."

Stepan paid no attention to either the change of tone or the apology. "Well, I don't like him." He scowled at Fadeyev. "I'm glad you're not my papa."

Fadeyev's flash of amusement disappeared. "Brat," he said. "What makes you think I'd want to be?"

"Stop it," I told the prisoner. "He's a child. You should know better. And Stepan, say you're sorry. You had no reason to be rude."

Stepan looked daggers at me, but after a while he mumbled an apology. Fadeyev nodded an acknowledgment, and the moment passed. After a while, he asked again whether the horde was holding him for ransom.

I watched him, searching for a trace of the humor that had so briefly lit his face—hinting at wit, kindness, even charm—but he hunched over and refused to meet my eyes. He resembled nothing so much as a tortoise pulled into its shell, and I sighed. Perhaps I'd imagined his interest. Or perhaps it hadn't survived his realization that I had a child.

"I don't make that decision," I said, referring to his question about the ransom. "Ask the khan. But didn't you say you worked as a junior clerk? Daniil Nikolaevich knows your family can't afford ransom. So rejoice that you aren't destined for the slave markets, and let your guards do their job. They're trying to protect you. The khan will let you go when the time comes, and not one moment before."

I heard the welcome clatter of the first guard returning. "Let's go, Stepan," I said. "Akbars is back." I reached for my son's hand.

"Thank you for your assistance, Honored Shaman," the second guard said in Tatar.

"Shaman?" Fadeyev asked. "Does he mean you? How so?"

I studied him, wondering how best to answer. What *was* the odd note I heard in his voice? Not anger this time, I thought, but fear. He worked with Tatar envoys in the Foreign Office—had minimal training in how to speak their tongue, even if it hadn't prepared him for the onslaught of everyday speech—so he must have heard the word "shaman." Surely he could guess what Akbars meant by addressing me in that way.

Maybe he didn't want to believe it. Anfim Fadeyev wouldn't be the first man repelled by a woman with the ability to communicate with spirits.

"Because my mama *is* the shaman, silly," Stepan said when I failed to respond. "What else would you call her?"

"*That's* what they mean by their spiritual mother? A sorceress? A pagan? Mother of God!" Fadeyev crossed himself three times, then made the sign used to avert the Evil Eye.

As I watched him, stunned into silence, a lump formed in my throat. All those times I'd yearned to return to my homeland, and here I saw in full color how that homeland would judge me. And for a few heedless moments, I'd thought I might like him. That could never be.

I took my son's hand, jerked my chin at the prisoner, said my farewells to the two guards, and left. "I'll send someone to help you," I told Akbars, remembering my promise as I reached the door. And I did, grabbing the first pair of youths I saw big enough to maneuver the heavy felts and not otherwise occupied.

If everything went as planned, I would never exchange two words with Fadeyev again. And from his reaction to learning my true position in the camp, I thought he'd be just as glad if I didn't.

While Stepan and I talked with Fadeyev, the men of the horde had completed their dismantling of my tent and moved on to the next. With my son in tow, I went to find out if any of my friends needed help. I steadied a chest while Guzel strapped it to her cart, then moved on to see how Nasan was managing. She had more servants than Guzel and I did, and I realized the moment I walked in that with so much assistance she'd already completed most of her preparations. I found her filling a cleverly designed box that contained compartments for her medical supplies. A pile of about half a dozen books sat next to the box. I'd seen the covers often enough during the diphtheria outbreak to recognize them as her treasured copies of Dioscorides' herbal and similar tomes.

My son said not a word the whole time, behavior so unusual for him that I wondered if he'd fallen sick again. When I asked, though, he denied any aches and pains. And when Daniil agreed to my request to lend us a pony, Stepan's high spirits returned with a bang. I had to catch him by the shoulder to prevent him from racing off right then.

"Borya and Irek are riding as well." Daniil patted my son's head. "You stay with me and the khan, though. Understood? Prince Timur will come with us too. Go to the corral, and Timur will show you which horse is yours. Tell him I sent you. You can help his man with the stirrups and the reins."

Stepan agreed with enthusiasm and ran off. "He forgot to thank you," I said. "Let me do it for him."

"No need," Daniil replied. "My son's no better when it comes to remembering his manners. Stepan looked a bit down, though, when you arrived. Did he think I'd say no?"

I shook my head. "We went to see the prisoner. At the guards' request, so I could explain in Russian about the move. He was cold to me at first, and Stepan got angry with him, but I think it was more than that."

I assumed Nasan had already told Daniil about the trance where I met Stepan and Stenka in the Russian forest, so I saw no need to repeat the story even if the horde hadn't been busy packing up. But I should say something. "He's started to wonder why he doesn't have a papa like the other boys. He asked Fadeyev right out if Fadeyev was his father. Because we spoke Russian? I don't know. I've explained that his papa died before he was born, but he doesn't understand what that means."

Daniil flicked the tip of the riding whip he held against the nearest rolled-up tent frame. "That's tough. Can't be much fun for you, either." He gave me the smile

I'd once loved. "We'll take care of him, you know. He's a good boy, and he'll make a fine warrior one day. Tell him he doesn't need a papa of his own. He can share Borya's and Irek's and Mergen's papas. All the fun and none of the annoyances."

I laughed and thanked him and went on my way, but I had no intention of telling Stepan anything of the sort. He wouldn't believe me, for one thing, and for another? Well, my skills as a shaman might terrify Anfim Fadeyev, but he wasn't the only man in the world. When the right one came along, I would be ready.

As I'd promised Fadeyev, the horde reached its new location and raised its tents once more in time for supper. At Guzel's suggestion, I had the men place my dwelling between her tent and Ruslan's, opposite Daniil's home and not far from the khan's. As she pointed out, Stepan spent so much time with one of their four families that it made no sense for us to live on the outskirts of the camp only because Suzukei had preferred that location. And as a woman alone, I liked the idea of having warriors around me.

As I settled my son for the night, I recalled his odd question that morning. "Why did you ask Anfim Fadeyev if he was your papa, darling? Was it because he speaks Russian? He's not someone Mama knows."

Stepan rubbed his forehead with his sleeve, his favorite gesture when bewildered or troubled. "When I was sick, I saw my papa. Don't you remember? We were there in the wooden house, and you got mad at him because he died. He looked a bit like the tied-up man, but he wasn't mean." He sniffled, and I saw a tear slide down his cheek.

"He said he'd always love me, but he couldn't live with us because he didn't have a body. I thought he'd found one."

He sounded doleful. "Oh my dove," I said. "I'm sorry, but that can't happen. Once people are dead, they stay dead. We can see Papa when we're sleeping, but not in real life."

Stepan sniffled and didn't answer. I murmured reassurances as I wrapped my arms around him and held him tight, treasuring the tickle of his soft curls against my chin and the solidity of his body against mine.

At the same time, I wondered. I'd never quite known how to interpret my soul journeys. When I lived with the Kolychevs, their chaplain told us about saints who flew to Jerusalem overnight, visits from the Holy Mother in dreams, monks tempted by demons. Haji Rahman had similar tales. He and the other Muslims talked of jinns and ifrits, and they too revered saints. Suzukei taught that the other worlds existed in their own spheres, as real as the lands experienced through our senses, and that we could reach them through trance. I was not a saint, but I had entered many trances. I had seen the effects of my journeys in *this* world. I had to believe in the power of the realms beyond our own.

And yet ... my Stepan was the first person ever to report sharing a vision of mine. As I sang him into sleep, I puzzled over that. He could have heard me talking to Guzel before I knew he was awake. Maybe he only thought he'd seen the Russian hut himself. Or perhaps his third soul did know that I'd gone after him and, thanks to the intervention of my guardian spirits, brought him home.

Shamanism runs in families, and he is my son.

More than any other possibility, that one gave me pause. If Stepan turned out to be a shaman too, I couldn't take him to Russia. Anfim Fadeyev's reaction left no doubt that my son and I would be shunned if we went home.

Stepan would prefer to stay in the horde, I suspected, but I? I was not so sure.

I loved the camp, the people in it, the generosity of its khan and khatun, who had welcomed my child and me into their midst. I loved my son and the life we lived here. I loved the steppe, even as a tiny part of me yearned for the forest scene I'd experienced in the other realm, for the past and Stenka, for the familiarity of the home that I'd left so long ago. In a horde that migrated twice a year, I remained a permanent outsider, the distance between my conflicting worlds wider even than theirs.

At that moment it felt like a bitter choice: never to see my homeland again, or to give up the person I'd become to return there. To sacrifice my son's future, if it turned out that the spirits had chosen him as well, or his heritage if they had not.

But it was too soon to tell what Stepan would one day become. Maybe he'd just heard me talking with Guzel and thought it was real.

Chapter Seven

THE NOGAI RAIDERS PASSED US BY, OVERWHELMING THE grasslands of our previous camp before moving on. A few sheep and goats eluded their herders on the drive south and disappeared, no doubt to fill the bellies of hungry warriors. My small flock arrived intact—fortunately, as I had no animals to spare. Ogodai set up a permanent guard at our new location and sent scouts to keep an eye on the invaders.

The day after we completed the move, the khan summoned me to a brief discussion that included Daniil and Ruslan. Afterwards, I visited Guzel. "The leaders want us to figure out how to protect the women and children in an emergency," I told her as soon as we completed our greetings. "For the moment, the Nogai are heading north, but suppose they circle back? We need a plan. I think we should come up with ways to occupy the boys and girls as well while we're waiting to find out what's going on. We have to keep them out of trouble, and we can't leave that job to their parents, because so many of the mothers and fathers are preparing to defend the camp. Nasan, for example, has her hands full with that group she's putting together."

"She certainly does." Guzel aimed a pretend arrow at the hearth fire, where embers smoldered under a hanging pot. Wisps of meat-scented steam rose from the simmering stew within. "She stopped by this morning to convince me to join her women's defense force. I had to prove to her that even though I learned to ride before I could walk, like everyone else here, I can't shoot straight to save my life." She relaxed long enough to send me a wicked grin. "Let me guess, she let you off the hook because she assumes that a Russian woman is hopeless with a bow."

"Worse. I'm hopeless with a horse," I said. "Warriors can't ride pillion into battle."

"So you're safe." Guzel stirred her bubbling pot. "Who's she recruited then?"

"Firuza will fight." I spoke slowly, struggling to remember what Nasan had told me about each woman in the camp. "Dina, too. They both ride as if they're one with their mounts. And they know how to handle a bow, although neither can shoot from horseback as well as Nasan."

"No one can," Guzel said. "None of the women, I mean. The khan and Daniil and Ruslan—they're on another level altogether. It's a pleasure just to watch them practice. Yes, Firuza and Dina will fight." She counted off a dozen others likely to join Nasan's defense force, and I added a few more names. Last I'd heard, the camp contained about sixty women between fifteen and old age. It sounded as if Nasan had recruited a good half of them, if not more.

"So who's left to keep an eye on the children?" Guzel asked after a while.

"You and I can supervise." I scrunched up my nose as reality hit me. "Otherwise it's concubines and servants."

Guzel dropped the wooden spoon she'd used to stir the stew. I'd seldom seen her so surprised. "The old bey's concubines?" she asked. "You must be joking. Most of them are ancient."

"And the rest spend their time sulking about Ogodai paying them no heed because he loves his wife," I added, laughing. "He keeps the whole lot of them in food, though, so let's tell the younger ones they owe it to the horde to help us out in these difficult days. We can ask the mothers of the old bey's children to take the lead. There are three of them in the harem, two with sons. I'm sure they want to get the boys out of their hair as much as any of us do."

"Yes, good idea."

I picked up the spoon, dunked a cloth in a nearby bucket of water, rinsed off the ashes that clung to the wood, and handed the utensil back to her. I waved away her mumbled thanks. "The nursemaids can help too. It's their job. That should give us around twenty, concubines and servants combined, and the older girls in the camp can assist them. So if we tell the harem mothers to split them into groups of five women with a couple of girls each, we'll have most of the day covered without anyone becoming exhausted."

As I'd guessed, the three mothers in the harem were happy to agree to any plan that gave their sons and daughter a steady stream of tasks to fill their days. Guzel and I had soon mobilized our force of twenty in the same way the khan deployed his troops. While Nasan drilled her hand-picked fighters, the mothers organized games and races, pressed every pony the warriors could spare into service, and sent the bigger children out with the herders, because monitoring sheep, goats, and the occasional cow was a task well suited to their skills as well as one they needed to learn.

Meanwhile, Guzel and I drew up plans for getting the children to safety if the raiders changed direction and again headed our way. The horrors of the diphtheria epidemic meant that most of the surviving youngsters were over six, and we could assign older girls and boys like Timur to watch over those aged seven to nine, freeing the mothers and nurses to focus on the littlest ones.

While Guzel took notes and drew maps, I kept long lists in my head of supplies. How many families could fit in a tent? How much food would we need, and of what type? How much clothing? Adults could get by with one set in an emergency, but rambunctious boys and girls needed extra shirts and trousers, or at least fabric, needles, and threads so that the women could sew patches as necessary.

And what of the animals? We couldn't drive them into the steppe. We'd lose them. We'd have to find more pasturage. That problem we handed over to the herders, who had a better sense of the terrain. But everything else, except for the defense force that Nasan had under her control, remained our responsibility.

With luck, we would never have to put the plans into operation. But if the worst happened, we were prepared.

As the Nogai raiders continued their ride northwest—to join the Crimean forces, Ogodai and the other leaders concluded—Nasan released her riders from all-day practice sessions, announcing that short daily drills would serve now that they had demonstrated the skills needed to defend themselves and the rest of us women and children if the men were called away. Life edged back toward normal, although the horde remained watchful.

A few days later, I approached my tent from the south. Stepan ran and jumped at my side. The morning had provided a lovely release from the ever-present sense of danger. We'd checked on our flock of sheep and goats, a task my son loved because he could practice counting. He shouted out a number with each leap—"nine, ten, four!"— as if still tracking animals.

I laughed as I watched him, because the sheep and goats thought of nothing but fresh grass and refused to stand still while he moved among them, so his jumping provided at least as accurate a count as the one he'd made an hour ago when the flock left the corral for the steppe. Or, rather, the one he might have made if he could get the numbers right, a detail that at six he hadn't quite mastered. But the herdsman knew his business and taught Stepan a little more each time we visited. And it was the perfect day for a walk: warm but not yet too hot for comfort, with enough billowing clouds to keep the power of the sun in check.

The usual mob of boys dashed past as we reached the edge of the camp, Irek and Borya in the lead and one of the mothers in pursuit. She looked rather haggard despite the early hour, and I sent her a sympathetic glance that she seemed too preoccupied to notice. I could guess how tired she felt, and day had barely dawned.

Stepan stopped jumping about and turned pleading eyes to me. "May I go with them, Mama?"

"Yes, but come back in time for dinner," I said.

"I will." He started to run after them, then skidded to a halt. "Look, it's the mean man. He's not tied up."

I followed the direction of his pointing finger with my eyes. "So it is." Ahead of us, Anfim Fadeyev lounged with his elbows propped against the wooden slats that at night contained the horses. The herders had driven the mounts not commandeered by warriors out to the steppe to graze alongside the other animals, so the corral stood empty except for a foal or two in need of special care. How had Fadeyev persuaded the khan to free him? Should I assume the leaders no longer considered him a threat?

I gave my son a gentle shove. "Go and play, Stepan. Anfim Fadeyev won't hurt me."

For a boy so young, Stepan could at times assume quite an imposing stance. He did so now, pulling himself up until he looked like a half-sized version of his father. "Are you sure, Mama? He wasn't nice to you before."

"I'm sure," I said. "He was scared and angry then. I'm sure he feels better now that Ogodai Khan has freed him. Off you go." He ran after his friends, but I noticed that he stared hard at Fadeyev as he went by. The man smiled at my son as he passed. Stepan stopped, his eyes wide, and smiled shyly in return before dashing off once more. Fadeyev ambled toward me.

Watching him approach, I tried to judge his mood. Despite the smile and my assurances to Stepan, my mixed experience with Fadeyev the last time we met gave me pause. Something he'd said or done had caused Ogodai, whose judgment I respected, to release Fadeyev from his bonds, but I didn't know the terms under which that change had taken place. Nor did I have reason to believe that Fadeyev had had second thoughts about my "sorcery," as he called it.

Although he looked good-natured enough at the moment. I'd urged Stepan to give him a chance. I could hardly refuse to do the same.

But let him prove himself worthy of it first. So as a test, when Fadeyev came close enough to hear me, I asked the question at the top of my mind. "Why did the khan free you, and when?"

"Yesterday eve." Fadeyev stopped a few foot lengths from me and tucked his thumbs in the sash that bound his coat. "Because I swore I'd not try to escape. Why would I? Crimeans on one side, Nogai between me and the place I want to reach—I've no wish to be captured a third time. One day my luck will run out and I'll end up dead. So I'll stay here until the crisis ends and the khan tells me it's safe to go."

He kept his voice level, despite my challenging tone. I warmed toward him, although my suspicions lingered. Perhaps he *had* just given into his demons that day in the tent.

I saw his brow crease. "Turns out your khan does speak our language. Like a native, in fact. He doesn't need that blond Russian to talk for him. Why did he pretend otherwise?"

"I don't know," I said. "If that's what you wanted to ask me, I'll be on my way." I started off down the path.

"It's not." He bowed, and I stopped. "I came to apologize. I was angry the last time we met. I didn't know what to expect, and that unsettled me. I said things I didn't mean—about you *and* your son."

I hadn't expected an apology, especially such a generous one. The surprise, and the appealing twinkle in his eyes, pushed me farther along the road to forgiving him. He sounded sincere, too.

"Thank you," I said. "I appreciate that." And I did. Yet I couldn't forget his violent reaction to the discovery that I was the camp shaman. The memory of the disgust on his face when he called me a sorceress still stung.

He dipped his head toward me. "Then will you let me show you I can do better? Few people here speak Russian. Let me not make enemies of those who do."

The bright sunshine revealed reddish highlights in his light brown hair and beard, both trimmed since I last saw him. Without the rigid posture, the tight set to his mouth, and the glare he'd bestowed on me before, his appearance was as pleasing as I'd expected. I sensed that he *did* regret what he'd said to me that first day, and his expression when he delivered his apology, like a puppy caught playing with a boot, touched me. When he smiled, his eyes lit up and his face crinkled in a way that appealed to me. It had been a long time since a man, especially a Russian man, had shown such an interest in me.

If I did want to go home someday, I could do worse than cultivate a person like Fadeyev, who could act as a suitable escort even if the existence of a wife and children and the difference in our social standing ruled out any closer relationship between us. No harm could result from asking him a few questions. And who knew when I'd get another chance?

So long as we remained outside, in public view among the rows of tents, we could stroll and chat without risk. "Very well," I said. "Shall we walk?"

In response, he extended his arm, crooked at the elbow. I placed my fingertips on his forearm, and we set off. The sensation of bunched muscles under my hand, like his general appearance, reminded me of long-ago strolls with Stenka. The sound of my native tongue caressed my ears like a breath of home. Each pure, liquid vowel eased my spirit like fingertips rubbing the tension from my shoulders.

"Tell me about your life in Russia," I said, to get him talking. To *hear* him talking in my native tongue. It was like listening to music. "You're a junior clerk, you said. For the Foreign Office. In Moscow?"

"In Moscow, yes. I live near the Convent of the Virgin's Nativity. Not far from the outer walls. Do you know the city?" He regarded me with warmth in his eyes, calling forth an answering warmth in me.

I blushed. For a moment, I reacted like the girl I'd been when I lived in Moscow eight years ago. A silly girl, in love with a man who, however passionate and charming, saw her first and foremost as a convenience. I hadn't realized that at the time, but in the end Daniil left me with no choice but to face the truth.

I gave myself a mental shake and shoved my memories back where they belonged. I'd left that girl behind long ago, and a good thing too. "Quite well," I said, my voice cool to counteract the heat in my cheeks. "Do you have relatives there? They must wonder what happened to you."

"Yes, I have family in Moscow." He gazed steadily at me, as if doing so would reveal what caused my blush. Or as if he couldn't take his eyes off me. I returned his gaze, not responding in kind but curious. "I don't know if enough time has passed for them to wonder. It's a long journey to Crimea. They won't be expecting word from me yet. But I worry about them. An elderly father and two children, a girl your son's age and a boy less than half that. Their mother died a few months ago, birthing a second son. The child followed her to Heaven a day later."

"May you have life," I said. The standard greeting to someone in mourning. My lingering suspicions dissolved in sympathy. And, I had to confess, relief. If he was a widower, his interest in me was easier to understand. Something I could consider without imagining that in doing so I threatened another woman's happiness.

"Had you been married long?" I asked. At least seven years, from the sound of it. That seemed a long time to me. Stenka and I had been together for less than two.

Poor Fadeyev. To watch his wife and son die, be forced to abandon his children for work, then endure captivity— so much misfortune in just a few months! Was it any surprise if he sometimes gave way to anger or fear?

"Eleven years." He sighed. "She was seventeen, and I nineteen, when our fathers arranged the match. We lost two boys almost right away. Then she had the daughter and son that lived. But this last time was difficult from the beginning."

"You miss her." The sadness I heard in his voice touched my heart. I tightened my fingers on his arm, expressing my sympathy. "I remember how it felt when Stepan's father died. I was devastated for months."

I bit my lip. I hadn't meant to reveal anything so personal. My tongue had run away with me. Because I understood how grief could sneak up on you when you were least expecting it, especially at first. At times, it ambushed me even now. But not as it had in the early days, when I'd walked around in a haze of sorrow, trapped in a cloud where only Stepan's constant need for care and attention tethered me to earth, my life cradled in the palms of a child too young to understand how he centered me with every anguished wail and contented coo. The thought of loving another man had seemed impossible then.

"You know what it's like," Fadeyev said, staring straight ahead.

I wondered if he would walk through the doorway I'd opened and ask me about Stenka's death, but caught up in his own past, he didn't.

I chastised myself for inconsistency. Did I want him to pepper me with questions? I'd already said more than I'd intended, and for no better reason than because I spoke, for once, in my own language and to a fellow countryman, someone raised according to familiar rules and principles. People in mourning were often self-centered. I had been, so how could I hold it against Fadeyev if he was too?

"She was a good woman, my Fevronia," he said, still gazing at the horizon, visible through the space that separated the last pair of tents. He spoke with the same even tone he must use at work, reading the lists of titles and place names that went into his documents. "A good wife. Obedient, even-tempered, chaste. Fair but firm in disciplining the children and the servants. I miss her, it's true." He turned his head then, looking at me. "But I'm also seeking another who can fill her place. Children need a mother, and households need a mistress."

I stared at him, stunned to hear my own vague longing for a companion made real. Another who can fill her place? After a few *months*? What kind of missing someone was that?

And that list, as if his wife had been a living version of the biblical passage Lady Natalya quoted at us servants whenever we displeased her. Had his wife never spoken a harsh word or made a face at him behind his back? She must have been a saint!

Then I saw how Fadeyev compressed the corners of his mouth, felt the tautness of his muscles under my hand, noticed the slight sheen in his eyes. He was hiding his sorrow behind stock phrases and a false tone, as men will.

One must not speak ill of the dead or weep like a child, even in the face of grievous sorrow.

I imagined his mind as a series of little blocks, stacked one on top of the other like the ones the herdsman made for Stepan when he was a baby learning colors and shapes.

Looking back, I realized I'd done something similar with my own man. After that first haze of despair lessened, I had pushed my hurt and loneliness aside, focused all my attention on our son, let myself recall only the good parts of our past. Not until I encountered Stenka in the other world had I released my anger, accepted how abandoned I felt by his death.

But I hadn't gone looking for another companion within months. I hadn't forced someone else to measure himself against a ghost. A ghost without flaws.

In that moment, I grasped that I'd been wrong to think that none of the men in the camp had ever taken an interest in me. It could be true, but I didn't know. I would never know. Because I'd made it so clear that I had no interest in them.

I decided not to challenge Fadeyev's view of his wife's perfection. It would be cruel, in a way. "How dreadful that you had to leave your family so soon," I said instead. "Did you miss the forty-day memorial because of your travels?"

He shook his head, as if clearing imaginary cobwebs from his brain. "No. My travel papers came a few days after the service. And I left my children in good hands. It's my father who worries me. His memory often fails him these days. I assigned a woman to watch him, but he's headstrong. Too sure of himself for his own good. If he runs out in the streets and gets lost, who can predict what harm might befall him?"

"I see why you're concerned," I said.

Again, I *did* see. My head filled with a picture of my own father the day he'd dropped me off at the Kolychev household. I'd not laid eyes on any member of my family since. Where was Papa now? Where was Mama? Did my brothers worry that Papa would wander off in the woods and get lost? Or had he died long ago, leaving his house and land, such as it was, to them?

Fadeyev reached out and caressed my cheek. Startled, I jerked away from him. For a wild moment, the sensation of his fingers against my face threw me back into that first trance, the one I'd entered in pursuit of Mergen's soul. The young man I'd met in the tent that day had tried to touch me in just that way.

"Stop that." I pushed his hand away. Only then did I realize I had no reason to react so strongly. Anfim wasn't the young man from my vision. A stranger, yes, and one moving too fast for my comfort, but not a demon in disguise.

I found him attractive. He might well sense that. He could even imagine that I'd invited his touch. I breathed slowly, deeply, to slow my racing heart. But I also took a step back, so that he'd understand I wasn't ready for caresses. When he clasped both hands behind his back and regarded me with his head tilted to one side, I decided I'd made my point and could afford to relax.

"You're a good woman too," he said. "I shouldn't have doubted you. My children would do well with a mother like you."

A mother like me? He knows nothing about me!

But I realized he did—enough, in any case, if he sought a bride mostly to care for his family and his house. I was Russian, so I could speak his language and bring up his children according to his customs. I had one son, so he could assume I might bear others. I knew how to listen. I'd offered him sympathy and support. I'd shown I returned his interest, even if I had pulled away when he got too close. And I didn't have a man of my own.

From my side, too, he offered exactly the qualities I'd sought. A husband, healthy and attractive and relatively young, with a good, steady profession and, judging by his clothes, an adequate salary. Unusual for a junior clerk, from what I'd heard, so he must have another source of income as well. He would be a father for Stepan. A companion capable of intelligence and humor. A way to return to my homeland, to pass on to my child the heritage my departure had denied him.

So why am I hesitating?

Fadeyev grinned, as if my shock amused him. "Don't worry," he assured me. "I have the means to look after you and your son. I've done well for myself in the Foreign Office, and I help out my two brothers with their overseas trading house. You could leave the steppe behind, live in Moscow, visit your relatives. You'd have to give up the sorcery, but you should do that anyway. Otherwise you'll burn in Hell. And that boy of yours would benefit from having a man in his life. A good Russian man who can teach him what he needs to thrive. He seems like a smart lad with a good heart. Strong in defense of his mother. He could learn the arts of administration from me—reading, writing, ciphering— instead of preparing for war. Think about that."

"I think about Stepan's future every day," I said, pretending that Fadeyev's outrageous not-quite-proposal had slid past me. Was the kind of marriage he offered really what I wanted at this point in my life? Or was my hesitation telling me something I needed to hear? "I'd better go."

"Until we meet again, then." He bowed. "I hope it's soon."

I dipped my head without speaking and walked away, my thoughts in a whirl. In a way, I had to admit, his offer was an answer to a prayer. He held out a solution to Stepan's need for a father, my desire to teach my son about the world I'd left behind, my longing for a man to share my burden and for the chance to create a family to replace the one I'd lost. If the spirits had sent him in answer to my pleas, nothing good could come from spurning their gift.

But *had* they sent him? And even if they had, it didn't necessarily follow that they wanted me to jump at the opportunity. Spirits love to test us humans by offering the very thing we think we want so we can learn for ourselves that it might not be the best choice after all. The path forward was still mine to decide, and it would determine the course of Stepan's life as well as my own.

When Anfim touched me, I sprang back. That told me something. I'd enjoyed my three years as Daniil's on-again, off-again lover and wept when he left me for Nasan. Stenka had been steady and comfortable, my feelings for him based on gratitude and affection, but intimacy with him had been pleasurable even so.

Fadeyev surprised me, and I reacted as I did because his gesture reminded me of my trance. Was there any more to it than that? As I thought about touching him, kissing him, lying with him, a certain heat and tingle did run through me. So the source of my hesitation must lie elsewhere.

In his reaction to his wife's death, maybe. Yes, that troubled me. I had no way to tell how deeply he'd cared for her, but one couldn't live with a "good woman" for eleven years and feel nothing at the loss of her and her child. He wasn't ready, whatever he thought, to enter a second marriage. He'd need to convince me that he'd mourned his Fevronia before I'd agree to take her place.

But that wasn't the whole problem either. I'd changed since Stenka's death. I'd become accustomed to living alone, according to my own rules. Was it possible that I no longer wanted a husband? Especially a Russian husband? I'd thought I did, that day when I saw Stenka in trance and he freed me to follow my heart, but then I'd believed no man had an interest in me.

Now, as I faced what had sounded like a proposal from Fadeyev, memories of the Russian men I'd grown up with in my northern village assailed me. Above all, they'd demanded obedience from their women. Fadeyev could be different, of course, but I shouldn't assume he was. If I agreed to wed him, I'd have to be prepared to put his needs first and accommodate myself to his demands, his views. I'd accepted such constraints as a girl, but after six years as my own mistress, I no longer wanted to shut up and follow someone else's orders.

And right there I saw the crux of the problem. Fadeyev had stated his one condition for our marriage in no uncertain terms. Accept him, and I would have to give up being a shaman—despite my five years of training, just as I was coming into my own. Marry him, and I'd leave the horde that had sheltered me without a healer to speak for its people in the upper and lower worlds or to search for them and plead on their behalf when they became frightened or lost. How could I betray those who had helped Stepan and me when we needed them and now counted on whatever assistance I could provide?

And what of the spirits? My commitment to their service was surely the subject that concerned them most. If they were testing me, what would they want to test more than that?

It couldn't work. It would be a huge mistake. Wouldn't it?

I worried the question like a dog with a bone as I headed toward home, but by the time I saw the patterns that marked my own doorway, I still wasn't sure of the answer.

Nasan caught me as I was passing her tent. "Come in. Firuza's here, with Dina and Guzel. I had Rasima brew that rose-hip tisane you like. We can sit and talk." Rasima was her cook.

"You want to know what that Russian said to me." I giggled at the amazement on Nasan's face. Why she believed she had the ability to hide her intentions from others I couldn't imagine: she approached life with the straightforward openness of a child. Even Stepan's rare attempts at deception worked better than hers, and his were no good at all.

"Yes, I do." She stepped back to let me in. "So do the others. We saw how he looked you over at that first meeting. And now inviting you to go for a stroll. Do you like him?"

"I'm not sure. I'm sorry for him: it seems that he lost his wife and child not long ago. But I invited him to walk with me, not the other way round." I greeted Dina, Firuza, and Guzel, who had arranged themselves in a line against the high-backed cushioned frame that Tatars called a sofa, then sat cross-legged on the nearest cushion and accepted a pretty clay cup decorated with splashy pink roses and fragrant with rose-scented tea. Flecks of dried apple floated in the clear liquid.

"You did?" Guzel asked. "Why?"

"Well, for one thing because he took me by surprise. I hadn't expected to see him wandering around the camp. I wanted to find out what made Ogodai decide to free him. And for another, he apologized for his rudeness the last time we met. I decided there could be no harm in talking with him so long as we stayed outside, so I suggested we go for a walk." I sipped the tea, which was delicious, as always.

"And did you?" Nasan settled into place next to me. "Learn more about him, that is?"

"Quite a bit," I told her. "As I mentioned, he lost his wife a few months ago. He has an elderly father, a former priest, who forgets things and wanders off, as well as a son of about three and a daughter Stepan's age. He works in the Foreign Office in Moscow and with his two brothers, who are merchants, and he's already looking for another wife. He seems to have settled on me, perhaps because I'm the only Russian woman here. He came close to asking me to marry him today—"

"What!" The women said, the four of them together like a village chorus.

"Will you?" Firuza added. "We'll give you our blessing if it will make you happy, but how can you tell if he's a good man? He's been with us not much more than ten days, and he's spent most of that time shut up in his tent. My husband says he's nice enough, now that he understands we don't intend to hurt him, but don't you deserve better than just nice enough?"

"I haven't decided what to do yet," I told them. "He can be pleasant—even charming. But I haven't spent enough time with him to know whether he's the right man for me. I suspect he's still in love with his first wife, because he hasn't had a chance to come to grips with her death. What he really wants is a housekeeper, which makes sense for him but wouldn't be much fun for the woman he marries. He didn't propose marriage outright, and I certainly didn't agree, but he told me I'd make a good mother for his children and that Stepan needed a father."

"That's pretty direct," Guzel said, "for a man you've seen ... what, three times?"

Do they really think I'm that stupid—or that desperate for a husband?

"And spoken with twice." I sipped tisane before going on. "The first time he looked me over, as Nasan said, but we didn't talk. The second time he called Stepan a brat and me a pagan sorceress. Today he apologized, so I gave him a chance to show me he meant it. I was shocked when he announced he was already on the lookout for a second wife, then hinted I could be the one."

"Would you like a husband?" Firuza asked. "I'm sure we can pick someone better for you. I didn't know that you'd consider a new man."

"Who in the horde needs a wife?" Dina asked. "Let's see. The imam just lost his. You get along with him, don't you?"

"I do," I said. "Very well. I have great respect for him, in fact. But an imam's wife has many responsibilities, most of which I couldn't handle, either because I don't know your scriptures or because I have important tasks of my own. He's also a good twenty years older than I am. And with three sons already, I'm not sure he'd want to take on another, especially a mischievous six-year-old with the energy of a colt."

"Not Haji Rahman, then." Dina counted on her fingers. "Who else? The fletcher's lived alone for years. He's a kind man. Rather set in his ways, though, and even older than the imam. You've waited so long; you don't want someone who could die any day or who's forgotten how to shoot a bow, if you know what I mean."

The rest of us groaned at that last comment, but Dina giggled, then continued unabashed. "You'd like more children, wouldn't you? Akbars is the right age, reasonably handsome, a good warrior." She winked at me. "Very respectful of the shaman. You know how you hate being told what to do."

"Maybe she'd prefer a Russian." Firuza waved her teacup, as if demanding the right to speak. "How about that captain who came south with Daniil? He hasn't married because most of our eligible women are Muslim, but you were baptized Christian. I'm sure he has too much sense to expect you to drop everything and wash his foot wraps. He knows you hold an important position within the camp. And after four years he has to be used to the *idea* of a shaman, whether he believes in what you do or not."

"That herdsman you and Guzel share is lovely," Nasan put in. "A much better fit for you than Anfim Fadeyev, and more handsome as well. And he already gets along with Stepan." She named half a dozen other potential candidates without stopping to draw breath.

"Wait, wait! You're moving too fast." Seeing Guzel open her mouth to add to the list, I grabbed the chance to intervene. They were having far too much fun with this, and I could see them going through every unmarried man in the camp before I had a chance to speak for myself. "We can talk about who's available later. I haven't answered Firuza's question yet. She's right: I wasn't looking for anyone. It took me a long time to get over Stenka's death. And I'm not certain I *do* want a husband. Especially a Russian."

I glanced at Guzel, the only unmarried woman in the group and hence the only one who might understand. "I've lived on my own for six years. I'd hate to find myself at the beck and call of a man who expects his wife to take orders and agree with everything he says. But in the last few months I have imagined at times that I would like a companion, especially someone who could act as a father for Stepan. No one in particular, you understand. I know the men you've mentioned, and they know me. So I think if anything were going to happen there, it already would have. But I was probably sending 'not interested' signals, so I won't rule them out altogether."

Guzel nodded. *Yes, she does understand.* Alexei had left eight years ago, and since then she'd kept to herself, even when Timur lived in Moscow. I'd thought she acted out of grief, but the expression on her face told me she shared some of my concerns.

"Any man in the horde would be a better choice than Fadeyev," Firuza said. "You'd know he was asking you because he wanted *you*, not a housekeeper or a nanny. What does it mean that he asks you the first time he talks to you? It can't be more than a fleeting attraction, if that; he hasn't had a chance to learn anything about you."

She had a point. I'd thought the same thing myself. And the men here respected the place I held. *They* wouldn't expect me to give it up, even if my power frightened them, which in some—maybe most—cases it probably did.

"I said I haven't decided," I reminded them. "Fadeyev has some appealing qualities, to be sure, but he hasn't mourned his dead wife even though he's angling for a new one. And he's convinced that my work on behalf of the horde is no different from witchcraft. I couldn't remain a shaman if I married him. That alone is a reason to turn him down."

"It's more than a reason. It's a necessity. You can't reject your gift." Nasan bent forward and clasped my wrist. "The spirits would punish you. You would sicken. You might die. What would happen to Stepan if you left him in an unfamiliar country without friends or family? Here we'd look after him." Firuza, Guzel, and Dina murmured their agreement.

"You're so kind." It was true: their concern touched me. I drank the rest of my tea in one swallow and set the cup aside. "And you're right. It's only ..."

I let the sentence trail off unfinished. I couldn't tell them Fadeyev had promised Stepan a safer career than that of a warrior, when war preoccupied their husbands and would one day consume their sons. They might hear it as disrespect, which I didn't mean.

"Only?" Guzel asked. I should have known she would pick up on my unfinished thought.

"It's only that I miss my family," I said, to avoid the more awkward explanation. "My parents may have died; I haven't seen them in ages. But my brothers and cousins? Some of them must still be alive. They should meet Stepan, and he should meet them, so he learns where he comes from and who he is. But not if they're going to call him a barbarian and me a sorceress."

"A Tatar could take you to Russia," Firuza said. "We go there ourselves from time to time. But are you sure such a long journey would be worth the effort? Suppose your family's moved on? Peasants don't stay in one place for more than a few years, from what my husband said."

"That's true. They don't. They exhaust the soil and clear another patch. And I'm *not* sure about the journey. I like my life here, and I love being your shaman." I'd stepped onto slippery ground again. I owed Ogodai and Firuza a huge debt for taking me in, and I wanted them to know how much I appreciated them. "I'd never marry someone only to go back to Russia. Still, I do have to think about what's best for Stepan."

"But why do you think going back to Russia is best for him?" Dina asked. "Besides, Nasan's right. You can't stop being a shaman. Stepan won't want to leave his home, either, for a place he's never seen."

Nasan poured another round of tea. "What Dina means is that we'd miss you both." She smiled at me as she handed my cup back, then looked at the others. "Enough," she said. "We've given her plenty to think about. Firuza, what has Ogodai told you about the couriers? Any word from Kasimov?"

"Not a peep," Firuza said, accepting the change of subject. "Still less Kolomna, which is farther away and unreachable unless they can get past Kasimov first. I hope Alexei and his men aren't under attack."

"I hope not," Nasan said. "Those damnable Crimeans. Whether it's Sahib-Girei or his princes acting up, I hope every last one of them develops boils under his armpits and saddle sores that last the rest of his life. Which with luck will not be long but will feel like an eternity."

She made such a face that the rest of us burst out laughing at the thought, and after that the conversation veered off into camp gossip for a while before I excused myself and went to prepare the dinner I'd made Stepan promise to come back and eat.

The women had indeed given me plenty to think about. So had Anfim Fadeyev.

Chapter Eight

Despite the odds and the barrier posed by Crimean and Nogai forces, the couriers arrived within a few days. Surrounded by twenty or so of our own men, the gold dragon-boat of Kasimov on its bright blue background waved in the center of the approaching force, provoking cheers and shouts of greeting from the defenders who guarded the camp. It was the first thing I saw as I joined those piling out of the tents, Stepan close behind me. Alexei Sultan's banner also rose and fell amid the onrushing horses, so some of the riders must hail from Kolomna as well.

A misty morning and a steady drizzle underlined the reality that August would soon end. Last week's heat had given way to cooler nights, and fall lay just around the corner. I spared a moment to wonder how long concerns about Nogai raiders would delay the onset of our own horde's migration to its winter grazing lands. The flocks would soon need the protection provided by the sheltering mountains, at present a good three to four weeks' journey to the east.

Stepan tugged at my hand, urging me forward, but I resisted his pull. "Stop," I said, and he stood at my side, shuffling his feet.

As the couriers' banners drew closer, I realized that several of the riders showed signs of injury. Blood-stained cloths tied around various body parts, arms strapped against chests, and at least one man who appeared incapable of controlling his horse suggested that the warriors had encountered enemies on their way to the camp.

"What's going on, Mama?" Stepan asked in piercing tones.

"I'm trying to find out." I stood on tiptoe to get a better view, but the number of horses and the speed of their advance made that difficult. Deciding that I'd learn more when they got here, I dropped back onto my heels. "Let's go tell Nasan Khanim. Some of the men are hurt." If I couldn't get a clear line of sight, it made sense that Nasan, being a good hand's breadth shorter than I, would have seen even less. I set off at a fast walk. Stepan skipped at my side, although I refused to release his hand. The last thing I needed was him dashing ahead and regaling Nasan with some garbled story.

Anfim Fadeyev stopped us as we passed his tent. "What's happening?" He sounded like an older version of Stepan, and I suppressed a smile at the thought.

"I don't know exactly," I told him. "Warriors from Kasimov and Kolomna. Couriers, I'd guess."

"Kolomna," he exclaimed. "Visitors from Russia here? Will the khan release me to return with them? And if I do, will you come with me? Marry me?"

So there it was, out in the open, unmistakable and unavoidable. Faced with the need to produce an answer, for a moment I felt tugged in both directions. Russia, a husband, a father for my son, and economic security versus a life I loved in a place I loved, with a community that valued me as its shaman. How could I choose?

Stepan yelped in protest. "Mama, you can't! I don't want him for a papa!"

"Stepan, hush. It's not your decision." I put a hand on his shoulder and looked over his head at Fadeyev, who bent one knee to look my son in the eye.

"Wouldn't you like to live in a house with other children?" he asked Stepan. "I have a little girl the same age as you. She'd be your sister and your friend. And I have a son who'd look up to you as his big brother. I'd take care of you and your mama. And I'd teach you to read and write, so you can get a good position and support a family of your own when you grow up. You've nothing to fear."

Stepan shook his head, but he looked at his feet and I saw his lips tremble. I guessed he might be having second thoughts. He so wanted a father.

But I'd told him the truth: it wasn't a decision to impose on a child, especially one so young. "Mama will always look after you," I told him. "No matter what."

When he continued to stare at the ground and shuffle his feet, I gave him a quick hug and turned my attention to Fadeyev, standing once more. "It's too soon for such questions," I said. "We've had one conversation. And I don't have time to discuss this right now. Some of the men riding in are injured, at least one severely. I need to inform Nasan Khanim right away. So whatever you want to know about the couriers, please ask the khan yourself. Let's go, Stepan."

I didn't have to tell my son twice. He set off for Nasan's tent at a run. As I hurried to keep up with him, I pushed Fadeyev's offer—and his reasons for making it—to the back of my mind. I did intend to weigh the good and bad of it again, but that would have to wait. At the moment, I had more urgent concerns.

The Nogai raiders had spared only a few of the riders from Russia, and several of Ogodai's men had hurts as well. Altogether I saw about two dozen warriors with everything from flesh wounds to broken bones, but only one whose spirit had fled in response to loss of blood, shock, or some other cause hidden from my middle-world eyes.

"We need to borrow the meeting tent," Nasan told her brother. He'd come to find her when it became clear how many patients we could expect. "Our regular living spaces won't hold so many—even yours—and where would we put the children while we were treating the men?"

"Agreed." Ogodai beckoned to Guzel, who'd joined us as soon as she saw the couriers riding in. "Send serving women to lay bedding in the meeting tent," the khan ordered. "Ask those who aren't on guard duty to move furnishings if needed, but leave the platform in place for my sister. She can lay out her supplies there, and those with lesser wounds can sit on it."

When Guzel left to perform these tasks, he turned his attention to Nasan. "Will that do? Firuza can oversee the raising of additional tents to house those with flesh wounds once you clean and bind the cuts."

"That's good," Nasan said. "Thank you. Grusha, you'll help?"

"We'll watch Stepan while you work," Ogodai offered. When I thanked him, he said, "Irek's in our tent, Stepan. You can play with him until your mama is free."

For once remembering his manners, Stepan managed a jerky bow before dashing off. I shook my head. "Well, he's getting better," I said, but Ogodai just laughed as he strode from the tent. He really was a dear, not haughty despite his exalted birth and title.

I turned to Nasan. "What should we do first?" I had my own ideas about how best to proceed, but since she had a better understanding of simple breaks, punctures, and sprains than I did, I usually let her take the lead.

"The one who's most injured," she said. "Do you need to see to him right away? The others can wait until the women set up the tent, but I'll ask for him to be brought in here if you think he's at death's door."

"Who will assist you, then? Guzel?"

"Dina," Nasan said. "She's good with wounds too. Guzel can drum for you, if you like."

I made my decision. "Yes. Please come and see to him as soon as you can: that wound in his thigh looks nasty. He must have lost a lot of blood. That's probably why his soul has fled, if it has. I can see him washed and bandaged, but I lack the skill to remove an arrow. Let's have him brought to my tent, though. Since Stepan is with the khan's children, no one will interrupt us there. And do we know the patient's name? It will help me find him if his soul has flown to the realms beyond."

"I'll ask." Nasan walked to the entrance of her home and directed a string of orders at someone I couldn't see, whose reply I heard only as meaningless sound.

Within moments, she returned. "Guzel will meet you in your tent," she told me. "Go start your preparations. I'll wait here for Dina."

I moved toward the door. "And the patient's name?"

"Mansur," Nasan said.

Mansur. The name meant "victor" or "conqueror," but the young man lying on the pallet of felts next to my hastily lit hearth fire looked incapable of conquering a rabbit, never mind death. Blood stained the dirty linen wrapped around the middle of his right thigh, where an arrow shaft stuck out from the center of the rag. More blood streaked his leather coat, torn in several places. Pallor gave his medium-brown skin a grayish tinge. I saw bruises on his face and suspected I'd find more once we removed his tattered clothing. I couldn't tell whether he'd received the bruises fighting or from the difficult ride south, tied to a trotting horse. When I bent to touch his cheek, it felt chilled beneath my hand.

I asked the two men who'd carried Mansur in to undress him, wash off the worst of the blood and dirt, and wrap him first in a soft robe Guzel had brought with her, then the coverings I'd laid out. While they performed these tasks and bandaged the leg injury with a clean cloth, leaving the arrow in place to avoid causing more harm, I turned my back to show respect for the patient's privacy. His soul might have retreated to the lands beyond earth and water, but he was still a Muslim man whose spirit would appreciate being spared the gaze of an unknown woman, even a healer.

As I waited, I smudged the tent in preparation for the ceremony to come and thought about what I'd seen. Had Mansur's soul indeed left for other realms? It seemed likely, given his wan appearance, the extent of his injuries, and the loss of blood I'd mentioned to Nasan. I would try to revive him first, but I must be prepared for a spiritual journey. Which raised a new problem: if I did need to search for him, what information did I have that would convince those in the lower world to help me find him, never mind persuade him to return?

His unwrinkled brow placed his age close to mine, and his dark hair and regular features appealed to me. It would be a shame if so young and handsome a warrior were to abandon this world before his time. I felt sure someone would love him, given half a chance.

Most likely, someone already did. If he was close to me in age, he must have been married for years. Happily, I hoped: remind him of a wife he loved, and I'd have a good chance of showing him that he had something to gain from coming back. A child, especially a son, would be a better lure still. But the warriors caring for Mansur at present came from our own horde. It seemed unlikely they could supply the details I needed.

"Tell me as much as you can about him," I said to the two guards when they assured me it was safe to look. Mansur lay at my feet, wrapped chin to toe in felt and wool covers except for a small circle around the arrow shaft. "Where he's from, for starters. Is he one of the khan's brother's men, or does he serve the khan's uncle Shah-Ali in Kasimov?"

"I can't say much, Honored Shaman." The speaker was the same Akbars whose name I'd forgotten the day I had my first conversation with Anfim Fadeyev. "I think he's stationed in Kolomna, but Alexei Sultan's troops stopped in Kasimov so that they could journey south with Shah-Ali's men—to have a bigger group, you know. So he could come from there."

"Yes, I suppose they'd have had even less chance of reaching us if they hadn't combined forces." I scrunched up my nose, thinking. "It's lucky you intercepted them, but you can't tell me even whether he has family—a wife, a child, someone his third soul might return for?"

Akbars shuffled his feet. He looked like Stepan when I challenged my son with questions he didn't want to answer. And this was a man Dina thought would make an acceptable bridegroom? "He must have a wife, Honored Shaman. He's not a child or even a youth. Most likely he has sons and daughters too, although who can predict what God will decree for each life? But the only thing I know for certain is his name. Mansur."

"Yes, that's the one thing I have heard," I said. "Nasan Khanim told me."

The second warrior had not spoken so far, but now he volunteered, "He's a good fighter. A good rider."

"And brave." Akbars looked brighter now that he had something definite to offer. "We didn't know he was injured until he collapsed over the horse."

A good fighter, a good rider, and brave. Typical male praise—probably true, but of little use in this mission I must undertake. How did they imagine I could convince Mansur's soul to return from the other world with a promise of more fighting and killing?

Then again, he too was a man and a warrior. Maybe he'd enjoy the praise. I'd start with the wife and family, though. That still seemed like the better argument.

"Very well," I told them, accepting that I'd heard everything they could tell me. "That'll do for now. Make sure no one interrupts me while I'm searching for him, if you please. I will be in a trance, and if one of you pulls me out of it too soon, I may lose him. The only exception is Nasan Khanim and anyone she brings with her. She's promised to examine his wound, and she knows not to disturb me."

"I hope you find him," Akbars said. He was a kindly man, and I smiled at him to show how much I appreciated his concern, even if the smile probably came across as rather distracted. I had already begun to retreat into the recesses of my mind. "He looks to be in a bad way," he added. "Like he might not make it."

"I'd better get started then," I told them. "Thank you again for bringing him in." The two warriors dipped their heads in agreement and left. I exchanged troubled glances with Guzel, then turned to observe my patient's stillness, which did indeed resemble death.

With luck, it wouldn't come to that. I knelt beside Mansur and again placed my hand against his cheek. What I saw and felt encouraged me. Now that we had him out of the wind and under coverings, with the hearth fire nearby, his skin had become noticeably warmer. When I raised the lantern, I saw his color improved to the smallest degree. His eyelids fluttered, and he muttered the Tatar word *fereshte*. Angel.

For a moment, I thought I might not need to search for him after all. I tapped my fingers gently against his face in the hope that he would return to the middle lands without my having to seek him out and plead with the spirits to release him, but he didn't awaken. Instead, he gave a deep sigh and relaxed against the hand I held to his cheek.

"If he wakes up while I'm in trance," I told Guzel, "bang the drum slowly and call me back." She nodded without speaking, her attention focused on the instrument she held as if not quite certain what to do with it.

"You'll be fine," I said to reassure her. "I can handle it if you prefer, but it will make it easier to enter the trance if I know you'll keep playing no matter what. I'll have enough trouble finding him as it is, and I have faith in you."

She picked up the clapper and hit once, paused, hit the drum again. "Like that?"

"Perfect." I marked the rhythm with my hands and feet, matching my movements to the beat of my heart. "Keep it as steady as you can until you want me to return, then slow it. If that doesn't work, put the drum down and touch my hand or my shoulder; talk to me as you did before."

She drew a long breath, and I understood that I hadn't completely resolved her doubts. But I trusted her. "You'll do fine," I repeated. "I have faith in you."

I bent to touch Mansur's cheek once more, and again he muttered the word "angel." Then, even more strangely, *yabalak*—owl.

Frowning, I stared at his unresponsive form. What thoughts went through his head? Lost in another world, perhaps he perceived my owl spirit. Or one creature with wings sparked pictures of another.

But he still didn't open his eyes, so I drew back and readied myself for the task of retrieving his soul. If the poor man was already seeing himself surrounded by heavenly beings, I'd better move swiftly if I wanted to prevent him from joining them.

While Guzel drummed, I smudged the area once more with sage and thyme and set the juniper burning in its holder. Then I circled the tent, chanting as I assumed my costume and took the slow, deep breaths that moved me into the trance state. I kept my eyes closed as much as possible, inhaling juniper and herbs. No throaty flute this time; with Guzel handling the drum, I could send myself into the next world on wings of imagination. When ready, I lay down near my unmoving patient and released my third soul to rise through the smoke hole.

My owl wings beat. My head turns impossibly far as I search for Mansur's first soul, his animating spirit. I don't find it. I send messages through my wingtips, asking the rocks and plants if any of them harbor his second soul. I feel certain both remain with him—my tufted and pointed ears pick up the sounds of his breathing, so the second soul can't have gone far, and the first would already be visible if it had left his body through the smoke hole as I just did. Nonetheless, I take this extra step to ensure that the more dangerous journey is necessary. When I seek the children of the horde, I already know their natures and their parents, their likes and dislikes, their favorite toys and tales, their siblings' names. Without such rich information about Mansur, tracking him depends on the clarity with which I can call on the spirits to help me, the purity of my heart, and the intensity of my determination to succeed.

I visit the local shrines, pleading with the resident spirits for aid. I fly north along the river, dive through the tunnel that leads to the lower world. I look for the golden tent, but instead I see nothing but thick, white fog swirling and billowing in every direction. No animal spirits, no forest or hut, not even a sight of Erlik Khan. Nothing but smothering fog.

I am an owl. I can fly through dead of night, but this fog hides landmarks, destinations, the target of my search. I must find a way to penetrate it. I think prayers to my helper spirits, call on the forces of wind and sun, concentrate my strength on creating a tree where I can perch. When it forms inside the mist, I settle on the largest branch and turn my attention inward. First I envision the Lord of the Underworld and send him pleas for Mansur's release. Not until I sense acceptance, borne on soft breezes that thin the fog to a drifting haze, do I turn my attention to the target of my search. "Mansur," I call in my mind. "Where are you? Your family needs you. Return to them."

It takes many repetitions, but after a while I perceive shapes—revealed, then concealed once more as the swirls lessen and thicken. Patches of gray sky appear within the mist and expand until they join together. A dim sun, no brighter than a lantern, hangs not far above my head. Only then do I take flight, dipping and swooping over earth dry as dust, each section indistinguishable from the next. In the many times I've traveled here, I've never seen the lower world as blank as this, as if my own lack of knowledge has affected the world itself. Even Suzukei is hidden from me.

It's not easy to do without dropping out of trance, but I try to remember the few things the guards told me about the soul I'm seeking. His name, Mansur. That he fights well and rides better. That he shows courage in battle. That he probably has a wife and perhaps children. Oh, yes, and that, more likely than not, he is stationed in Kolomna under the leadership of Alexei Sultan—or if not there, in Kasimov.

The last is something I can use. I passed through Kolomna on my journey south to join the horde. Kasimov, too. I picture them in my mind as I soar over the dull brown countryside and watch grass and trees come into being before my spirit eyes. The Oka River glitters as the rays of the pale yellow sun strike the water. The minarets and turquoise-tiled mosques and white stone palace of Kasimov appear above their earthen rampart, and I circle the town until the swirling fog surrounds me once more and I know I must fly on.

At last the river leads me to a red brick fortress on a hill. Massive bastions loom at each corner, and the mouths of cannons show through slits high in the walls. I hear church bells for the first time since my departure from Moscow and admire the round white towers, each topped with an exquisite gold or sky blue cupola bulbed like an onion. Intricate crosses pierce the dull, storm-laden sky.

The sound of priests singing fills my mind, yet as I pass the brick walls and stucco churches, I hear instead the Muslim call to prayer, so familiar from my years on the steppe. The sound comes from the center of a square paved with wood, its planks barely visible amid rows and rows of round tents. Here, after I don't know how much time, I see the first evidence of living beings—or rather, beings that once lived. Souls flit from tree to tree, smoke hole to smoke hole. They flicker like candles against the gray background of the lower world. The heady aroma of juniper surrounds me, cradles me, wafts me on its scent like currents of warm air under my wings. And in the distance I see an owl, the color of snow, with round black eyes.

The owl draws me, one bird to another. Sensing a powerful but gentle spirit, I fly straight for the smoke hole where my fellow owl perches on the rim. My wings are tired from the long journey, and my talons grip the bent wood with the last of their strength.

"I'm looking for Mansur," I say as I land. "Can you help me find him?"

"I am Mansur," the snowy owl replies. "And you?"

"Grusha." His response releases a flood of relief in me. I have found him at last. Now to make use of my helpers' wisdom and convince him to follow me back to the middle lands. "The shaman of the horde you were traveling to reach. We have a capable physician to care for your wounds, but she can do no good if your spirit remains apart from your body. Will you not return with me? Your family needs you. Your lord needs you."

He turns his head, swiveling it fully to the right and then the left, not answering, and I find myself at a loss. I've learned how to persuade a child. But a man with whom I have not exchanged two sentences in real life? Surely he can decide for himself whether he has fulfilled his purpose in the middle world.

"You seem young," I say. Each word clinks like a pebble falling to earth. "I know little of your life, but you have a family that loves you. And however great the success you've enjoyed as a warrior, there must be goals you have yet to attain. To know your grandchildren or advance in service to your sultan, for example."

His head swivels once more. "My family," he says. "You speak of them with such confidence. What do you know of them? Are you so sure they need me still?"

"Of course," I tell him, because what else will persuade him? "How can you think of abandoning them before your time?"

Grief flickers at the tips of my wings as I recall the family that didn't hesitate to send me away from them, but I push the sorrow away. No time for that here. It can only distract me from my present task, and that's proving difficult enough. "Alexei Sultan, too, would regret your death. You're a brave warrior, I'm told. A strong fighter, a good rider—what lord would not want to retain a man such as you?"

Again Mansur gazes into the distance, not responding to my question or even acknowledging it.

I wait, too tired to think, certain that my spirit helpers have deserted me. Where is Suzukei? Why have I not seen her during today's journey, for the first time since she left me for these realms beyond?

An image of my son's blond head forms before my eyes, and I blink away tears of exhaustion. I need to get back to him, and soon. I refuse to desert him as others have deserted me.

I chide myself. That's fear talking. The spirits brought me to Mansur when I called on them. They will give me the power I must have if I'm to persuade him and return home, to Stepan. I will always take care of my son, whatever Mansur decides to do about his own wife and children.

If he resists the lures I've held out, though, I'm at a loss. What else can I offer him? I imagine music and art, beautiful horses, fine clothes and trappings. But I don't know him well enough to guess which of those things he might like, and if he wants them, he can have them here in the lower world. Only experiences require a physical body. I cling tight to my perch, watching as he surveys the town—Kasimov?

My mind blurs, and I see white stone, turquoise tiles, gold paint, minarets. I shake my head quickly, and my vision clears. It's a warning. I can't stay here much longer.

This isn't Kasimov. I flew past Kasimov on my way here. This town is Kolomna, its brand-new fortress and bright red bricks not yet aged by weather. The town where Mansur is stationed.

"It's your choice," I tell him. The silence has dragged on so long I sense my owl self fading, hear the slow beat of the drum. "Shall I go?"

"Let's go together." The snowy owl spreads his wings and takes flight. I follow, then summon my last burst of strength to dart ahead and show him the way home.

When I opened my eyes, my head buzzed with fatigue and my arms dangled as if Guzel had tied weights to them while I lay in trance. Pins and needles ran through my legs as I sat up. My fingers trembled as I untied my headdress, bound the plaits back from my face, and looked around, wondering why I felt tired, even dizzy.

My drum lay a safe distance from the hearth. The scent of juniper, sage, and thyme mingled with the dung odor of the fire. I opened my mouth to ask Guzel to extinguish it, then shivered as a chill breeze blew through the smoke hole. I wrapped my arms around my waist, pulling the robe close.

How long had I been away from my body? Looking up, I saw the first hint of stars amid the purple haze of twilight. The morning drizzle had faded into memory, but lingering drops of moisture splashed and sizzled in the rising flames. My journeys had never before lasted half a day.

Guzel brought me the rose-hip tisane, and I drank it gratefully. "Mansur. How is he?" I asked when I could croak.

"Better," she said. "Not awake, but his skin has become less ashen. And Nasan stitched and dressed his wound. It's serious, an arrow deep in his right thigh, but with Daniil's help she managed to extract it without causing more damage on the way out. So unless infection sets in, Mansur should recover now that you've retrieved his soul." She glanced anxiously at me. "You did retrieve it?"

"I did. Erlik Khan released him. And he agreed to come back, although it took a lot of persuading. More than I'd expected." My head ached as if it might split in two. "How could so much happen and I remain in trance—Nasan and Daniil, the removal of the arrow, her treating the wound? I had no idea any of that was going on! And you, poor thing, did you keep drumming the whole time?"

"Most of it." Guzel rubbed her eyes and temples. I could only guess how tired *she* felt. "You were gone so long," she added. "Was he hard to find?"

"Very." I frowned, trying to make sense of what I'd experienced. "I've never seen the lower world like that. At first there was nothing but fog, then flat stretches of earth in every direction. As if my own confusion, my lack of knowledge about Mansur and where he came from, showed itself in that way. Maybe it did, because when I hunted for the horde's children I saw a beautiful tent, and with Stepan I found myself outside a Russian hut ..." I let the words trail off, too exhausted to finish the thought.

"You didn't know what to look for, so you saw only nothingness?" Guzel sounded perplexed. I couldn't blame her. "How did you find him, then?"

"I begged Erlik Khan, and then my spirit guardians, for help. I called to Mansur himself, although he didn't respond at first. After a while I remembered Akbars telling me Mansur rode in from Kolomna. I've passed through the town, so I was able to picture it, although it took me forever to get there. Once I did, though, I had no trouble tracking him down. He's an owl, like me. I saw him as another helper and went to ask if he could point out Mansur to me. That's when he gave me his name. But it took ages to convince him even then. I tried everything I could think of, but it wasn't until I offered to go that he agreed. By the end, I was so tired I expected to fall out of trance any minute. Then I would have lost him for good."

I waved at the darkening sky visible through the smoke hole. "It's a first, though. Me being out for so long, I mean. Time doesn't exist there, of course, but still ... it's never happened like that before."

Right then, Stepan pulled the door open and ran in. "Mama, Mama, Mama," he cried. He raced across the room and hugged me. "Nasan Khanim said she would tell me when you woke up, but she didn't and didn't, and I got scared. So I begged to come and see, and she said I could so long as I didn't make any noise. But you're not sleeping!"

I returned his hug with all the strength I could muster— not much right then, but he didn't seem to notice. "Run and tell Nasan I'm fine, darling, and that I found the warrior and brought him back. Then come home right away so we can have supper and get ready for bed. I've worn Guzel out with my long journey, so I want to let her go to her own tent."

"Will you tell me a story?" Stepan asked, his gray eyes pleading. "I haven't seen you since morning. I've been good, I promise."

"I will." I hugged him again. "We'll have to be quiet because our guest is sleeping, and he needs to rest so he can get well. But if you don't shout and you eat your supper, I'll be happy to tell you a story before you go to bed." He jumped and clapped his hands, then ran out of the tent once more. I decided not to mention that leaping and clapping, although not shouting, also made noise. He was only six, and he was trying.

"You want him to stay here, then?" Guzel pointed at Mansur, unmoving on his pile of felts even though the raised lantern she held showed me she'd told the truth: his color did look more normal.

"I think he must until he recovers, don't you? It would be dangerous to move a man with so deep a wound, and until he awakens, we can't be certain that his soul not only returned but will stay." I rubbed my forehead once more. "Anyway, I need rest, and so do you. Let's not have people roaming in and out this evening. It's not as if he can do us any harm. And it will take every scrap of energy I have left if I'm not only to feed Stepan but tell him a story."

"Nasan would let your son stay overnight, I'm sure." Guzel's shoulders slumped, and she sighed. "Or I can ask Timur to keep an eye on him."

"No," I told her. "It's a lovely offer, but not fair to you. Or to them. Nasan has patients to see to, you spent the whole day drumming for me, and Timur has better things to do than watch other people's children. I'll be fine once I eat.

And I'd like to spend time with Stepan. He hasn't seen me since morning, but neither have I seen him!"

Guzel laughed. "True enough. I'll leave you till tomorrow, then." And with my thanks and goodbyes following her out, she went through the door.

Chapter Nine

STEPAN RETURNED FASTER THAN I EXPECTED. HE BREATHED hard and stopped, gasping, as he crossed our threshold. I guessed that he'd run the whole way to Nasan's tent and back.

During his absence, I'd had time to strip off my shaman's costume and place the pieces in the chest where they belonged. I'd dug out flatbread and cheese curds, some dried apples I'd saved for a special occasion, and the jug of water I'd dragged from the river yesterday and boiled in time for last night's supper.

Every so often, I glanced at Mansur, lying quiet on his makeshift bed. From time to time, I saw Stepan gazing at him as well.

Mansur looked peaceful, his features and body relaxed. I saw no signs he would soon awaken, but no reasons for concern either. Somewhat to my surprise, because my son didn't usually keep his thoughts to himself, Stepan asked no questions about our guest, not even whether this was his missing papa. Perhaps Mansur's Tatar appearance and name convinced my son that this couldn't be the father he imagined, just as Anfim Fadeyev's resemblance to Stenka and use of Russian had done the opposite.

I did wonder what Stepan made of the strange man sleeping in his tent, but I chose to set that question aside for a time when I felt less weary. Instead I fed my son supper and made sure he washed his hands and face and rinsed his mouth before bed. Then I sat on the floor, propped my back against the chest closest to his pile of felts, and settled him on my lap.

"Which story would you like?" I could already guess the answer, because he wanted the same one every night, but it was part of the game for me to pretend I didn't know.

"'Ivan and the Gray Wolf'!" he announced, just as I'd expected.

"Are you sure?" I asked, teasing him. "I didn't think you liked that one."

"Mama!" He tugged at his hair, still unruly despite the water I'd slicked into it with my comb. "It's my favorite!"

"Sh-shh," I reminded him. "All right, 'Ivan and the Gray Wolf' it is."

It was a long story, far too long for telling by a mother recovering from the effects of a trance that had lasted half a day, and much of it struck me as poorly suited for a six-year-old—especially when Ivan's horrid older brothers kill him and steal the treasures he's collected throughout the story and try to pass them off as their own. But after so many retellings over so many nights, I'd developed a version I felt certain I could finish before I fell asleep where I sat.

"Well, here we go," I said. "Once upon a time a tsar had three sons. He was a very rich and powerful tsar, and he had a tree in his garden with apples made of pure gold." I stopped to sip some water. My throat still rasped, as if scraped with sand.

"But every night," Stepan prompted.

"But every night someone stole one of the golden apples. That made the tsar mad, even though he had lots of apples left. Alas, he wasn't a very good person, this tsar."

"Like the prisoner," Stepan interjected. "You're not going to marry him, are you, Mama? I don't want to go live with him in Russia. I want to stay here."

"We'll talk about that another time," I said. "I know you'd rather be with your friends, but you have family in Russia. You might like it there." Stepan looked unconvinced, so I let the subject drop and went on with the story. "The tsar had everything he could possibly want, but he got so angry about someone stealing his apples that he ordered his two older sons to hide near the tree and catch the thief. He told them whoever did that would become tsar after him."

"But they fell asleep! And Ivan went to stop the thief instead. He didn't fall asleep, so he managed to catch a firebird by the tail." Stepan wriggled on my lap as he said this, and I had to laugh—quietly, so as not to disturb the sick man nearby. Glancing Mansur's way, I thought I saw his eyelids flutter, then decided I'd made a mistake.

"You know the whole story," I said to Stepan. "You should be telling me."

He shook his head. "No, Mama. I like it when you tell it. The firebird got away."

"Yes, it got away, but Ivan kept one of its feathers. So everyone knew it was the firebird that had been stealing the apples. And the tsar wanted it even more after he saw the feather, which was the color of flames." I pointed to the sullen hearth fire, clinging to life despite the renewed assault of rain from above but producing only an occasional outburst of red-gold sparks. "So he sent his older sons to find it, but they got confused. Do you remember why?"

"They came to a stone, and it said bad things."

"Yes, that if they went one way they would be hungry and cold. If they went another way their horses would die, and if they went the third way they themselves would die. So they couldn't choose, and they did nothing. When they didn't come back to the palace, after a while the youngest brother, Ivan, asked his father to let him try, and when he got to the stone, he thought about the choices it gave him. He didn't want to die, and he didn't want to be hungry and cold. He didn't want his horse to die either, but if it did, he was young and he could walk. So he went straight ahead, and a wolf attacked his horse and ate it right up."

"A gray wolf, Mama." Stepan rubbed his nose, as he did every night when we reached this point. "Why did the wolf eat his horse, Mama? That was wrong."

"He couldn't help it," I said, as I also did every night. "It was the prophecy, so the wolf had to do it."

"Well, I wouldn't let a wolf eat *my* horse." He glared at me. "If I had a horse, I mean."

"One day you'll have a horse. And until then, you can ride Daniil's pony; he said so." I tapped his scrunched-up nose. "Shall I go on with the story, or have you had enough?"

"Yes, more," Stepan said. "You didn't get to the good bits yet."

"Ivan went to look for the firebird. But when he found it—"

"Mama! You forgot the part where he rides the wolf!"

"Sh-shh." I sighed. I heard a soft chuckle that could only come from Mansur, but when I looked in his direction, his eyes were closed. I must have imagined the sound.

I returned my attention to my son, tugging impatiently at my sleeve. "So I did. Ivan walked for hours, and his legs ached and his head drooped and he wanted to do nothing but sleep." Like me. "But when he'd walked as far as he could, he found out that the wolf had followed him the whole way. By then Ivan was so tired that he fell on the ground and didn't care that the wolf might eat him too. That's when he found out that the wolf could talk. The wolf told Ivan that he was sorry he'd eaten Ivan's horse and said that Ivan could ride him to where the firebird lived. When they got there, the wolf told Ivan not to touch the firebird's golden cage. He should take the bird and run if he wanted to live. Only Ivan forgot, because the cage was so beautiful. He took the bird, but then he tried to grab the cage as well. As soon as he touched it, bells started ringing, and people came and caught him, and he was in big trouble."

"That's right." Stepan sounded drowsy at last, and his head drooped like Ivan's in the fairytale. I heaved another sigh, of relief this time. With luck, my son would tumble into sleep long before the end.

But only if I kept talking until he did. So I went on, following the fairytale Ivan as he pursued a magic horse with a golden mane to trade for the firebird, then a beautiful girl to trade for the horse and the horse for the firebird. At last, after more rounds of help from the gray wolf, Ivan succeeded in leaving the forest with girl, horse, *and* firebird. But by then, saints be praised, my son's head had dropped onto my shoulder, his breathing slow and steady and his eyes closed. I shifted into the lullaby that I always used to ease him into sleep. I'd learned it from my mother, who'd learned it from her mother, and so on down the endless trail of generations. As happened each evening, my throat tightened for a moment as I recalled that long tradition, started by women I couldn't have known and passed on to me by the mother I expected never again to see in this life.

Then I shook my head, dismissing the unwanted sorrow, and allowed myself to think only of my son.

When I reached the end of the song, I shifted Stepan onto his pile of bedding and wrapped the felts snugly around him. The skies had cleared again, so with luck no raindrops would threaten the fire for the rest of the night. The air remained chilly, though, so I added a wool rug to Stepan's bed and another to my own.

As I approached Mansur's sleeping place with a third rug in hand, ready to spread it over him, he opened his eyes—wide and dark, like those of the snowy owl of my vision. He gazed at me, his expression unreadable. His forehead creased in puzzlement. His brows drew together over a straight nose, his mouth firm between the dark mustache and trim beard. He moved his hand under the coverlet as if feeling the bandage that Nasan must have tied there, then flinched—as he touched the wound, I assumed. But his eyes didn't leave my face.

"*Fereshtem*," he said. My angel. "*Yabalak*. Shaman." Each word came out slowly, as if it required great effort for him to think and to form them.

Angel, owl, shaman. Was he talking to *me*? *I* was his angel? I stared at him, shocked anew by the possibility that some reality beyond my ken connected me to one spirit or another—Stenka, Stepan, and now Mansur?

"Grusha," he said, quite clearly. "You got your wish. I came back."

And as I continued to stare, bereft of words, his eyes closed once more, and I was again the only person awake in my tent.

"Thank you," I told his sleeping form when I could speak again. "Welcome home."

I didn't expect a reply, and none came. I spread the rug over him, picked up my cup of water and drained it, then walked to my own bed, next to my son's. But despite my exhaustion, I watched the stars beyond the smoke hole for a long time after I lay down.

Stepan roused me by dragging the rug off me and emitting a piercing shriek that he probably thought of as a whisper. I groaned and pushed myself into a sitting position, tugging the rug toward me and wrapping it round my shoulders. The fire had turned into a pile of embers overnight, leaving the tent with no defense against the chill breeze entering through the smoke hole.

"Why?" I asked my son. "It's barely dawn. What do you need?" Indeed, the pearl gray light descending through that same smoke hole revealed little more than shapes. I might as well have been back in the lower world. I squinted, but it didn't help.

"The sick man woke up," Stepan said. "And Nasan Khanim wants to look at him. She told me to ask you, Mama, if she can come in."

I groaned again and pressed a hand against my brow. My quick survey had revealed no signs of wakefulness in Mansur and no Nasan, and therefore no reason for my son to be bouncing around like an over-eager wolf cub so early in the morning. I felt stupid with lack of sleep, and every muscle ached, as if I'd truly flown throughout the previous day instead of lying flat on my back in trance.

But Stepan's words gave me pause. "Is Nasan Khanim outside?" I said. He nodded.

"Then ask her to come in." When he went to do as I bade him, I pushed the rest of my covers aside and straightened my clothes. I bent to relight the fire, because restoring heat for our patient came first. While I placed another round of dung on the embers and watched the fire blaze into renewed life, I cast a sideways glance at Mansur and discovered his eyes fixed on me once more. This time he didn't speak, even to repeat his odd phrase about angels and owls—or, for that matter, my name.

So Stepan had told the truth. I still didn't know what had my son up so early in the morning—Nasan's knock? a sound from Mansur?—but he'd done the right thing to wake me, even if I did wish I could crawl back under the wool and felts and sleep for a week, at the very least.

Mansur's gaze didn't falter. A shiver of desire ran through me, stronger than anything I'd experienced in years. I turned away, embarrassed. The man had returned for his family, so Akbars' guess had been correct. Mansur did have a wife and children. I had no right to yearn for a married man.

Nasan arrived in a bustle. Stepan followed her, his hair wilder than the night before and his shirt slipping off one shoulder. I caught him as he passed, straightened the shirt, and dropped a warmer tunic over his head, pulling his arms through and whispering in his ear that he was a good boy. "Let's have some bread and cheese," I told him before greeting Nasan. "Will you join us?"

"Soon," she said. "I'd like to examine our patient. Feed your son first, though. And I'm sorry. Stepan wasn't supposed to wake you, only to find out whether you were already up and about." When I nodded my understanding, she tipped her head in the direction of Mansur. "Can you help me with him?"

"Gladly." I took Stepan's hand and led him to the side where I kept our food. "One moment." I placed a flatbread and some of last night's cheese on a wooden platter, said a quick prayer over it, put it in front of him, and went to join Nasan. She was already kneeling near the fire, murmuring information and reassurances in Tatar. Mansur looked wary, even scared, but he didn't protest.

"You are Alexei Sultan's man?" she asked him.

"I am." His voice, deep and rich—perhaps under other circumstances soothing—had a hard, rasping edge of unexpressed emotion.

"I'm your commander's younger sister, Nasan." She held out her hand to me. "This is Grusha, our camp's shaman. She brought you back from the lower world."

"I know," he said.

Perhaps the harsh edge came from thirst. I fetched a cup of water and supported him while he drank.

"*Yabalakam*," he said. My owl. Nasan sent me a questioning glance, which I ignored, and Mansur whispered his thanks for the water. I offered him more, but he refused.

"I need to look at your wound," Nasan told him. "Will you permit us to examine you? Only the injury to your thigh, I mean. I'd like to check it for infection. I won't unwrap the bandage. I can ask my husband for help if you prefer to have a man present. He'll stop by later to assist you with washing and other personal matters, but he's talking with the khan about how to handle the raiders who attacked you, and I'd rather not delay until they finish."

Mansur hesitated, then said, "I will permit it." He smiled at Stepan, who had abandoned his food at the sound of the patient's voice and stood not more than a foot's length from Nasan's shoulder. "Besides, I see a young man here. What's your name, young man?"

Stepan's eyes widened, and he straightened his shoulders, pulling himself up to his full height as he returned the smile. I'd seldom seen him look so proud. "Stepan," he said. "What's yours?"

"Mansur. It's good of you and—is this your mama?" He extended his hand toward me, and Stepan nodded. "It's good of you and your mama to take care of a stranger in your tent."

I felt a flash of gratitude toward Mansur, who, although ill and in pain, had spared a moment to acknowledge and support my son. He was a kind man. I was glad I'd persuaded his soul to return. His wife was a lucky woman.

And would no doubt be delighted to have him back in her arms. I suppressed a sigh.

At Nasan's instruction I folded back the coverlet over Mansur's right leg, taking care to expose no more of his body than was essential before us, a pair of women. A thick bandage covered the upper half of his thigh, and as promised, Nasan did not remove it. Instead she checked the surrounding skin for signs of infection and released a long, relieved breath when she didn't find any. "You will heal well, *inshallah*," she told Mansur.

His tense face relaxed at the news. "*Inshallah*," he repeated. God willing. He looked at me, and for the first time I saw a glint of humor lighten the suffering in his eyes. "I wouldn't wish your shaman to have journeyed in vain." Before I could respond—if I'd known what to say—he turned his head toward Nasan. "What now, Khanim? Am I to impose further on the hospitality of this fine woman and her young man?"

Perhaps Nasan would order him taken somewhere else to heal, freeing me from temptation. I should encourage her to do that, should I not? At the thought, my stomach lurched and the word "no" howled in my mind. I bit my tongue, annoyed with myself, and the moment passed.

What was happening to me? I was losing my common sense. I hadn't reacted so strongly to Anfim Fadeyev, and he at least wanted to marry me. But whatever the cause, I must resist. I would *not* pursue a married man—or accept the status of someone's second wife. I deserved better than that.

Nasan, alas, was oblivious to my inner struggle. "I'm afraid you must, Elder Brother's Warrior, because it would be unwise to risk reopening so dangerous a wound by moving you too soon. But have no fear. Grusha is a charming hostess, and you won't want for visitors now that you're back among the living." She patted Stepan's tousled head. "This young man, too, will have a thousand questions for you, I vow. So you'll have lots of entertainment while you heal."

As if to prove her point, Stepan, apparently believing himself released from his promise to keep his voice low, clapped his hands and said, "I can tell you a story, if you like."

"Can you now?" Mansur looked at me, then at Nasan. "Am I allowed to sit up, even a little?"

"Are you sure?" I asked him. "We want you to conserve your strength so that you'll heal quickly and well." And move out of my tent while I still have a shred of sanity left. I bit my tongue again to keep the rebellious words inside.

"I'm sure," Mansur said. "Your son reminds me of my youngest brother. I've heard many such stories, and it will feel like home. So long as I can listen to it without staring at the roof cover the whole time."

"I think we can arrange that." Nasan beckoned to me. "Grusha, can you help me raise his shoulders? And Stepan, bring those cushions over there. Yes, the red ones will do nicely." We soon had Mansur settled.

My fingers tingled as I pulled away, and I scolded myself once more. The appreciative glance Mansur sent me did little to restore my inner calm.

"I'll see if Guzel has some broth," I said, eager to get out of the tent. "It's too soon to serve our patient cheese, but broth and flatbread should stay down."

"Good idea," Nasan replied. "I won't leave till you get back."

"Thank you." I bent to tie on my shoes. "In a pinch, I'll ask Dina and the cooks, but I saw Guzel making stew yesterday, so she probably has broth somewhere."

"If not, Rasima does. In fact, go there first."

"I will." I dug my fall cloak from the chest and wrapped it tightly around my body, then headed for the door.

"And which story are you going to tell me?" I heard Mansur ask Stepan.

"Would you like to hear about Ivan and the gray wolf?" my son chirped. "Mama tells it in Russian, but I can say it in Tatar."

"Very much," Mansur said. A hint of amusement tinged his voice. I remembered the fluttering eyelids and suppressed laughter from last night and wondered how much of my story he'd overheard. We'd conducted this conversation in Tatar, but he must speak some Russian if he served Alexei Sultan in Moscow and Kolomna.

"Good," Stepan said. Glancing over my shoulder, I saw him settle into place next to Mansur. He looked serious, unusually grown-up for such a little boy, and I had a sudden, startled vision of how my son, my eaglet, would look when he became a man.

If he became a man. I quickly made the sign against the Evil Eye and murmured a petition to my helper spirits to keep Erlik and his demons well away from my child.

"It's my favorite," Stepan went on. "Once upon a time a khan had three sons ..."

I was halfway to Nasan's tent before I realized how extraordinary it was that my son had not only learned the story by heart but could translate it. And translate more than the words: I knew from watching him play with the other boys that he could, if he wished, convert the whole essence of the story from forest to steppe. I'd be amazed if, when I got back to the tent, I didn't discover he'd done just that for Mansur.

The thought stopped me in my tracks. I recalled Dina asking me why I believed I owed it to Stepan to raise him in Russia. Was this not his native land, and Tatar in a sense his native tongue? What right did I have to force him into the world of *my* childhood, only because I missed the family that had cast me out so long ago? Was that not what my own parents had done: pushed me into the life that best suited them?

Catching sight of the tent that housed Anfim Fadeyev— the man was fortunately not lounging outside as he so often did, because I still had no idea how to respond to his proposal—I pushed my feet into motion once more and hurried to Nasan's home as fast as I could go. A quick exchange and explanation, and I was again scuttling past Fadeyev's lodgings, now with a covered clay bowl of broth.

My desire to avoid him caught my attention. Why couldn't I decide whether to accept his proposal or reject it? Not because of Mansur. My attraction to him must be left over from my trance. I couldn't be so stupid as to fall for a married man before I'd exchanged a dozen words with him. That would be worse than clinging to Daniil, who had at least been my lover *before* he met Nasan. I'd grown up since then. Hadn't I?

But I didn't know much about Fadeyev either, and some of the things I did know bothered me. I wasn't sure I wanted a husband. I certainly didn't intend to give up my life here to become his housekeeper, warm his bed, and bear his children while he yearned for the woman he'd lost. He might accept the rules we'd both learned in childhood—marriage is practical, a union aimed at securing money and children—but I'd outgrown such arrangements long ago.

If I no longer cared about moving to Russia, I had no reason to accept Fadeyev's offer because he was a man of means or even a potential father for my son. I earned enough here to support Stepan and myself. I had a community to ensure we never lacked for food, clothing, or shelter. Daniil had offered to watch over Stepan as my son grew to manhood, and I knew Ogodai and Ruslan would do the same if I asked them. Fadeyev would have to offer more than money to win me.

Love, then?

No. That's not enough. He'd have to accept me as a shaman.

And then I understood—in my bones, beyond a doubt—that I couldn't deny my gift, even if the spirits permitted it. I loved the shift into trance, the journeys to other realms. I loved the fulfillment of healing bodies and minds, restoring lost family members. I liked making a difference—to my patients, to the horde—by opening my own soul to channel the wisdom and the power of those who lived in worlds beyond this one. When Mansur called me his angel or his owl, when he spoke my name and affirmed that he'd returned in response to arguments funneled through me, a glow of happiness suffused my chest.

I heard my mother's remembered voice, scolding me. Had I learned nothing in my years away from home? Only a fool let herself get warm and tingly inside because an injured—married!—stranger called her his angel while out of his head. Even if he spoke kindly to her child and listened to that child's story.

My mother was right. I was daydreaming, as surely as if I'd swallowed Suzukei's mushroom potion.

But dreaming or not, I couldn't marry Anfim Fadeyev unless he changed his mind about my "sorcery," as he called it. Because while I might never have Mansur, and might not want him once I learned more about him—which I would have to, wouldn't I, so long as he remained in my tent?—I would always be a shaman. The spirits had chosen me as their own, and whatever else happened in my life, a shaman I would remain.

Chapter Ten

East of the Don, September 1542

TWO DAYS LATER, I WOKE TO THE SOUND OF STEPAN'S terrified wails. The ground shook under the felts, and the tent swayed back and forth in an alarming fashion. In the distance I heard thunder.

What is it? An earthquake? A storm?

I reached out both arms for my son, who flung his body against mine, whimpering. I clung to him, shaking the last wisps of sleep from my brain.

A man's voice cut across my disordered thoughts. "A raid," the voice said. "Hide, both of you."

Stepan pulled away from me. His breath came in sobbing gasps. I twisted my head toward the voice, recognizing it only then as Mansur's. In my confusion and dismay, I'd forgotten he was staying with us.

Thunder—hooves, not a quake. Who ever heard of a quake on the steppe?

A raid. Our emergency plans: the ones Guzel and I had so carefully drawn up. We'd imagined the raiders returning southward, but we hadn't counted on having no warning of their coming. I had to get to her right away. From the sound of those hooves, I suspected it was already too late, but I wouldn't know until I saw how close the horses were.

And what about Mansur? He couldn't run. Even getting him on a cart would be a challenge.

"We can't move you," I said. "I haven't the strength to lift you, and anyone who does will be fighting." Stepan struggled to his feet and staggered toward Mansur, as if the mere presence of a warrior reassured him.

"Leave me," Mansur said. "If attackers take the camp, I'm done for anyway. They'll kill me because I'm the enemy. Save your son and yourself."

I didn't intend to abandon him, whatever he told me, but I didn't waste time arguing. Instead I grabbed Stepan's outer tunic and dressed him, pulled my shaman's robe over my woolen tunic for warmth, and tied on our shoes. "Let's find out what's happening, Stepan," I said. As I took my son's hand in mine, I looked at Mansur. "I'll be back as soon as possible."

"Leave me," he repeated. "Save yourselves." The exhaustion I heard in his voice revealed how the injury still weakened him.

No time for such thoughts. "As soon as possible," I told him and pulled Stepan with me through the door.

Outside, I saw preparations for war wherever I looked. Nasan sat in full armor, already mounted on her favorite mare—Firuza on one side, Dina on the other, and their troop of women arrayed behind them. The khan, flanked by Daniil and Ruslan, had already passed the border formed by the outermost tents. Every warrior capable of mounting a horse followed them, the banners of Kasimov and Kolomna flying free amid our own. I didn't see Timur, but he was still fourteen, not yet a man. Ogodai loved Timur and had probably ordered him to stay with his mother, although whether Timur appreciated being left out of the fighting, I couldn't guess. Boys his age were often war-mad, and I'd seen no signs Timur was an exception to that rule.

But it was the approaching banners that turned my throat to the texture of summer dust. Long panels of black silk embroidered in sets of yellow circles radiating out from a single center, they revealed that Ogodai's attempts to conceal the camp hadn't survived the assault on the couriers.

I knew what those banners meant. I'd seen the captured ones hanging in the khan's tent from his last encounter with their owners, a few years back. The Nogai raiders had found us.

All the plans Guzel and I had made were for naught. We had no time to escape. The attackers would be on us before we could run. I had no skill with sword or bow, so if the enemy broke through, I couldn't cut them down. But I was a shaman, and I had other means of defense.

I looked down at my son. "Run, Stepan," I said. "Run as fast as you can to Guzel's tent. Ask her and Timur, if he's there, to join us. Go now."

He ran. Much as I hated to let him out of my sight, I didn't wait for him to get there before racing home to start my preparations. I lit the burners, attached my ribbons and mirror with trembling fingers, and tugged on the false plaits I'd made of wool after two occasions when I'd had no time to braid my own hair. I'd sewn them to a piece of netted cloth, and the beaded headdress would hold them in place. I needed as much help as I could get on this journey. Least of all could I afford to anger the spirits of wisdom.

"What are you doing?" Mansur asked as I walked in my sun-wise circle, smudging the tent as I reached the point marking each new direction. "I told you to leave."

I'd forgotten his presence as I moved into my trance, and his question dragged me back into the here and now. "Hush," I told him, not bothering to hide my annoyance. "I have a task to fulfill. Stepan will be back in a moment with another woman and perhaps her son. Tell her to beat the drum for me. She knows what to do; she drummed while I rescued you. Explain to them why I'm visiting the lands above." I gave a short description of what I'd seen. "It's too late to escape, so I'm going to beg the spirits for aid. But the enemy is moving fast, and so must I. Don't interrupt me again."

For a moment, I thought he might argue with me. He didn't, though. Instead he tipped his head toward me. "Yes, Honored Shaman," he said.

I'd finished my smudging by then, so I settled my burners in their holders. I placed my drum and its clapper where Guzel couldn't fail to notice them, then lay on my back and released my third soul to roam free.

This time I have no need to enter the lower world. The steady beat of my owl wings propels me through the smoke hole, and Suzukei's eagle waits on the other side. As one, we soar above the steppe. Beneath us, the clash of swords and snap of bowstrings releasing, the screams of men—and women, for I see Nasan's defense force in the thick of the fray—reveal attackers and defenders engaged in mortal combat. I shudder at the sight but turn my owl eyes away, so that fear for those below can't distract me from my mission and prevent me from securing the help they need.

Ahead of me, a golden curtain shimmers in the mist like the most delicate of silks. It marks my destination, the first of the upper realms where I can beg the spirits for assistance. If they refuse, Suzukei and I must fly higher, farther, through the seven kingdoms of God. I can only hope we reach our final destination before the enemy destroys everyone I love.

A whoosh, and another traveler joins us. Before I even turn my head, I know what I will see: the snowy owl that to me represents Mansur's soul. And indeed, when I look he is there, the strength of his flight unaffected by his injury, driven by the power of his spirit. Suzukei calls a greeting, then with a single flap of her powerful wings she speeds ahead of us, parting the golden curtain in the space of a breath. Mansur and I fly on, together.

We are in luck—or perhaps Suzukei has already spoken on our behalf. We no sooner pierce the barrier to the first of the upper worlds than we see a beautiful young woman. Tall and slender, winged like us, she glows with the pure light of a sweet and loving nature. All around her stand trees with branches twisted into impossible shapes, odd rock formations in shades of blue and green and purple never seen in the middle lands. The sky above her has the rich hue of turquoise, and clouds white as Mansur's feathers drift back and forth. A soft fragrance like that of wildflowers in spring wafts past my beak.

I alight on the nearest tree and touch my wingtips together to show my respect. Mansur settles next to me, his snowy feathers bright against my earth-tone brown. His presence reassures me. Having two of us to plead improves our chances of success. My talons grip the twisted branch, which bears me up and supports me.

I sway gently back and forth as my branch moves in a passing breeze. "Gentle Peri," I say to the spirit before me. Her layers of rose pink gauze hemmed with silver thread swirl in the fragrant air. "The horde of the Winged Horse, where we live, is under attack. If our warriors can't repel the enemy, many brave men, many women and children, will die. My own child will die, and this owl beside me. I too will die, for there is no hope of escape. The raiders have reached the doors of our tents. We come to beg for your help."

"You are the student of Suzukei," the peri replies after a pause that twists my stomach into knots. "You have rededicated yourself to our service in recent days, resisting temptation. I applaud your strength of purpose."

By deciding that I would accept Anfim Fadeyev only if he could in turn accept my gift. That must be what she means. I dip my head, pleased that the spirits noticed. That I did not mistake their intention in sending Anfim to test me. When I glance at Mansur, I find him studying me. I wonder what he sees, then remember that it doesn't matter. However close he feels to me when we fly in other realms, he has a wife already.

I turn my attention back to the peri, who continues without waiting for my reply. "This owl Mansur I also know. I am pleased to see him here, responding at last to our call. Illness has freed him, it seems, to follow the path laid out for him."

"Path?" Mansur says. "As a shaman? I heard no call from the spirits!"

"It went out." The peri speaks with a firmness strangely at odds with her fragile appearance. "You failed to listen, so you received a life-threatening injury. But you heeded Grusha's plea to return to your body. That was good. Now you have another chance to find your way."

I twist my head sideways. Now it's my turn to study him. So he is a shaman, like me but as yet untrained. No wonder he can fly at my side. No wonder I feel close to him. The thought fluffs my feathers with joy, as if the warm gusts in the trees blow through them. Yet I sense resistance in him, perhaps fear—a communication between souls, not in words or expression.

I send him soothing thoughts. Maybe they reach him, for the aura of anxiety surrounding him lessens.

The peri is still talking. Again she addresses me. "Your eaglet too is precious to us. He will serve us well when he grows up. We must nurture him—and you, if you are to succeed in your tasks. I will help you."

She raises her hands, spreading the fingers wide, and from each tip a bolt of lightning flies. The bolts explode the golden curtain, unleashing a torrent of glittering sparks, and crash into the middle lands beyond.

Mansur and I tumble over each other mumbling our thanks, but without another word, the peri disappears in a puff of smoke, blending into the sky behind her. The tangled branches snap free as the tree trunks dissolve under us. Without a word, Mansur and I race toward the sea of glittering sparks as if we were one undivided soul.

When we break through, we discover that sheets of drenching rain pierced with flashes of light obscure the steppe below. I see no people, no horses, no signs of the battle that raged when the first sweep of my wings lifted me through the smoke hole and Suzukei joined me in flight. This rumble of thunder comes not from horses' hooves but from the unleashed anger of the heavens. It sounds like the steady bam-bam-bam *of my drum.*

"What happened?" I sat up and looked around at a tent crowded with more people than I'd expected. Anfim Fadeyev crouched as close to the lattice frame as he could get, right next to the door. When I spoke, he made the sign against the Evil Eye, then crossed himself three times, as he had that first day in the tent next to mine. From the appalled expression on his face I gathered he was again having second thoughts about me. The odds that either of us could overcome our differences seemed slim.

I sighed, mourning the death of something that never had a chance to form. Like a stillbirth. I didn't want him, exactly, or I would have accepted him already, but I did regret seeing opportunity die.

As if pulled by the thought, I glanced at Mansur. When I went into my trance, he'd been awake and talking—giving me orders, even—but now he lay as still as when I'd first seen him three days ago.

I reached for him, intending to check for breath, a pulse, anything. But then Guzel spoke, and her words jerked my attention back to her. "A great storm arose without warning, and the onslaught of lightning and thunder sent the raiders into flight," she said, answering my question about what had happened here during my journey to the upper realms. My journey with Mansur. "The camp is saved for the moment. It's a good thing the nomads fear God's anger. Was that your doing? I saw you were on a spiritual journey when I came in." She set the drum aside as she finished, and Timur, who'd been holding Stepan back, released my son to run to me.

I pulled my child close. "Were you scared, dearest?" I asked him. He didn't like thunderstorms, and the battle must have frightened him too. He burrowed his face in my shoulder and didn't speak, which I interpreted to mean that the events of the day had terrified him into silence. "Mama's here." I patted his back. "The bad men ran away. You're safe. Everything will be all right."

After a while, he drew a long sobbing breath and released his grip around my neck. Only then did I reply to Guzel's question. "The spirits chose to help us," I said. Without thinking, I answered in Russian, the language I'd been using with Stepan. "Suzukei pleaded with them, I think. I met her as soon as I left the tent. But I also begged for their aid—supported by another soul I encountered there. In response, they sent the storm. In that sense, yes, it was my doing. But they were the ones who saved us."

I didn't mention Mansur by name. His state of stillness fit my sense that he'd accompanied me into trance—an unfamiliar experience for him—and it had worn him out. That would explain why he again lay as if dead. But telling others about his gift must be his decision, not mine.

When Guzel stared at me blankly, I realized what I'd done and repeated the whole thing in Tatar.

"How is he?" I indicated Mansur with an outstretched hand. "He looks as if he's clinging to life. And what happened to the rest of our people? When I left, I saw fierce fighting. Did we lose many warriors? Are there injuries we must heal?"

As I again reached for Mansur, pressing my fingertips against the pulse in his throat to answer my own question as to his state of health, Fadeyev surged to standing and waved his right arm, cutting off any response Guzel might have made. "You're saying *you* prevented the raiders from overwhelming the camp? Are you a servant of the devil, that you have such power? And to think I considered you as a possible mother for my children!"

No one could mistake the horrified rejection on his face. I swallowed a sharp, indrawn breath. Guzel and Timur hissed. Stepan leaped to his feet, brushing tears away with short angry strokes. "You're mean," he said. "You can't talk like that to my mama. It's rude."

"Oh, can't I?" Fadeyev scoffed. "She's damned anyway, and by her own choice. So shut your mouth, boy, before I shut it for you."

"Show more respect. This woman and her son have done you no harm." Mansur's voice, hard-edged with fury, caused me to jump. Had he been awake the whole time I'd thought of him as beyond human reach? And he'd answered in *Russian*! I'd guessed he must speak some, but why hadn't he used it until now?

Not the world's most important question, especially right then. I shoved it aside for another time and promptly forgot about it.

"No harm?" Fadeyev asked. At the incredulity in his voice, I suppressed a shudder. How could I ever have dreamed of taking my precious son to live with people as narrow-minded as this man!

"Enough," I said, as clearly and calmly as I could. "Anfim, I'm a shaman. I have no intention of giving that up, for you or anyone else. So if that's what you want, find someone else to marry." Stepan cheered, and Fadeyev turned his glare on my son.

"Hush, Stepan." I sent him a glance at once admonishing and sympathetic.

Guzel caught my son around the waist and pulled him down next to her. I concentrated on Fadeyev, looming over me with clenched fists. I refused to let him bully me.

When he didn't retreat, I stood. With great deliberation, I untied my headdress and removed the false plaits so that he would receive the full effect of my stare. "I am chosen by the spirits," I said, emphasizing each word. "If you disrespect me, you disrespect them. You dishonor the horde. We have protected you. You have no right to treat us as less worthy than yourself."

I extended my palm toward Guzel and Timur. "My friends brought you here to shelter you from the raiders.

You dishonor them too. Since you don't like what we do, remove yourself from our presence. Leave my tent."

Fadeyev took three strides in my direction, his arms raised before him, wrists together in the shape of a crude cross. For a moment, I expected him to attack me. I heard Mansur's voice raised in warning, saw Timur catch Stepan as my son hurled himself forward. Guzel grabbed the clapper she'd used to beat my drum and held it high, her pose threatening.

I didn't flinch. Remembering how Suzukei used to draw the forces of other realms to her, opening her soul to channel them into the middle lands, the here and now, I lifted my hands toward the smoke hole and tipped my head to face the heavens, summoning the spirits, creating lines of entry with my upswept arms.

Their energy flowed into me, sending rippling rivers of light through my body like the lightning bolts flung by the peri. Their rage at Fadeyev's contempt for them and for me, their servant, strengthened and deepened my voice.

I tipped my head forward once more and held his gaze with my own, forcing him to see the power of the ancestors shining through my eyes. "Chosen by the spirits," I repeated. "I do God's work, as much as any priest. Don't you dare raise a hand to me. Or say so much as a harsh word to my son. The angels of Heaven will join forces against you, and you will perish. Now leave my tent. You are not welcome here."

To my eternal surprise, he turned on his heel and left, scowling. "*Fereshtem*," Mansur murmured. Guzel and Timur cheered. Stepan stared at the closing door as if he didn't know what to make of what he'd seen. In a corner of my mind, I sensed Suzukei applauding. And I smiled.

I glanced at Mansur, who raised both eyebrows at me. I couldn't read the expression on his face. It looked like a mixture of pride, amazement, and approval, but it could have been any of those—or all three. Again I wanted to ask him whether he had flown with me on my journey, whether he could accept the spirits' call to become a shaman, but here, surrounded by others, seemed like the wrong place, the wrong time.

Stepan rushed to me and wrapped both arms around my waist. "I hate that man," he said. "He's *worse* than the tsar in the story."

So much for those moments when I'd thought my son might be warming toward Anfim. Another reason to rejoice that I'd turned down the Russian's proposal. Still, I didn't want to encourage hatred. "He was scared," I said. "That's why he behaved badly. But don't worry. Mama doesn't plan to marry him. I like being a shaman, and the spirits would be angry if I stopped."

I realized then that in the fracas caused by Fadeyev Guzel hadn't had a chance to answer my questions. I asked again. "What happened to those who fought? Were *they* terrified by the sudden storm? Were many injured or killed?"

Guzel dropped her head, gazing at the drumstick she still held as if it contained the strength and wisdom of the worlds beyond. Timur watched her, his face troubled, and I knew before they shared their news that I wouldn't like what I heard.

I sat beside Mansur and waited. Stepan dropped down next to me, and I wrapped my right arm around him.

Mansur reached for my left hand, and in my anxiety I let him take it. The three of us clung together, like a family—and where did *that* thought arise? I couldn't have forgotten he had a family already!—but still Guzel couldn't find words. I saw her wipe a sleeve across her cheek, touch her throat as though it ached.

At last she pulled herself together and spoke. "We lost fifteen good warriors," she said. "Dina and Firuza were captured by the raiders."

"Oh no!" Capture was a dreadful fate for a woman, worse than death in some ways. "Can't our men retrieve them?"

"We hope so," Guzel said. "They will try. And there's a good chance they'll succeed. Although who knows what Dina and Firuza will have endured by then."

I didn't have to ask what she meant—rape by their conquerors, forced marriage, servitude. No matter that both of them had husbands and children already.

I shuddered at the thought. On the whole, Tatars respected strong women. But not those they captured, who became the property of the victor, whether they liked it or not. Dina and Firuza might end up in the slave markets of Istanbul, although their high rank made forced marriage more likely.

Guzel was still talking. "Ruslan is livid, Ogodai more so. He's sent messengers to the beys of the hordes that recognize him as khan, ordering them to report for battle without delay. To his relatives too, asking for cooperation against these invaders. It's all-out war. The two of them won't rest until they recover their wives and see the captors dead on the field. And if they discover their wives have been violated ..."

She left the sentence unfinished. I didn't ask her to complete it. The thought of how Ogodai and Ruslan might punish enemies who raped their beloved wives turned my stomach, however deserved the punishment. "That's terrible," I said instead. "I feel so badly for our friends. And their husbands. The children too, since they can't understand where their mothers have gone."

When Guzel nodded without speaking, I went on. "As soon as I can, I'll beg the spirits for help. Maybe I can find out where our friends are. How they are. But tell me more. Who else needs our care? Fifteen warriors died, you said. What of those injured?"

Again Guzel paused before she answered. I saw her exchange glances with Timur. At last she took a deep breath and said, "There are many wounded. I don't know how many exactly, but only one requires a visit from you right away."

I was already on edge, suspecting the worst. Even so, something in her tone warned me. A break in her voice. A hesitation, as if she knew the name of the one most endangered would affect me more than others. It couldn't be my son, curled at my side, so who else among the horde was most important to me? Not Firuza or Dina—she'd already broken the news about them. Not Guzel or Timur, sitting before me. Not the khan or Ruslan—if they were gathering the steppe to fight the raiders, I doubted either of them had suffered a significant injury. That left whom? Daniil?

Oh no. The name popped into my head, and I thrust it away. *She's a healer. She's invincible. She always comes through without a scratch. She can't be the one.*

I sounded like a child begging to be excused from a necessary task. As if not wanting something to be true could ever make it false. I pulled myself together and said, "Who?"

"It's Nasan." Guzel stuttered the words and burst into tears.

Chapter Eleven

"STEPAN CAN STAY WITH ME," MANSUR SAID. GUZEL AND Timur had gone, she to rest if she could and he to find his uncle Ogodai. The three of us—Mansur, my son, and myself—were again the only ones in the tent.

"He'll tire you," I objected. Mansur looked strong enough at the moment, as if our voyage to the other world had invigorated him, but I hadn't forgotten how weak he'd appeared to be when I first came out of my trance. "I'll take him with me and see if Nasan's nursemaid will watch him while I work. Should I ask Daniil to visit you if he's there?" To help him relieve himself was what I meant, but I hesitated to discuss anything so personal with a man not my own, however close to him I felt at times. I was sure he understood my question.

"I want to stay with Mansur!" Stepan said, but I ignored him.

"If he has time." Mansur spoke in firm tones—referring to Daniil, I assumed, rather than my son. "If not, I'll manage on my own. As for your son, he won't tire me. Find me a board, and I'll teach him the basics of chess. Or he can tell me stories."

He grinned at Stepan, who was shouting, "Yes, Mama, say yes!"

"See?" Mansur said. "He won't give me any trouble. Will you, Stepan? And I'd like to do something to help you, as you've helped me. You can trust me to send him to the khanim's tent if he wears me out. I'm not a child."

I wasn't wholly convinced. Although Mansur's wound continued to heal without infection, only three days had passed since I retrieved his soul, and not so much as an hour since I'd last witnessed how quickly unexpected demands could sap him of strength. He'd reached the point where he could push himself into a sitting position, but chasing a playful six-year-old remained well beyond his power.

Still, he was right: he was a grown man and could make his own decisions. And I liked his willingness to consider my needs as well as his own.

"Does it hurt?" I pointed to his thigh, hidden by the felts and the rug. "Any throbbing or redness?"

He turned back that portion of the covering, revealing a bandage with no hint of the radiating streaks I feared. "See for yourself. You and your khanim do good work."

"Very well," I said. The mention of Nasan recalled me to my immediate priority. "Stepan, come with me. We'll ask if you can borrow a chessboard and, if they say yes, you can bring it back here. But be good for Mansur, and if he gets tired or asks you to stop, then you must."

He nodded, his face solemn, as if this heavy responsibility weighed him down. I laughed and flicked my fingers against his cheek. "You can still have fun," I said. "So long as it's quiet fun." I turned to Mansur. "Don't hesitate to send for help if you need it."

"I won't." Whether he meant he wouldn't hesitate or wouldn't need help, I couldn't guess. But he was smiling, so I thanked him and left, the warmth of gratitude lighting my heart. Not to mention another kind of warmth that I refused even to name.

To my surprise and relief, I found Nasan sitting up when I entered her tent, her back supported against the frame of the sofa by a pair of large tasseled cushions and her lower body covered in three or four light silk-covered quilts. More piles of felt, rugs, and coverings lay beneath her. Someone had brought in a wooden table, carved with flowers and vines, and placed it next to the sofa. On it sat a clay bowl, a flask, and a roll of plain white cloth suitable for bandaging. "Grusha," she said as I entered. "Did you see that amazing storm? It seemed to come out of nowhere!"

"You're awake." Thank the saints, I wouldn't have to retrieve *her* soul. I sighed with pleasure, my shoulders dropping for the first time since Guzel had told me the news. If Nasan had needed that kind of assistance, I would have gone after her without a second thought. But two such trance journeys in such a short time would weaken me for several days, so I was glad that the heavenly forces had spared me—and even more to see her alive and alert.

"Mansur is going to teach me to play chess," Stepan announced at top volume.

"Shh." I put a hand on his shoulder. "Greet Nasan Khanim properly, and speak more quietly. Remember you promised to behave well with Mansur? Nasan Khanim is sick too. I'm here to see if I can make her better."

Stepan produced his jerky bow and murmured a greeting and an apology, which Nasan received with a graceful tip of her head and a twinkle in her eyes. "That's very kind of Mansur," she said. To me she added, "How is he?"

"He seems stronger today. Most of the time. When I first came out of trance, he lay so still that I feared he'd had a relapse, but he soon proved me wrong. And saints be praised, I see no signs of infection. I'm not sure he should be watching Stepan, but he insisted he would stop if Stepan wore him out, so I said yes. Which reminds me, we need to borrow a chess set, if you can spare one."

"Of course," she said, as I knew she would. "Stepan, ask Sara." Sara looked after her children. "Tell her I said you may borrow it."

To my amazement, he remembered to bow again without prompting. "Yes, Khanim," he said. "Thank you, Khanim."

"Good boy," I told him as he ran off. "Don't forget what I told you about Mansur!"

Watching from the doorway, I soon saw Stepan on his way back to our tent, clutching a rolled-up marked cloth (not really a board) and tied pouch containing the stones that stood in for men. Sending a quick prayer skyward that he wouldn't pester Mansur into exhaustion, I could at last focus my full attention on Nasan.

While asking for details about her symptoms, I examined her as best I could. Her skin, usually porcelain flushed with rose, looked as if she'd applied bright bands of rouge above each cheekbone against a too-pale undertone. Her eyes seemed unnaturally bright, and when I clasped her wrist to check her pulse, it felt hot and dry.

"Yes," she said in the matter-of-fact tone she used when discussing patients. "I have a fever. I suspect the raiders tipped their arrows with wolf's bane, because my arm feels numb in places and I have a headache. I collapsed from the shock of being hit, I think. Fortunately, the wound"—she pulled up her right sleeve and showed me a long, jagged gash—"isn't much more than a scratch. I don't think it would let in enough poison to endanger me. It didn't even require stitching. But it looks inflamed, so we should apply some mint and vinegar."

"Goodness." I sat back on my heels and regarded her as if she'd grown a second head. "How did you get all that out? Have you been directing your own treatment since the moment you woke up?"

"You have to ask?" Daniil said from behind me. "She's been keeping us hopping—driving us mad, in fact, with her demands that we prepare this and apply that." I heard laughter in his voice, so I knew he was teasing her, but I also heard concern.

I turned to greet him without leaving Nasan's side. From the full armor he wore and the weapons he carried, I concluded he'd stopped by to see how his wife was doing before heading out on whatever defensive or offensive action he and Ogodai had discussed. When I asked him, he confirmed that was the plan. "The beys will arrive within a week," he said. "Then we'll have five times the number of men. Until then, we can only stand guard day and night. Lucky that storm arrived when it did, but it won't hold the raiders for long. We need to distract them, but we can't spare warriors for a diversion until we have more of them."

"The spirits of the upper world sent the storm," I said, giving credit where it was due. "They want us to succeed. I'll plead with them on behalf of Dina and Firuza too, but later, after I see to Nasan." I hated to think of my friends bound or under assault even now. A shiver ran through me as I remembered Guzel talking about all-out war. More injuries, more captives, more deaths. And our plans to protect the women and children still unfulfilled.

I realized I could discuss my concerns with Daniil. He probably already knew that Ogodai had asked me to think about what steps we'd need to take, because the two of them worked closely together. And since I had patients to care for, he and Ogodai would be the ones to set the plan in motion if they thought the situation called for it. I excused myself to Nasan and explained, as briefly but clearly as possible, what Guzel and I had decided. "Will you bring it up with the khan?" I finished. "If nothing else, he'll want to talk with the herders to hear what they planned for the animals. The beys' forces will bring many horses, and you will need more pasturage. Whether it makes sense to move the women and children, I don't know, but if it must be done, we discussed how best to go about it—which older children should look after the younger ones, which families could share tents, how to make the best use of available supplies, things like that. Guzel has lists."

"A good idea," Daniil said. "For a few days to a week, though, I expect Ogodai would prefer to keep everyone here. Today's attack changed the game. We moved out of their way before, only to have them come after us. Now we're going after them. We have enough warriors to surround and protect the camp and those who live here, although not enough to launch a major attack. It's safer if everyone stays put; otherwise we'd have to split our forces. And we're watching for trouble, so the raiders can't surprise us again."

He was right. That was what had disturbed me about the previous raid: our failure to predict the attack. We'd had no hope of moving anyone by the time the raiders appeared. If I hadn't convinced the peri to aid us ...

I let the thought go. "Why were the raiders close enough to attack us?" I asked. "I thought they passed us weeks ago because they were traveling north to join the Crimean forces. Did they follow the couriers south? That makes no sense."

"They did go north," Daniil said. "We tracked them. I assumed they ran into the couriers by chance. But you're right. Why turn back to chase a party of couriers? Even if they recognized the banners as belonging to their enemies, the prize wouldn't be worth the effort expended or time lost from pursuit of their main target." He spoke slowly, as if balancing the alternatives against the knowledge he already possessed. "If they're retreating south because the Russians have won a victory, they'll be on the run, and that will improve our odds of defeating them. Maybe we can find out. I'll talk to Ogodai."

I noticed Nasan hadn't offered an opinion. Her silence troubled me. "I should tend to your wife," I said.

He dipped his head in acknowledgment. "Thank you."

"It's nothing," I told him. "You're my friends. I'm glad to help."

He laughed and shook his head. "If you encouraged the spirits to send the storm, believe me, you've done more than help. You saved the horde."

Again I experienced that flash of pleasure. I made a difference here. I belonged here.

Daniil looked as if he was about to leave, so I said, "If you have time to stop by my tent on your way out, I think Mansur could use some assistance with personal matters. If not, could you send a man to see to him? He insists he can manage alone, but he can't stand or walk, and I wouldn't like him to open that cut again. Meanwhile, I'll wash out and purify Nasan's injury. If she's right about the wolf's bane, her symptoms should heal over the next few days. But I must act fast to counter any infection."

"Of course." Ducking his head, Daniil crossed the small space between the door and Nasan, then dropped to one knee to kiss her. "Get well, wife of mine. I'll be back by evening. And please do what Grusha asks for once, instead of arguing with her." He shot me a mischievous grin, and I guessed he could predict the unlikelihood of Nasan doing my bidding—or anyone's.

Nasan groaned. "I *do* know what I'm talking about, you two. Dioscorides writes about wolf's bane, and I've seen Ogodai's men make the poison myself, even if they don't use it on people."

"She does know," I said. "I'll listen to her. So long as she also listens to me."

"Thank you," he said again. "We're lucky to have you." And with that he left.

Alone with my patient, I lifted the clay bowl on the carved table and sniffed it. "Willow bark? That should help with the fever. I need clean water to flush any impurities from the gash made by the arrow, including traces of the wolf's bane, and more water that I can use for protection. I'll prepare the mint and vinegar potion and apply it, then make a spirit doll to trap any evil beings that have entered the wound. After I get rid of them, I can bandage your arm. Agreed?"

She nodded and slid down into her coverings. When she closed her eyes, I saw the lines of strain on her face and understood what worried Daniil, even as he teased her to keep her spirits up. As a rule, Nasan stepped forward, took charge, put the needs of others first. Even injured, she'd exerted herself to spare those close to her, but now that I'd convinced her I knew what to do, she could relax and trust me to take care of her. It was an attitude I understood, but it meant that I should ignore her claims that she'd overcome the effects of her injury or even that the pain did not trouble her.

Like Mansur, when I thought about it. The pair of them were two of a kind. I had to keep an eye on him too, and not accept every declaration of health at face value.

I called for a servant and Rasima came running—another sign that those close to Nasan feared for her safety, as the cook should have been supervising preparations for dinner now that the storm had driven back the raiders. I told her how to make the mint and vinegar potion and learned that she already knew the proportions; as cook, she often aided Nasan with her medicines. While she chopped and stirred, I asked another servant for a fresh bucket of water, which I poured freely over Nasan's wound, catching the liquid in a second bucket to avoid drenching the floor.

By the time I felt certain that no traces of dirt or wolf's bane could remain—even though they had already done damage I had yet to heal—Rasima had finished her mixing. She handed me a bowl and a clean cloth, and I daubed the potion on as thickly as I dared, covering the long slash in Nasan's arm and extending the mixture out beyond the cut. The vinegar was so strong that I wrinkled my nose as I spread it, and the sharp scent of mint filled the air. If they didn't cause evil spirits to think twice about attacking my patient, I couldn't imagine what would.

Still, it was not the time to overlook any potential remedy. "Keep her still," I told Rasima. "I'm going to gather dried grass. There must be some between here and the corral. As soon as I find it, I'll be back. I can make the spirit doll here."

"Yes, Honored Shaman."

When I stood, she took my place, her eyes fixed on her mistress as if she could heal Nasan by the strength of her gaze.

I walked at a rapid pace toward the penned horses, scanning each side of the path for patches of grass. I needed only handfuls, but people and horses had flattened the pathway, and the four central tents stood close together. I saw a few clumps near the place where the khan had chosen to house Anfim Fadeyev, but I wasn't in the mood for another confrontation with him. I quickened my pace.

As I passed my own home, I heard Mansur's deep voice and Stepan's lively chatter intermingled. I poked my head in the door. "How are you two doing?"

"Mama!" Stepan waved both arms above his head. "Look at me. I'm winning!"

"He has a gift." Mansur pointed at the squares laid out on the fabric chessboard. The arrangement of stones meant nothing to me, as I'd never learned the game, but I chose to treat Mansur's comment as truth and praised Stepan. From the glee on my son's face, I could believe he was winning, if only because Mansur was allowing it, and I liked to encourage him.

"Did Daniil Nikolaevich stop in?" I asked. "He promised he would."

"He did," Mansur said. "All is well. And what of you? How is the khanim?"

"Better than I feared," I told him. "Her souls remained with her, and her injury is less severe than Guzel's description led me to believe. But she thinks the raiders poisoned their arrows, which would explain why we had so many deaths." I hadn't realized the last point until that moment, which showed me how fast events had piled one on top of the other. "I've dressed her wound and will bandage it soon, but I need to purify her and the tent to drive out evil spirits first. Otherwise I might shut them in where they can do more harm. It shouldn't take long once I find dried grass, but I have to look for it and perform the ritual before I can join you for dinner. I hope. Is there anything you need before I go? Food? Water? Someone to look after Stepan?" My son yelped in protest at the last.

"Stepan and I are doing fine." Mansur patted my son's curls, and Stepan quieted. "He'll get food and water for us if we need them. Stepan, do you know where your mama can find dried grass?"

My son screwed up his face, thinking. "There's some near Timur's tent," he said after a short pause. "I saw it yesterday."

So close. Right next door, in fact. "Thank you," I told them both. "I'll return as soon as possible. But eat if you're hungry. Don't wait for me." As they chorused their agreement, I left.

The dried grass was exactly where Stepan had told me to expect it. I pulled several handfuls and, to save time, twisted them into the rough shape of a person as I made my way back to Nasan's bedside. Except when again forced to pass by the tent occupied by Anfim Fadeyev, I walked more slowly than before, preparing myself for the ritual to come. I would not enter a full trance, but I had to be calm, open, and receptive to whatever suggestions came to me from above and below. With each twist and tie of the grass, I prayed to my helper spirits for guidance and touched the mirror that hung around my neck. It would play an important role in the healing ceremony, revealing the presence of otherworldly intruders and redirecting them to the lower realm where they belonged.

I stepped across the threshold of Nasan's home and looked around, verifying that I had every piece required for this simplest of rituals. For once, I didn't need the drum or my elaborate headdress, so I propped them against the tent frame and ensured that both my hair and my patient's were tied back. I lifted the mirror from around my neck and placed it on the table near Nasan. I pulled a feather fan from the bag of supplies I'd brought with me and put it, with the grass doll I'd made, next to the mirror. Rasima got up as I approached and asked me if she could leave for a while to supervise the preparations for the midday meal.

"Yes," I said. "But please send someone with nine twigs—small and dry enough to break—and a jug of boiled water. And make sure no one comes in until I tell you I'm done. If there are spirits troubling the khanim, I don't want them to bother other members of the horde."

She agreed and left me alone with my patient. While I waited for the twigs and the water, I prayed to the spirits above and below. I lit my burners of juniper and thyme and passed each one three times around my body from east to west, then held it above the crown of my head and again over the inner eye in the middle of my forehead. The beads and shells attached to my robe shushed and jingled as I moved, creating a soothing, pleasing sound.

After I purified myself with the sacred smoke, I repeated the ritual over Nasan, who lay still on her bed, her injured arm bright green from the mint-vinegar potion and her eyes closed. I made an extra pass over the injury, taking care not to touch her body or drop ash from the burners. When I was done, I placed the burners near enough that I could reach them as needed but not so close that I might knock them over.

A pretty, dark-haired girl of about twelve ran in with the twigs, a jug, and a clay cup about the height of my thumb. I recognized her as Rasima's oldest daughter. "Thank you, Kiraz. You may go," I said as I took the objects from her. She scurried out without a word, and I laughed gently as I watched her go. No need to wonder what animal form her soul would take. She looked just like a mouse.

Outside, I heard the noise of the cooks preparing food, children playing, animals lowing and baaing and neighing. Deep breaths and a focus on my inner eye gradually caused these sounds of daily life to fade, until they had no more weight than the beads and shells that jangled whenever I moved.

When I felt calm once more, I sat next to Nasan and picked up the magic mirror. I held it shiny side down over the burners, infusing it with sacred smoke to unlock its power. I let my thoughts drift on the scent, chanting softly to my helpers, calling the animals with their sounds and the others with my praise and thanks for their many gifts. "Look down on Nasan," I begged them. "She is a healer like you, brought low by wicked men of another tribe, men who didn't hesitate to poison their arrows even though they were hunting people, not animals. Restore her strength. Give her back to us. And help me find and remove any of Erlik Khan's subjects who have come to prey on her weakness."

After a while, I drew enough helpers to me that I felt comfortable moving to the next stage. I turned the mirror toward Nasan and passed it over her body, again not touching her. At the same time, I extended my left hand, palm down, and used it to follow the mirror's path. As I reached the patch of air over her wound, I felt the prickling and heat that indicated a troubled spirit, and the mirror showed my inner eye the rough outline of its shape, about the length of my forearm, narrow and wispy. I didn't address the problem right away but instead continued my exploration until I had covered her entire body, from head to feet and back again. The results pleased me. I had arrived in time. I had seen only one intrusion, in the wound itself, so I needed to banish only that one.

I placed the mirror on the table and put the fan and the grass doll in my lap, where I could grab them quickly. I picked up three of the twigs and lit them as one from the hearth. When I saw that the flame was well established, I snapped my arm forward as fast as I could to startle the unwanted spirit with the sudden appearance of fire. I let the twigs burn down halfway, extinguishing them by pressing them against the stones that surrounded the hearth before the flame could singe my fingers, then repeated the action twice more with the remaining twigs, three at a time. Each time the twigs burned brighter, showing me that the spirit was withdrawing in fear. When I'd gone through all nine twigs, I raised my mirror once more and saw that this part of the ceremony had worked: the spirit had left Nasan's body.

Now the hard work of persuading the intruder to return home began. First I pressed the mirror to the floor of the tent, near the hearth fire, to remind the spirit where it belonged: in the realms below. Moving with ritual slowness, I stood, picked up the jug of water, and poured a small quantity into the clay cup. I stopped next to the hearth fire and tossed the water in the air to nourish the helper spirits. I went back to my seat, placed the jug and cup in front of my crossed feet, closed my eyes, and spoke to my helpers. "Grandmothers, ancestors, spirits of air and water, earth and fire, fill me with your power. Use my breath as your own. Turn this water into sacred liquid, able to heal and to cure. Save this descendant of yours. Make her whole again. She has much good that she may yet do for you and yours."

I waited, hands turned palm up in my lap. I sensed Suzukei perched on the smoke hole, imagined the tigers and other animals from my drum circling the tent where I sat. I thought of the grandmothers and the many, many generations they represented, back to time immemorial, the beginnings of the Tatar people.

At last I sensed their approval, their strength lifting me like the warm breezes beneath the wings of my spirit owl. The moment had come. I raised the jug to the level of my chin and blew three times across the surface of the water, infusing it with holy energy. I filled the clay cup halfway and drank, savoring the clean, cool taste before setting the jug down.

Only then did I pick up my fan and the grass doll. With the fan and lots of encouragement—because spirits, I've found, most often turn to evil when lost, angry, and confused—I urged Nasan's intruder into its temporary home. When my helpers assured me that the spirit had entered the doll, I felt safe allowing my thoughts to return to the present. Nasan lay quiet on her pile of coverings. The willow bark had reduced the redness of fever in her cheeks, and she appeared to have fallen into a natural sleep. I would bind her wound as soon as I released the captured spirit into the wild.

Leaving the magic mirror at her side to protect her from further attacks, I picked up the burned twigs and the grass doll and walked with swift steps to the edge of the camp and beyond. At the bank of the river, I placed the doll on the ground and spoke to it. "It's time for you to travel to the hunting grounds below. The grandmothers await you. You will see again the loved ones whom you lost to death. Here you are troubled and lonely, cut off from life in every realm; there happiness and rewards await you, an eternity of bliss. Go, and I will send you food and koumiss via the hearth fire. Here I can do nothing for you."

After a while, I sensed the intruder's essence departing, like a mist hanging in the air, then sinking into the earth. The doll again became simply a bundle of twisted grass. Pulling back my arm as far as I could, I flung the grass into the center of the river, where the current ran strongest, then broke each twig in half and threw it, too, into the flowing water.

When I could no longer see the pieces, I ran back to Nasan's tent, leaving the spirit to complete its journey to Erlik Khan's kingdom. Once I reached my friend's side, I wrapped the clean cloth around her arm. I praised my helpers and picked up chunks of meat and bread left uneaten by Nasan. I tossed the food into the hearth fire as a reward for them and for the departed intruder. I sprinkled koumiss on the air for them to enjoy. I purified the tent, Nasan, and myself once more with the smoke of juniper and thyme. I left the holy water for her to drink when she awoke and every day until she healed. On my way out, I stopped by Rasima's cooking area.

"The khanim is sleeping," I said. "I removed the spirit that was troubling her and sent it home. Then I bandaged her arm, which I think will heal well. When she wakes, give her another dose of the willow bark potion, as well as a cup of the holy water I left for her, and more again early in the morning. She should continue to drink the water twice a day until it's gone. I'll check on her tomorrow— not at first light but as soon as seems least likely to disturb the household. Until then, don't touch her wound or the bandaging unless she complains of burning or great pain or the prickling sensation she reported before. If any of that happens, send for me at once. Day or night, it doesn't matter. I will come straightaway."

"I will, Honored Shaman." Rasima ladled several portions of goat-meat stew into a clay tureen—enough for half a dozen warriors, at least—and covered the dish with a matching top. She took a stack of flatbreads and placed them in a leather pouch.

"It's too much," I said. "You can't spare such a large amount from your household's dinner."

She held out the pouch for me to take. "The fall slaughter has begun, so there's plenty. And you saved our khanim. Everything we have is yours." She frowned at the bag I already carried over my shoulder, containing my shaman's tools, and the drum I held in my right hand. "But you can't carry it," she said. "Wait."

She bustled off and soon returned with a strapping lad of about fourteen, one of the boys being trained to form Timur's personal bodyguard. "Barak will carry the food for you," Rasima said. "Barak, take these things to the shaman's tent."

"Thank you," I told her. "Your generosity overwhelms me. Tell Daniil Nikolaevich, please, what I said about checking on the khanim tomorrow. And send for me at once if anything goes wrong."

She agreed, and I left, rejoicing that the spirits had arranged such a good outcome. After all the work I'd done today, I was eager to reach home. As I led Barak across the short distance between Nasan's tent and my own, I allowed myself to hope that Mansur had somehow managed to tire Stepan out instead of the other way round, but I had to admit that seemed unlikely.

Still, it would feel good to eat, to rest, and to tell my son "Ivan and the Gray Wolf" yet again. It had been a long and eventful day.

Chapter Twelve

AS I APPROACHED THE TENT, I HEARD NO SOUND—ALWAYS A source of alarm if a six-year-old is present. I held up a hand to ask Barak to wait, pressed open the door as quietly as possible, tiptoed over the threshold, and stopped openmouthed on the other side. Stepan lay fast asleep on his bed, curled up like an infant, his curls and expression angelic against the sky-blue silk under his head.

I glanced at Mansur, who regarded me with a distinct air of amusement. No longer in the half-sitting position that had made it possible for him to play chess with my son, he lounged against the pillows, looking a great deal more relaxed than I felt. To him, too, I held up one hand, signaling "wait," then placed my drum and bag of shaman's tools next to the chest where I stored them and went back through the door. There Barak stood, showing impressive patience for a boy his age. I took the covered clay pot and the pouch containing the bread from him, thanked him, and let him go. Then I returned to my own tent.

I set the pot and pouch on the floor next to Mansur. "Did you eat?" I asked as softly as I could and still be heard. "Rasima insisted I take enough goat stew and flatbread to feed a small army. Please say you'll have some."

"Stepan gave me bread and cheese after the noonday prayers," he said. "I'll eat Rasima's stew with pleasure."

I fetched wooden bowls and spoons, a ladle, and a platter to hold the bread. Only after I'd watched Mansur prop himself up again, served us both, and sat cross-legged next to him did I speak. "I'm impressed that you managed to get Stepan to sleep. I hadn't expected that. In fact, I feared the opposite: that I'd return and find you in exhausted slumber and him romping about like a lamb in springtime."

I hesitated as a thought occurred to me. I wasn't sure I wanted an answer, but really, why not ask? I'd have to face the truth sometime. "Is it because you have sons of your own?"

The spoon fell from his hand, plopping into the stew. I'd never seen him so shocked. "Sons of my own? Not that I ever heard. I don't have a wife, so why would you think that?" He stared at the spoon, his smile rueful. "All right, I'm not an infant. I have had women, but if any of them became pregnant, they didn't tell me. And I'm sure they knew I would support a child if I had one."

"You're not married?" I must look as startled as he did. He shook his head. "But ..." I stopped, trying to recall why I'd felt so certain of something that his reaction told me couldn't be true. Had he ever mentioned a wife? A child? Where did the story come from?

"Oh!" I clapped a hand over my mouth and hurriedly lowered my voice. Waking Stepan was the last thing I wanted to do at that moment. "It was Akbars who told me, that first day when I went to retrieve your soul. I was trying to find out more about you, so I could convince you to return. I thought you'd come back for a wife or a child, and he said you must have one. But of course, he didn't know.

187

Then, when I found you, we talked about your family. I just assumed ... If you don't have sons, though, how is it that you're so good with Stepan?"

He laughed, also softly. "Didn't I tell you I have younger brothers? Two, to be precise, and a sister. My father died in battle when I was eighteen, so as the eldest I had to support my mother and help her with the younger ones. That's why I don't have a wife: I couldn't afford to take on any more responsibilities. I've started to think I might marry, but I've yet to find the right woman." He gazed at me as if his words had a special significance, and the desire that so often ran through me when he watched me sent tendrils of flame the whole way to my toes.

He didn't have a wife. He didn't have children. But he might marry, if he found the right woman. The mere thought thrilled me.

"Even though you're supporting your brothers and sister?" I asked, clinging to whatever straw of sanity presented itself. What had he said to me, there in the lower world? *Are you so sure my family still needs me?*

"I'm not supporting them anymore, only my mother. My sister has a husband, and the boys have also joined Alexei Sultan's service. But to get back to your original question, I can handle Stepan because I remember what it took to raise them. Children are like candles at this age. Boys and girls both, but especially boys. They burn until the wick gets low, then poof—they go out for a while. Make them think, let them run, feed them, and they collapse on their own. Don't you have brothers and sisters? You didn't grow up here in the horde, I think."

"I didn't grow up here, no." I hesitated. The memory of my lost brothers, my lost parents, still hurt. For a moment I gave my weaker self its head and hid my awkward truth. "I should check your wound again before you sleep."

"If you wish." He sounded unconcerned. "My leg still aches, but otherwise it seems about the same as this morning. Looked the same too, when Daniil Nikolaevich stopped by. Thank you for sending him. How's his wife doing?"

"Better." I chewed a mouthful of tender meat before continuing. It was delicious. Rasima was an excellent cook, and I was hungry. I realized then that I hadn't eaten since the previous night. "When I got there, she'd already recovered enough to sit up. In fact, she was ordering everyone about, telling them how to treat her." He laughed again at that. "She has a slash on her arm—not deep, fortunately, because she thinks the arrow was poisoned with wolf's bane. I cleaned it and dressed it, chased away an evil spirit, and purified everything. I think she'll heal well, but I'll go back tomorrow and as often thereafter as needed to check on her."

"I'm glad to hear it," he said. "She cared for me. I'd hate to think of anything bad happening to her."

"So would I. We've become good friends." I tore a piece of bread into quarters and placed a spoonful of stew in the center of one. Together they tasted even better.

Mansur studied me, his head tipped to one side, his eyes dark as those of his owl spirit. "You didn't answer my question about brothers and sisters. Is it a painful topic? Should I not ask?"

Caught in my own cowardice, I hesitated once more. But why not tell him? We were near strangers even now, although I dearly wanted to know him better—and to be known. That wouldn't happen if I refused to answer his questions.

"It is a painful topic," I said. "But not one you need avoid. I'm a peasant girl from a village near Kostroma. I have two brothers, both older than I am. But I haven't seen them or my parents in ages. I don't know if they're still alive."

My throat tightened, and I stopped, blinking hard against an unexpected onslaught of tears. "What happened?" Mansur asked when I didn't go on. His voice almost undid me, it was so gentle.

"Famine," I said. My voice sounded choked. I cleared it, trying to pay attention only to the facts, not the feelings they evoked. "It's a northern area with poor soils, and in years when the rain comes too often or not enough, people starve. We had such a famine the year I turned twelve. My mother was making bread from acorns and stew from nettles to keep us alive, and then even the acorns ran out. That night I heard my parents talking by the stove, but not what they said." I stopped, staring at my shoes, swept into the past as if into one of my trances.

"Did that frighten you?" A reasonable question. Did I know the answer? I wasn't sure.

"I don't think so," I said. "Not then. I couldn't imagine what they would do. But the next day my father took me to a nearby estate, owned by the Kolychevs. Daniil Nikolaevich's parents, you understand."

Mansur nodded. "So that's how you know him."

"Yes, but we didn't meet until later. He wasn't at the estate that day—only his mother, Lady Natalya, who'd heard about the famine and come from Moscow to check on their people. Alas, we were neighbors, not dependents, or I'm sure she would have supplied grain to us too. As it was, Papa made me stay outside while he spoke to her.

When he came back, he told me to be good and that I'd have a better life there than he could give me. I was still trying to find out what he meant by that when he walked away." I stopped, fighting for control. The tears I'd not shed in fourteen years threatened to become a cascade, and I didn't want to disgrace myself by weeping.

I'd heard Mansur's sharp intake of breath and expected more questions, but he waited without speaking for me to go on. When I could speak without sobbing, I did. "I found out only later that my parents had sold me to the Kolychevs because they couldn't afford a dowry and they decided it made more sense to keep boys old enough to drive the plow than a girl who would soon marry out. If life improved and they needed more women, my brothers could take wives. Meanwhile, at least they'd be able to afford food and seeds for the next year's crop."

I'd seen Mansur's eyes widen during this last part of my story, and as I stumbled to a halt, he placed his bowl on the floor and reached for my hand. "But that's dreadful," he said. I heard the sympathy in his voice, and the warm clasp of his fingers comforted me. "Your father sold you as a slave and didn't have the guts to tell you himself?"

The tears spilled over despite my best efforts, and I scrubbed at them with my sleeve. "He told me he loved me," I said in scattered bursts. "I suppose I should have guessed he'd done something dreadful, because he wasn't a man who talked about feelings, who kissed or hugged. He'd never said that before."

"You were twelve," Mansur pointed out. "How could you have guessed?"

With difficulty, I blinked back another onrush of tears. "You're right. Anyway, Papa said he loved me. Then he left.

It was Lady Natalya who explained the rest. She was a good woman. She took me into her household, brought me to Moscow, and trained me as a servant. I lived there for six years. Then I met Stepan's father, Stenka, who was working for Lady Natalya's nephew at the time."

And wasn't *that* a tale for cold winter nights, if far too long for a single sitting.* "After a while, I went off with Stenka. The family could have chased me, because I belonged to them, but instead they let me go. They were good people, as I said."

"And how did you end up here?" Mansur's face showed none of the rejection I feared, only calm curiosity.

I breathed slowly, deeply, trying to restore control. "Later I ran into the Kolychevs again." Another long story.** "Nasan, in particular—she married Daniil not long before I ran away, and she was the one who persuaded her mother-in-law to free me and the khan to bring me here. She assisted the midwife during Stepan's birth, and she took a personal interest in us after that."

Waiting on tenterhooks for Mansur to respond, I realized I wanted to feel his arms around me. I yearned for a hug.

I pushed the thought aside. I liked him, he had a gift with my son, *he wasn't married*, but I'd known him such a short time. He'd been warm, calm, accepting. He'd understood how my father's unwillingness to break the news himself had hurt me. He still clasped my hand. I shouldn't hope for more.

I did, though.

Slowly, Grusha, slowly. Stepan is sleeping nearby.

---

* A story told in *The Golden Lynx*.
** As told in *The Swan Princess*.

I expected Mansur to ask how I'd convinced Nasan to help me when I was an escaped slave from her mother-in-law's household. Instead, he squeezed my hand and changed the subject. "And how did you become a shaman? Isn't that unusual for a Russian girl?"

"Ah." I smiled, relieved to hear a question that I could answer without weeping. "I suppose. But the Kostroma region has many shamans. The Cheremis live there, and they worship the trees and the bears, animals of all sorts. They can tell you everything you want to know about herbs and mushrooms and medicines, spells for healing and love and goodness knows what else, and some of them live in or close to most of the hamlets. I was baptized by the midwife who brought me into the world, but my family's homestead lay far from any church. I spent every spare moment with our local wise woman. Lady Natalya was appalled at my ignorance when I first arrived at her house."

I giggled at the memory. I'd had great respect for Lady Natalya, but her piety and her embrace of rules both large and small had been legendary. Appalled didn't begin to cover her response to my upbringing, or what she saw as a lack thereof. "I recognized some of the icons, but I knew far more about spells and plants than I did about Jesus and His Holy Mother. She summoned her chaplain, Father Job, right away and ordered him to teach me—and he did, to the best of his ability. He was a dear man; I hope he still lives. But when I met Suzukei, I felt as if I'd come home."

I picked up my bowl again. "Enough about me. I must tell you that when I retrieved your soul, I saw you as an owl. A beautiful snowy owl. And when I went to plead with the spirits to save the horde, I saw you again. We flew together, and the peri who sent the storm said that you were a shaman too, that the powers above had called you and you hadn't responded. Does any of that sound familiar to you?"

For the first time since I handed him the food, Mansur turned his head away. The color of his skin concealed any blush, but his unwillingness to meet my eyes suggested embarrassment.

"I don't know," he said after a long pause. "I haven't heard a call, but now I wonder. Since I woke up in your tent that first day, much in my mind is a blur. I remember the arrow that felled me and a beautiful pale-skinned woman I saw as an angel, with wings like an owl. I believed those things were dreams."

How could he not have heard the spirits summoning him? They weren't shy. They appeared right in front of you and called your name, and if you didn't respond or fled in fear, they hunted you down and tormented you in mind and body until you either gave in or died. Such behavior was what Nasan and Guzel had in mind when they warned me that I couldn't give up being a shaman on the day I'd told them of Fadeyev's hinted proposal.

So I didn't believe Mansur had missed the call. I *did* believe he preferred not to hear it, due to fear of a shaman's strangeness or some other reason I couldn't guess. The need to support his family, maybe. A lord like Alexei would reward his warriors generously, whereas a shaman depended on the kindness of people who often had few worldly goods to share. I must convince him to admit why he hesitated—or at least that he'd set off on a dangerous path. It was good that he'd reached us when he did. That too must be part of the spirits' plans for him.

For the moment, I spoke to the comment about what he recalled from our first encounter. "That was before I went to retrieve your soul," I told him. "Those things you saw or imagined probably weren't dreams so much as visions caused by your slipping in and out of wakefulness. I heard you talking about angels and owls. I was watching you to see if you'd come around on your own. If you did, I wouldn't need to search for you. But you didn't." I gave him a brief description of my journey to the lower world, explaining how I'd approached the snowy owl because it was a spirit like me, only to learn that it was his soul. He nodded as if he understood. He didn't question my story, but he listened with the distant courtesy I'd expect if we talked about a stranger. As if the snowy owl had nothing to do with him.

Repeating myself wouldn't convince him, so I decided to approach the same point from a different angle. "What happened to you this morning, during the raid?"

"During the raid." Mansur spoke slowly, his brows drawn together as if he struggled to recall the sequence of events. "After you went into trance, I waited as you'd told me to do for Stepan to arrive with the woman and her son. The ones you talked about."

He stopped, as if waiting for information. Had I told him their names? I couldn't remember. "Guzel and Timur," I said. "He's the khan's nephew, Alexei Sultan's son. You've never met him? Alexei's married to a Russian noblewoman now; they have two children. But he and Guzel lived together for years before he left this horde, and he sent Timur to his uncle for fostering."

Mansur nodded his understanding. "I hadn't met Timur. I joined his father two years ago. It must have been close to when Timur came south. He was twelve? He looks about fourteen now."

"Yes, fourteen. Two years sounds right. He'll be leaving soon, I think. His father has promised to visit us once his assignment in Kolomna is done. I expect he'll take Timur back with him." The khan and his brother had not confided the details of their plans to me, shaman or not. I spoke on the basis of Guzel's fears.

"So I would have met you then anyway," Mansur said with a smile. "The boy's mother won't like that, though, I expect."

"Not one bit," I agreed. "It's a difficult situation for them, living so far apart. For Timur, too, because he can be with only one parent at a time. But you were telling me what you recall during the raid."

He frowned again, as if conjuring up the memory. "Yes, the raid. After you lay down, Guzel and Timur came in with Stepan and that Russian. I saw the four of them arrive. Then Guzel picked up the drum and began to play it."

"Did it affect you? The rhythm is supposed to encourage the trance state." I marked the slow, steady beat with my hands, as I'd done while teaching Guzel how to play. When I realized what I was doing, I stopped.

"Not right away. The fumes from your burners got me first. They stung my eyes, so I closed them; the scent overwhelmed me." He scrunched up his eyes as he talked. I could see he was remembering the sting caused by the juniper.

He went on. "Then the drumming lifted me out of myself. I sensed my soul separating from my body. I tried to stop it from happening, but I couldn't. After a while, I found myself sitting on the smoke hole. I looked down, and my feet had become claws. I saw talons gripping the rim. I looked up, and there was the steppe extending in all directions. My head swiveled so far I could tell what was happening behind me. At the time, it didn't seem strange, but that does sound like an owl, doesn't it?"

"It does," I said. "What then?"

"I heard the battle—saw it, too, from above." He released my hand and flapped both sets of fingers as if they were wings. "A blast of wind blew me off the smoke hole, and I was flying. I saw an owl and an eagle, and I felt drawn to them, so I flew toward them. The eagle screeched and left, but the owl stayed with me. We flew on together. After a while, I realized you were the owl—I don't know how I figured that out—but I didn't recognize the eagle. Did you?"

"The eagle is Suzukei. My teacher." Sorrow spread through me. I still missed her daily presence, even though I could reach her in the other worlds. "She died a few months before you came here, after she drank a potion that contained poisonous mushrooms. Until her last day, she was the camp shaman, and I served as her assistant. What else did you see?"

"May you have life," he said.

Startled by his use of this Russian expression, even in his own language, I released a short, sharp breath. Where had he learned it?

Then I remembered he was stationed in Kolomna. He must have heard it there.

Mansur continued. "There was another pale woman with wings, who looked like my angel; she could have been a peri, I suppose. The whole thing felt fuzzy, unreal. Again I wrote it off as a dream. After a while, I heard the drum again, beating slowly; then everything faded. The next thing I recall is that Russian shouting. I wanted to jump up and hit him for his disrespect, but I could hardly move. Are you telling me some of what I experienced was real?"

"In a sense." I raised the empty bowl that had contained Rasima's stew. "Perhaps not in the same way as this dish is real. But the spirits do talk to me, and the things I see in trance have *meaning*. They aren't random; they answer questions I'm asking or show me where to find help when I need it. So I do believe that reality extends into realms beyond those we can see, hear, and touch. It must, because when I retrieve souls, those near death recover. When I banish spirits, sick and injured people heal. But I don't usually ask my patients what they saw and heard while I was helping them. I just want them to get better."

"So the whole thing exists in your mind, like a dream?" He sounded hopeful, as if he needed a reason to doubt his own impressions. "No one confirms what you see in your visions?"

I wrinkled my nose, looking for words to explain what I'd learned in a way that would be honest but not encourage him to reject his gift. "Stepan remembered parts of the trance I went into when I retrieved his soul. That too was before you came, and I talked about it with Guzel. So he may have overheard me without being fully awake. I can't be certain, although he seemed convinced he'd seen a wooden house—which he didn't know was a Russian hut, having lived on the steppe since he was three months old. But he's the eaglet the peri mentioned, and she said they've already chosen him to serve them, which suggests that Stepan will one day become a shaman too. Or a sacred storyteller, more likely; he does love stories."

"That he does." Mansur fingered the chessboard, rolled and tied next to his bed, as if recalling his games earlier today with my son. "I remember the peri talking about an eaglet. She meant Stepan? I can imagine him as an eaglet."

"Me too," I said. "More with each day that passes."

"And you don't think he can already see into other realms without understanding that's what he's doing?"

I thought about how to answer his question. There was no real way to tell what a child so young might have the capacity to do. "Yes, perhaps," I said after a while. "It's the reason he dislikes Fadeyev: because Stepan saw his father in the trance and hoped he'd come back as Fadeyev—they look alike. When I explained that couldn't happen, Stepan was bitterly disappointed."

"Fadeyev," Mansur said. "That's the Russian?"

"Yes. Anfim Fadeyev." I gave him a brief account of how Anfim wound up in our camp. It hadn't occurred to me until that moment that the two men hadn't met before, because Mansur had arrived already injured and still wasn't strong enough to leave my tent.

He wrinkled his nose as I reached the end, as if he smelled something rotten. "Stepan's instincts are sound. I detest the man myself, and I've only had to deal with him once."

"You've seen him at his worst. My power terrifies him."

"It sounded as if he'd asked you to marry him," Mansur said. I listened for hints of emotion in his voice, but if anything he sounded too casual, as if deliberately concealing what he felt. "Why did he do that, if you terrify him?"

"He doesn't understand what it means to be a shaman. He thinks I could set it aside to look after him and his children." I shrugged. Mansur had been honest with me. If I wanted him, and I did, it behooved me to respond in kind. "It doesn't matter, anyway. I toyed with the idea for a while, because I thought I'd like to go back to Russia—search for my family, show Stepan where he comes from. But once I realized that I couldn't deny my gift, and he couldn't tolerate it, I knew I would turn him down. He brought it up today, so I did it today, but I would have told him soon no matter what."

Mansur nodded without speaking, and I grabbed the chance to get the conversation back on the path I wished it to follow. "But although *Stepan* could either have overheard what I said or experienced it in trance, your situation is different. I may have described you to Guzel as an owl after the first time I saw you; I don't really remember. But I haven't told her or anyone else that we flew together today. I said only that another soul helped me. I wanted to talk to you before I gave them your name."

"I see." He frowned.

"Anyway, the peri I met said quite clearly that the spirits have summoned you. It's dangerous to resist them." I pointed to his wound. "The peri insisted your injury was intended to get your attention. If you'd like to learn more about shamanism, I'd be happy to help."

"I'll think about it," he promised. "I'm a warrior. I've been good at it, and I've enjoyed it, for the most part. It kept my family in food when we had no other means of survival. I owe service to my sultan, too. But my brothers can help me ensure that my mother wants for nothing in her old age. And if God intends me to follow a different path, I'd be foolish to resist."

I released a long, relieved breath. He was willing to see reason. I needn't fear for his future.

Then he spoke again. "But do your spirits indeed have such power over a Muslim? I rather doubt it. I didn't grow up on the steppe either, but I spent plenty of time in a horde like this one, visiting various relatives. I haven't seen the dire results you describe. I respect what you do, but I don't feel the need to do the same. My uncle's camp survived quite well without a shaman."

My hopes for a simple solution dashed, I swore under my breath. Persuading him was going to be difficult. The peri had not minced words, and I feared the worst, even if I did understand that Mansur, raised as a Muslim, had the same loyalty to his religion as Fadeyev had to Christianity and I to shamanism.

I should think before I urged him to betray his conscience. Such a plea would almost certainly fail, and if it didn't, he might hold the decision against me later. I didn't want that. After such a stress-filled day, my mind couldn't stretch to consider new possibilities, but if I waited, another solution might present itself, or at least a more convincing argument.

I let the bigger question go to pursue a smaller but perhaps no less important one. "You didn't grow up on the steppe? Where *did* you grow up, then?"

From the expression on his face, it was clear that my surprise amused him. "Where do you think? In Russia. My family hails from Kazan, but my grandfather fought alongside Kudai-Kul Sultan—the one who became Tsarevich Peter, the old grand prince's brother-in-law—so they were captured together and taken to Russia decades ago. After the old grand prince released Kudai-Kul, Grandfather summoned his wife and son to join him in Moscow. That's where my father married and I was born. When Kudai-Kul died, my father accepted service with Shah-Ali, your khan's uncle. I was nine then, and we followed Shah-Ali from one post to another, including back to Kazan when they chose him as their khan and up to the north when he was incarcerated there."

I stared at him, at a loss for words. He'd grown up in Russia, among the Muslim Tatars who served the grand prince. Like my son, Mansur was both Russian and Tatar. No wonder they got along so well. Had the spirits sent him to us, then, not only because he needed us to help him find his way but because they knew we needed *him* to find ours?

I couldn't voice these thoughts. He'd think I'd lost my mind. When I'd mastered my shock, I said the first thing that came into my head. It happened to be the most idiotic comment possible. "So you do speak Russian."

He laughed, then—not a quiet chuckle but an open, hearty laugh that caused Stepan to twist and turn amid his sheets. "Sorry," Mansur said in my native tongue and a softer tone. "Yes, of course I speak Russian. I've been surrounded by it for as long as I can remember."

"And you never mentioned it? Never spoke it to me? Why?" I could barely get the words out in any language, I was so amazed.

He shrugged, although another sideways glance indicated he was less indifferent than he seemed. "I didn't see a need. You and Stepan always used Tatar in my presence, except that one time when you told him the story about the gray wolf."

So he *had* heard me that night. I felt my cheeks flush. I couldn't help myself. It had been a ridiculous question. "I see," I said, eager to cover up my embarrassment. "And how did you meet Alexei Sultan?"

"Through his uncle," Mansur said. "Shah-Ali is enormously fat, as you may have heard. He's an excellent general, but no horse can carry him, so his bodyguard mostly stands around during battles to prevent stray arrows heading his way. Not the best use of a warrior's skills. A couple of years ago, Alexei came to Kasimov and I realized that service to him would be a far more satisfying position, so I asked if I could switch. He and his uncle agreed, and I found myself back in Moscow." I still saw laughter in his eyes as he finished. "That I spoke Russian like a native was one reason Alexei took me on. Most of his men came with him from Crimea, so they struggle with the language and the customs. I act as their interpreter, among other things."

"That's quite a story," I said, struggling for a suitable response. His tale had overturned my whole sense of him and who he was, and I didn't know where to start. I'd believed him to be a married Tatar warrior of the steppe, and instead he knew as much about my homeland as I did (and he had no wife or children, although he did have a family for which he felt responsible). And he spoke my language as if born to it, because he had been. "But you will consider becoming a shaman instead of a warrior? I would hate to see you suffer, and I do believe it's dangerous to resist the spirits' call." I stopped then, sure that I'd already said too much.

"Yes, I'll consider it. I already told you that." He hesitated, and for a moment I expected him to continue, but he didn't. Instead he handed me his bowl and pulled the supporting pillows from behind his head. "Thank you for the food. I should sleep, and so should you." He sighed, then gave me a mischievous smile. "Your son will wake us early enough."

"Very true." I piled the dishes on top of the food and rose, wishing I hadn't spent quite so much time sitting cross-legged, first at Nasan's house and then here. My ankles hurt, and my feet were on the point of falling asleep before I did. "Perhaps you could become a sacred storyteller, as Stepan may do. You could honor the spirits without giving up your beliefs. But let's discuss it tomorrow—or if not tomorrow, then soon."

"I look forward to it," he said as I carried the dishes to the section of the tent reserved for food storage, close to the frame so that the cold air from outside could do its work of preservation. "Thank you for your patience, *fereshtem*."

I turned to stare at him once more. *Fereshtem*, my angel. The beautiful, pale-skinned woman with the wings of an owl. He *had* meant me.

Indeed, hadn't he called me that after I routed Fadeyev? The events of the day had moved so fast, and I'd been so happy about persuading the peri to save the horde, that I'd had no time to savor the details—even this most precious one.

Mansur gazed back at me, his eyes solemn, in contrast to the smile playing about his mouth. Another rush of desire flooded my body, and only the sight of my sleeping son stopped me from reaching out. Humming under my breath, I set my burden down, placing the pot and pouch near the lattice frame and stacking the dishes for washing in the morning.

Maybe I'd do a better job of convincing him next time. But before I slept, I had one more task to perform. I must try to discover what was happening to my friends Dina and Firuza and, if possible, intervene with the spirits on their behalf.

Chapter Thirteen

I DIDN'T HAVE THE STRENGTH TO ENTER ANOTHER TRANCE, something that would also be hard to attain without the juniper and drumming. That would wake up Stepan and Mansur, not to mention the rest of the camp, except for those already in a state of armed vigilance. I might as well start a fire; under the circumstances, I couldn't cause much more trouble if I did.

Fortunately, I didn't need to go into trance again to ask my questions. I could achieve the state of communion with other worlds that I used for healing through no more than steady breathing and a willingness to receive whatever revelations the spirits chose to send me. Lying flat on my back, covers pulled to my chin and my hands palms upward beneath the layers of wool and felt, I closed my lids, opened my inner eye, and addressed my helpers without speaking the words aloud.

"Great Ones," I said in my mind. "Thank you for the assistance you have already given us today. You saved so many of our people. Please accept our gratitude."

I waited, testing the air around me for the ancestors' presence. When I felt a cool blast through the smoke hole,

I sent a picture of Dina and Firuza as I'd last seen them, in full armor on horseback.

"These two descendants of yours are missing," I told the grandmothers. "Captured by the enemy. I fear for them—and for the rest of the horde, who will retrieve them at whatever cost in lives and health. Can you tell me where they are, reassure me of their safety, in the hope of saving lives?"

Again I waited, eyes closed, hands cupped to receive the essence of the realms beyond. For a long time I sensed nothing.

I became concerned. Then, like a fire bursting into sparks, I saw three pictures in my head, one after another in swift succession: Dina and Firuza, unbound, together in a tent with no one else around; the two of them galloping at top speed—Firuza on her beautiful palomino mare, Kubelek, and Dina on her Moon Shadow; and, last and most disturbing of the three, Firuza and Dina lying as if slain, draped in the banner of Alexei Sultan.

I jerked bolt upright. My breath came in gasps as I gazed at the silent tent. I was sitting on my own bed. The light cast by the hearth fire revealed Mansur lying across from me, Stepan curled in sleep to my right. They both looked peaceful, untroubled. I could imagine them blessed by happy dreams.

I couldn't say the same for myself. What had the spirits shown me? Were these visions part of one story or three possible futures?

Firuza and Dina captive, Firuza and Dina escaping, Firuza and Dina dead. I didn't know which one to believe.

Still less did I know what I should tell the khan.

In the end, I told Ogodai nothing. Every time I saw him, he seemed caught up in military matters—strategy and planning and equipment checks, drills and messages. To disturb him with the shadowy, partial, and ultimately alarming impressions I'd managed to wring from my spirit helpers struck me as a poor use of his time.

Then, less than a week after I'd sent Nasan's intruder to the nether world, the thunder of hooves again woke the camp at first light. As before, I tumbled from my tent half-asleep, Stepan's hand clasped in mine. Mansur limped behind us, holding on to my shoulder for balance, then stopped where he could grasp the edge of the carved door for support.

Roars of greeting assailed my ears. I blinked without understanding at the horizon, where a line of armed men on horseback obscured the rising sun.

Run? Hide? No, too late. They'll be on us in a moment. But what is it, another raid?

It couldn't be. No one around me showed the least sign of anxiety. Even Stepan, who'd managed to scramble onto a nearby cart without releasing my hand, shouted, "Mama, Mama, look!" I grabbed him around the waist and lowered him to the ground before his unrestrained leaps broke the unfilled traces.

"What do you see, Stepan?" Mansur asked from behind me.

"Horses," Stepan said between pants. "Thousands and thousands and thousands of horses." He sucked in his breath. "Ours, Mama. Look. I've never seen so many!"

"Ours?" I asked. "Are you sure?"

He nodded as if his efforts had robbed him of speech. With more care than he'd shown, I stepped on the cart wheel and balanced myself on the seat.

From the edge of the camp to as far as the eye could reach, galloping horsemen and unsaddled reserve mounts filled the steppe as a felt mat covers a tent floor. But it wasn't until I saw the banners—black winged stallions embroidered on white silk backgrounds—that I grasped what was going on.

Stepan was right. The horsemen were "ours." The beys of the khan's council had answered Ogodai's call. And judging by the numbers, they'd committed every man and beast to his cause.

Suzukei never attended meetings like the one scheduled for that morning, which would focus on military strategy and whatever intelligence Ogodai's scouts had obtained since the day before. So I didn't expect an invitation either. Even Nasan and Firuza, if the first were well and the second freed from captivity, left that kind of planning to the men.

I could have eavesdropped, I suppose, since the leaders made no attempt to keep their voices down. But it hardly seemed appropriate behavior from the camp shaman, so instead I put in several hours to ensure that Mansur and Stepan had whatever they might need for the rest of the morning and went to check on Nasan. I'd found her improved on every visit, and I expected her to be restored to her usual state of boundless energy soon, but I stopped by once a day just in case. And in truth, on this particular day my motives were not wholly pure. I had few doubts that she would have coaxed Daniil to tell her as much as possible about the horde's plans and might even have sent him off with suggestions for her brother.

I found her up and dressed, one wide sleeve folded back to display the bandage, and sitting on the sofa. Only the wealthiest members of the horde could afford them, and for the first time, looking at it, I admitted to a touch of envy. It would be so much easier for Mansur to play chess, converse, and eat if I owned a sofa. Although his staggering as far as the door this morning confirmed that his wound had healed to the point where he could move about on his own without my fearing the bleeding would recur—and, saints be praised, without infection setting in—he remained limited in what he could do.

Nasan greeted me as I came in. She sounded quite cheerful, and the color of her cheeks had returned to its normal hue of rose over ivory. "You look much better," I said, delighted to see her so restored. I touched her forehead and detected no signs of fever. "Have the effects of the poison faded?"

"Mostly." She raised the bandaged arm. "I tire more easily than I should, as if the wolf's bane continues to sap my strength. And I still feel some tingling around the edges of the wound. The surrounding skin looks clear, though, and the gash has scabbed over. I'll have a lovely scar to remember the raiders by, but it would have been much worse if you hadn't stepped in when you did. Thank you."

"Is that the bandage I put on yesterday?" I didn't see how it could be, since she had described the appearance of the skin beneath.

"No, Rasima redid it this morning so I could take a look." She grinned at me. "I know, I should have waited for you. And I do trust you. I couldn't have managed better myself. I finished the sacred water you left for me, too. I'm sure that helped. Curiosity got the better of me, in truth."

I shook my head at her, but I was so glad to see her almost healed that I didn't complain. "The beys arrived this morning," I said. "They're busy discussing strategy now. Or will be, once they finish asking after one another's great-grandchildren." Nasan laughed at that. She knew how long it took, even under urgent circumstances, to finish the preliminaries and get to the matter at hand. "Do you know what your husband and brother have in mind?"

She waved at the sofa. "Most of it. Enough, in any case. If there's more, I'll find out when the meeting ends. Have a seat, and I'll ask Rasima to bring us some tisane."

"I'll take care of it. If your arm still tingles, you should rest. I'm glad the wound has closed, but let's not risk undoing our good work." When Nasan didn't object—a sign she wasn't as much recovered as she pretended—I went to the door and dispatched Kiraz, who happened to be the first servant I saw, in search of Rasima and the promised refreshments. When Kiraz bowed and scurried off, I joined Nasan on the sofa.

For a few moments after I saw her sitting up, I'd considered sharing my vision of Firuza and Dina with her. But my sense that she might be pushing herself before she was ready gave me pause. If I had useful information, I'd take it straight to the khan. But I didn't. Alarming Nasan could do her no good. It wouldn't help anyone else, either.

Instead I asked, "Did the khan's scouts find out where Firuza and Dina are being kept?" The answer might help me pick the right image among my three possibilities.

Nasan shuddered, and I again had second thoughts about encouraging her to talk. "I hate to think about what will happen to them if we can't get them back," she said. "I'm so glad the beys have arrived. Even though it means more fighting, we can hope to free Dina and Firuza now."

"You should have seen the men riding in," I said to encourage her. "They covered the steppe from here to the horizon. I thought my heart would stop when I first caught sight of that massive line of warriors against the sky. I've never seen so many in one place at one time. I kept expecting Stepan to explode from excitement, the way he shouted about the thousands and thousands of horses."

That last made her laugh again, as I'd intended. "I bet there are thousands," she said. "Bring five hundred warriors and you have fifteen hundred horses. There must be many more than that. Ogodai will have to move them out fast, or they'll eat every blade of grass from here to the Volga."

"It was an impressive sight," I agreed.

Kiraz arrived right then with a steaming jug of rose-hip tisane and a fragrant basket that turned out to contain *chek-chek*, deep-fried balls of dough dipped in honey. I— and especially Stepan—loved *chek-chek*. They reminded me of Russian donuts with their light, fluffy insides and crisp, sweet outsides. I'd have to save one or two for my son, or he'd never forgive me. I should probably save one for Mansur, too.

When Kiraz put down the refreshments and left, Nasan picked up the story. "We learned that the raiders took Firuza and Dina north, to the camp where they intercepted the couriers coming from Kasimov. And that our enemies never did join forces with the Crimean princes, because Alexei's troops got in the way. So we can guess that the men were angry and frustrated, and when they recognized some of the couriers' banners as his, they gave chase. Most likely, they took our women to teach us a lesson. They made a big mistake there, because Ogodai and Ruslan will stop at nothing to punish them, and Alexei is pursuing them as well, even though he doesn't know about them capturing Dina and Firuza. But desperate men make stupid decisions."

"How do you know all this?" I asked.

"Our scouts captured one of the raiders and dragged the tale out of him by brute force." She pounded a fist against the quilt, as if demonstrating.

It was my turn to shudder. Even enemies feel pain. "I suppose he wouldn't have told them the truth otherwise, but I do feel bad for him. I'd feel worse if I weren't so worried about our friends. He didn't say what happened after they took the women north?"

"He did." Nasan poured tisane as she talked, although the glare she inflicted on the innocent *chek-chek* threatened to set them ablaze. "Up to a point. The leaders decided to keep them both as a gift for Sheikh-Mamai. Their bey, you know. He ordered the campaign, but he didn't want to take on the Russians himself. So like the Crimean khan, Sheikh-Mamai is pretending that these raiders are renegades. Nothing to do with him."

"Sheikh-Mamai again." I snorted in disgust. "What a menace that man is." Sheikh-Mamai led the forces that had once carried the captured banners now adorning our horde's meeting tent. "I'm amazed he managed to raise a new army after Ogodai defeated him so badly the last time. But it means we must rescue Dina and Firuza before his men can turn them over to him. He won't treat them well. He'll see them as weapons to use against this horde and its leader."

"Agreed," Nasan said. "But it also means that we have a chance to rescue them before any harm comes to them. They haven't been given to anyone else."

My breath escaped in a rush. "You mean they may not have been violated? Oh, I'm so glad to hear that!"

Nasan passed me the cup of tisane with one hand and clasped my wrist with the other. "Not yet, assuming the information is true. We do have to act quickly, so it's good that the beys have arrived—and in force. If the raiders move our friends to their main camp, a rescue will be much more difficult. But there's reason to hope. Remember I said the raiders weren't able to join forces with the Crimean princes because Alexei got in their way?"

I nodded. "How could I forget? There's more?"

"Much more. The Russians halted the Crimean advance. Kolomna and Kasimov are safe, as is the whole Oka riverbank. And while the other generals harry Sahib-Girei's forces to ensure they continue to retreat, Alexei is marching his troops east, against the men holding Dina and Firuza. He wants Ogodai and his beys to come up from the south so the two of them can act as pincers and catch the raiders between them."

"Which they will, because it's what they planned to do anyway." Thoughts spun through my head like thread on a distaff. It was a great plan. Even I, unfamiliar with military strategy, could see that. Alexei probably didn't know that his brother had raised the steppe and had a huge force at his command. For certain, the raiders hadn't had time to discover it. It would be a pleasant—or in the case of the raiders an unpleasant—surprise. But I also understood that was another reason for Ogodai's troops to move fast, so the raiders had no advance warning. "They'll leave soon?"

"The moment the noon prayers end, my husband said." Nasan picked up her cup and drained it. "I think you're right: I should rest for one more day. Can you come back tomorrow? Take the *chek-chek* for Stepan. I know how much he loves them."

"Of course," I said. "And thank you."

As I walked back to my tent, I saw that the meeting had ended. The leaders must have gotten down to business faster than I expected, because I hadn't spent that much time chatting with Nasan. As she'd predicted, the troops would set out soon. They were already massing. The glint of sunshine from so many steel helmets was blinding.

I stopped, surprised to see Haji Rahman mounted on a beautiful white gelding. He must have decided to ride with the warriors.

After thinking about it, I decided that made sense. Who but an imam could ensure God's blessing on the campaign, send the men into battle in full compliance with their Law, comfort the wounded, and minister to any who fell in the fight?

As I watched, Rahman's three sons took their places behind him, forming a tight-knit family group within the surrounding army. Once the men left, only a small rear guard—including the remnants of Nasan's defense force, led by one of the younger women until its commander healed enough to resume her position—would remain to protect those unable to fight.

With so many warriors and horses, the beys' combined forces could not move out as a single unit, but columns had formed and lines of cavalry showed against the distant hillside. I looked for Stepan's blond head amid the tight knot of children his age milling around at the edge of the campground and didn't find it. About to investigate, I recalled that I'd left him in my tent in response to a suggestion from Mansur—who as usual appeared to have kept my son under good control. At a minimum, it made sense to check there first. If Stepan had somehow managed to escape Mansur's oversight, I had a pretty good idea where to search for him. Every boy in the camp would be riveted on the sight of the departing warriors and their horses.

Fadeyev stopped me halfway. I was cursing him in my head until I noticed that he again had the hangdog expression that indicated a desire to apologize. I hugged the basket to my chest and waited while he begged for forgiveness.

"I do forgive you," I said when he stumbled to a halt. "You were afraid. Many people fear me, because I talk to the spirits. But you must see for yourself that we don't suit. You need a different kind of wife, and I need a husband—if I need a husband at all—who understands what I do and appreciates it."

"Can't you give it up?" he asked.

I wondered at his persistence. He'd never hinted that he desired me. But if he saw the match as a practical solution to a problem, why push? The world was full of women who would leap at the opportunity to become his wife.

But then, did it matter whether he desired me? I thought about that for an instant, then realized it didn't. He was still insisting I give up my "sorcery."

"No," I said. "That's the whole point. I can't. The spirits choose those they want, and they insist that we serve them. I wish you well, but I can't change myself for you."

He seemed to get it then, finally. At least, he stepped away from me and bowed, and with an answering tip of my head I left him standing in the pathway.

When I ducked through my own doorway, Stepan greeted both me and the *chek-chek* with delight. He grabbed the basket from my hands. "Slowly," I said. "Be polite and offer one to Mansur first."

"Yes, Mama." Stepan made a face, but he did as I asked, picking up a wooden plate that still held crumbs of flatbread and a curd or two and handing it to Mansur. Then, with the air of a traveling magician, he pulled back the cloth that covered the sweets and held the basket out to our guest. "Would you like one? They're Rasima's. I can tell from the patterns on the basket. They're awfully good."

"Thank you." Mansur accepted a *chek-chek* and regarded me with that quiet smile that indicated hidden amusement. "Your mama might like one too."

I picked up a clean plate and accepted a sweet. "I would. I love them almost as much as Stepan. I didn't get to taste them earlier because Nasan had news I wanted to hear, and then she needed to rest, so I made her comfortable and left. She looks much better, though, and she gave me some valuable information. Stepan, you did that beautifully, so help yourself now. You may have two." While my son happily gobbled his *chek-chek*, I filled Mansur in on what I'd learned from Nasan.

"And the thing is—I didn't want to say this to anyone in the horde because I don't know what to make of it—a few nights ago, after the spirit journey we took together and the healing ceremony for Nasan, I had a vision of Firuza and Dina. Three visions, in fact. I can't tell whether they are one story or several disconnected ones. Alternative possibilities, you understand." I glanced at my son, thinking about how to describe what I'd seen without either scaring him or giving him a tale to tell that, if he shared it, would frighten others. "I haven't wanted to raise hopes—or dash them—when my impressions are so vague. None of my efforts to clarify things have worked."

"Another vision?" Mansur prompted. "You went into trance again? Three times is too much for one day, surely."

"It would be, but the healing ceremony doesn't require a trance. Nor did this one. I just lay still and let the pictures form. Like this." I closed my eyes, sitting, and turned my palms upward. I hoped I might get a clearer sense of which picture to trust, but the three continued to waver before my shut lids, as if interchangeable.

"I have a lot to learn, it seems," Mansur said.

I opened my eyes to find him still regarding me with that steady gaze. The warmth of his expression aroused a similar heat in me. I saw yearning in his eyes but also affection—admiration, even. I liked that. "You've decided to accept your gift then," I said. "I'm glad."

"Not exactly." Mansur glanced at Stepan. "I'm still considering what to do. I like your suggestion that I could become a storyteller rather than a shaman. But I'm not my own man. I have obligations to my lord and my family. I can't assume that Alexei Sultan will release me from service or that my mother will agree to live here in the horde: she didn't grow up on the steppe any more than I did. I have to ask them. So long as I'm here, though, I'm willing to learn from you. It will help me decide later. And convince them, if necessary."

"Your mother would be welcome here," I said, eager to encourage him—not just to become a storyteller but to stay with us. The mother of so charming a man could not be other than charming, surely. "Still, I understand your position."

I did, too: despite a pang of disappointment, it reassured me that he cared about the commitment he'd made to his lord and about his family's well-being. It gave me hope than one day he might care as much about me and Stepan.

"It's not a good time to bring her, anyway, even if she agrees. Better if she joins us after the fall migration," I told him. "If you leave soon, you wouldn't know where to find us until we reach the winter grazing lands. The khan will no doubt order the move as soon as he rescues his wife and Dina."

I crossed myself, out of habit, and shivered at the memory of the two women lying side by side. "So long as he does rescue them, that is."

"He will," Mansur said. "If they live, he will rescue them. I have great respect for your khan. And I appreciate your words about my mother. But you tremble. Is that because of your vision? Tell me what you saw."

I shivered again at the memory, but the kindness in his eyes, the quiet strength of his presence, convinced me that I could safely share my muddled thoughts with him. I described the conflicting pictures the spirits sent me: Firuza and Dina in the tent, the pair of them riding, the two bodies wrapped in Alexei Sultan's banner. With Stepan nearby, I didn't talk about their pallor, the stillness so characteristic of death.

The frown of concentration I'd come to expect from Mansur when I presented him with a problem creased his brow. For some reason, his intense focus on my words comforted me. "But my lord's on his way here," he said. "You told me that when you came in." He gestured in a circle, his hand pointing to the smoke hole above his head. "Not here to the camp's present location, but here in the sense of meeting Ogodai Khan on the battlefield. That Alexei Sultan sent messengers asking his brother to join him against the raiders. That the troops had already begun to move out while you were on your way here."

"I did, yes." Where was he going with this? What did it mean for Dina and Firuza?

He produced a shrug, extending his palms outward as he raised one shoulder, his expression almost apologetic. "Do visions mean only the obvious? Could the banner be a sign that your friends' rescue depends in part on what Alexei Sultan does? If he attacks the raiders' camp as planned, he will find the women and free them. They're the wives of his half-brother and his sworn brother. He will recognize them, even if Ogodai Khan hasn't had a chance to share the news of their capture."

I bit my left thumbnail, considering. Mansur could be right—except for the way the women lay, as if dead to the outside world.

But suppose the women weren't dead but sleeping, and the banner a sign that they had reached a safe place? Wasn't that how a storyteller would show the chain of events Mansur had described?

"Perhaps." I clenched my hands together and rested them in my lap, as if I hugged my friends tight. "I hope so."

And I did hope so, more than I could express in words.

Chapter Fourteen

ANOTHER WEEK PASSED. NASAN RECOVERED COMPLETELY, and Mansur's injury healed to the point where he could hobble around the camp with the aid of a crutch. Not easily, but well enough to take care of his own needs and walk short distances with Stepan and me. He talked about moving out of our tent, but I suggested he wait. The camp might gossip about us—although I doubted it, because I'd not heard much speculation about anyone else, and I knew that not every couple here had signed a marriage contract. Assuming the members of the horde even imagined Mansur and me as a couple, which I wasn't sure they did, given their respect for me as their shaman and his injured state.

A more convincing reason for delay was that so many of the warriors had ridden off with Ogodai and his beys. The only place Mansur could stay would be with Anfim Fadeyev. When I pointed that out, I received a refusal so emphatic that I had to hide my smile as I turned away. For a while, I thought I'd successfully put a stop to the whole idea, but after a few days Mansur raised the possibility again. So I accepted that it was important to him, although I didn't understand why.

Indeed, I couldn't imagine where he thought he might go. Of those who remained in the camp, most were women, children, sick and wounded, or so elderly that they had less ability to feed and care for an injured man than I did. And with the number of guards reduced to the essential minimum, Ogodai had told Guzel and me before he left to implement the emergency plans we'd drawn up, filling each tent to capacity to reduce the need for fuel and sending two-thirds or more of the herdsmen off to keep an eye on the cows, sheep, and goats as they migrated. In the midst of battle, the raiders would have no time to steal animals, and the faster horses could catch up with the flocks and herds later, so it made no sense to keep the cattle in one place while the days shortened, the nights turned colder, and the over-grazed grass became ever sparser. With Mansur already assigned to my tent, Stepan and I had no reason to move to more cramped quarters or take in additional members of the horde, but the changes meant that no other tent had room for Mansur.

At least, that was what I told him. In truth, I didn't ask because I didn't want to lose him. After six years alone with my son, I'd forgotten the pleasure of sharing the day's events with a person my own age. And Stenka died before I could appreciate the different approach to children, especially boys, taken by men. I loved my son as I loved no one else, but I couldn't teach him to think like a warrior by mastering the chessboard, to draw a bow or aim an arrow or clean saddles and stirrups. For Mansur, these things were the most natural pursuits in the world, and he instructed Stepan as he had his own younger brothers.

Under normal circumstances, I'd have discouraged Stepan from becoming close to a man who had yet to commit himself to either of us. But since it was already far too late to worry about that, I chose to take advantage of Mansur's presence and hope that the growing closeness among the three of us would make him more eager to stay with us—or at least return to us. Each day I watched my son blossom under my guest's gentle handling.

Look at them now. Stepan, his curls as untamed as ever but with a look of intense concentration on his face, stood sideways a few foot lengths from me. At Mansur's suggestion, I'd asked Nasan to lend me a child's sword, about the length of Stepan's forearm. My son held it straight out in one hand as though it were an enormous eating knife that he planned to use to pierce a loaf of bread.

Mansur was laughing, his eyes alight with affection and perhaps a certain pride. "Two hands, Stepan," he said. "You have more control if you hold the hilt with two hands. Right now you look as if you're about to skewer meat."

A sharp breath escaped me. Swords skewered men, not meat. For the briefest instant I recalled Anfim Fadeyev promising to train Stepan for administration instead of war. Surely I owed my son that chance: to live without killing, without risking death in each battle. Stepan might become a shaman or a storyteller, but suppose he didn't? What then?

Mansur caught Stepan's hands and showed him how to place them, how to raise the sword and bring it down, how to turn it against an enemy. Above my son's head, his eyes met mine, brows asking a question.

I gazed at him, troubled. "He needs to learn how to defend himself," Mansur said. "Even a storyteller can't prevent every attack on those he loves."

"I know," I said. And I did. Fadeyev would no doubt want to teach my son to defend himself too. It was the way of the world—especially for men, especially here on the steppe. I wasn't having second thoughts. Not really. Yet I did wish for a life focused on peace and on healing for myself and my son—and yes, for Mansur as well.

Maybe it would happen someday, but not today, not on the steppe. Not even in Russia.

"I like the songs," Mansur said. It was the afternoon of the same day, and I'd sent Stepan off to play with his friends so that I could talk to Mansur. My excuse was that I'd promised to teach him how to contact the other worlds, to help him decide which direction his life should take. In truth, I prayed the ancestors would persuade him, and not only so that he'd stay with me and Stepan. I hated to think of him tormented by vengeful spirits whose power he didn't believe in. They might even kill him, and then what would happen to my hopes for a life together?

He sang a few lines in a rich, warm voice. "'The princess placed her sword on the ground, / Walked to the tent door and looked all around, / Then called those she saw to entertain the forty heroes.'" He treated me to his mischievous smile. "You would know about that, *fereshtem*, although you've entertained only one."

"Oh, so now you're a hero, are you?" I pushed playfully at his arm.

He pointed at his healing wound, still bandaged. "Well, what else would I be? Wounded in the line of duty." He laughed as he said it, so I could tell he was joking.

"You have a beautiful voice," I told him, because it was true. I'd noticed it even when he spoke, but when he sang, the purity of his tone sent shivers down my spine. "I should call you *my* angel."

"Then why don't you?" His lips twitched. "I wouldn't mind a bit. *Batyram* would please me too."

Batyram. My hero, another reference to his jest. I hadn't flirted in so long that I wasn't sure I remembered how to go about it, but I did my best. "*Batyram,*" I said. "It's good that the songs and stories speak to you. You have the voice for it, and I'll enjoy listening to you address the spirits. You'll need to find someone else to help you learn the epic tales, though, since women don't tell them. I can teach you how to become a channel between the other worlds and this one. You must have the ability, or the spirits would not call you."

He took my hand and raised it to his lips. My palm tingled, and a warm glow spread through my center like a flame banked for the night. Stepan was elsewhere, leaving us for once alone in the tent. Without quite intending to, I leaned toward Mansur, inviting a kiss. But he was answering my question and didn't notice.

"I know many of the sagas already," he said. "As a boy, I dogged the footsteps of the bards who visited my uncles' tents. But yes, teach me how to contact the spirits. And to drum, perhaps? The drum accompanies stories as well as chants and trances."

"I'll be happy to." I straightened in my seat, suppressing my disappointment as best I could.

Why didn't he kiss me? Did I misjudge his interest? Did he miss my signal? Was he afraid Stepan would walk in and find us? Does he not care for me?

I couldn't just come out and *ask* him. Good women didn't do such things. So I forced my thoughts into another channel and spoke as calmly as possible. "Let's start with the simplest way to reach the realms beyond this one. Lie down and stretch out. Hold your hands palms up, and close your eyes." To show him what I meant, I lay flat, looking up at the smoke hole, then turned my head sideways to check whether he'd mimicked my pose.

He had. I pushed thoughts of kissing out of my head, faced the center of the tent once more, and closed my eyes. "Breathe in," I said. "Out. In. Out. Let your thoughts drift. Open your inner eye. See yourself as an empty cup and, without using words, invite the helper spirits to enter. Be very clear: helpers only. You don't want to accept any spirit looking for a body or a home. Few are truly evil, but they can be angry or fearful and difficult to get rid of. Once you've thought the invitation, wait. If you have a question you'd like answered, send it to the heavens on the wings of a bird. But for a first time, it's enough to explore your own sense of readiness, of waiting, of stillness."

I took deep breaths of my own, letting the beauty of the moment fill me. Even without the kisses I'd longed for, I had to admit it was thrilling to move from student to teacher, to pass on the secrets I'd absorbed from Suzukei and the Cheremis women before her, to explore the heavens with this appealing man by my side. Although Mansur saw himself as a storyteller rather than a shaman, I'd learned, long before I met Suzukei, that these things are not as distinct as most Russians imagine. Storytellers lead the entire community in appreciation of the ancestors and the otherworldly forces that listeners might encounter, and that effort, too, depends on the teller's ability to channel messages from the upper and lower realms.

I didn't intend to enter a trance, but my third soul had other ideas. A pair of connected questions formed unbidden in my head, and as I'd instructed Mansur, I imagined them taking the shape of an owl, then released them to rise on the column of warm air that connected the hearth to God's Heaven.

Does Mansur care for me, not only as a friend and a teacher but as a man cares for a woman? Do the two of us have a chance?

As I rise through the smoke hole, I turn my head left, right, left. I don't know what I'm seeking. An image of the future? Suzukei's eagle? Mansur's snowy owl? My clawed feet brush the rim as I spread my wings, tips pointing skyward. I see no other beings, except the souls who cluster amid the spirit banners, each lost in its own concerns.

I soar on gusts of warm air, circling the camp. In one direction my eye is caught by the flocks of sheep and goats, the herds of cows, the riders in constant motion keeping the animals moving eastward and redirecting those that stray too far from the rest. As I reach the other side, at a great distance I see the thousands of horses, the host of armed riders, the winged-horse banners rippling in the afternoon sun that casts its glow on steel helmets and chain mail vests.

Ogodai's warriors. Am I supposed to follow them?

I don't think so. A force I can detect but not identify draws my owl self toward the low hills that border the river. My wings propel me past the borders of the camp. There, in a clearing, I descend.

When I alight, I notice that my talons don't touch the grass. I look down and see hands in place of wings, slippered feet, a soft flowing skirt like the peri's rose gauze but made of scarlet silk embroidered in intertwining flowers formed from gold thread. A white silk under-tunic billows at the edges where the scarlet panels meet. The dress is tight at the waist and full at the hem—a wedding gown. My head turns only as far as my shoulder on each side. I catch a glimpse of red gauze as I twist my neck back and forth, and when I lift a palm to touch my hair, I find a flat round cap, the gauze a veil floating from its back.

A collection of stones adorned with bright ribbons of many colors marks the shrine of a forgotten ancestor. I greet the spirit of that place, wondering what—or who—has summoned me here. I turn in a circle, searching.

Ahead of me stands a tent, covered in cloth of gold. In shape, it matches the tent from Erlik Khan's kingdom—and of the horde in which I live, for that matter—but it is smaller than the one I share with Stepan and, for the moment, Mansur. Here, freed of the dim gray light that defines the lower world, the tent glitters in the brilliant sunshine. The door opens, as if inviting me to enter, and on a thought I am there, stepping over the threshold.

Inside, I find Mansur. Not his owl self but his true appearance. Like the tents of the underworld, this one glows from within. Without needing to be told, I know it is ours alone. I run to him, and here in this other realm he doesn't hesitate. He sweeps me into his arms. I press against him as our lips touch. His hands roam over my body. As one, we tumble onto a pile of felts. Heat flows between us and around us, enclosing us in a bubble of passion. We need no flame to banish autumn's chill; each of us warms the other. We exchange no words, and we need none. Our togetherness is enough.

A harsh cry shatters the blissful moment. Like a demon grabbing me around the waist and tugging, the sound rips me away from Mansur. He and the tent dissolve into a sparkling mist, leaving only the decorated shrine and the quiet glen that surrounds it. I am alone. Again.

Disconnected images assail my senses: a deserted courtyard; a three-story wooden house; a graveyard isolated and uncared-for amid trees as tall as cathedrals; a dark street and a young girl—myself—scuttling toward a place she fears, dreaming of a man no longer hers. In a wooded clearing filled with huts, Stenka's blood-drenched body lies on a cart bed. One corpse among many. Cruel laughter mocks my grief. Too late, too late. Stenka is gone.

I squeeze my eyes shut and press both hands against my temples to push the unwanted sights—memories? visions?—away. When that doesn't work, I force myself to look, to turn in a circle, seeking ... what? Mansur, Suzukei, the shrine and its spirit—anything that will ground me in this place.

I hear the whirr of beating wings. Feathers spread before my face. Again my owl self takes to the air. Even from above, I don't see Mansur. The man I want to spend my life with. Shaman and storyteller, together, kindred souls.

I stare at the sky, as if it holds answers to my questions. I must be mad. To fall in love with Mansur after such a short time. Without even a declaration from him that he cares for me. How could I be so careless as to let that happen?

How could I not? He is charming, compassionate, good with Stepan, desirable, responsible, amusing, affectionate ... It's no wonder that his presence has become essential to me. But I don't need a message from my helpers to know that road leads to heartbreak. It's a road I've already traveled twice, and this time not only I will suffer. Stepan will miss Mansur too.

I search for Suzukei. That jarring shriek, harsh and strong enough for an eagle, demanded my attention. She must have seen the danger to my heart and sought to warn me.

I turn my head in every direction, but however hard I search, no eagle fills my gaze. The cobalt sky gleams like a mirror, reflecting only puffed clouds. Mother Sun blows a gentle kiss past my cheeks. Winged horses chase the horizon, racing one another across the sky from dawn to dusk. No threatening presence lurks in their midst. No guardian or helper rides on their backs.

The clearing forms around me once more. Again I am a woman rather than an owl. Yet still I catch no sight of Mansur. Spirits flit and perch near the shrine. Except for them, I am alone.

Alone with spirits—who, because I'm a shaman, will always remain at my side. Unlike the man to whom I've so foolishly given my heart. I fall to the ground, wrap my arms around my head, and keen.

In the midst of my grief, I hear the slow beat of the drum. The drum no one is supposed to be playing. I curl into myself, resisting the call. But the soul of the drum refuses to take no for an answer.

How can I return? What happened here today is everything I fear. That all those I love, leave. And that however close I come to connection and companionship, only the spirits will remain true in the end.

Against my will I returned to my body, trembling amid a sudden onslaught of chill air. I looked to my left, where Mansur lay—his face serene, his palms cupped, his breathing steady. I saw no signs that he'd been the one to call me back from the other world: I hadn't even taught him the right rhythm yet, and my drum lay in its usual spot near the chest that held my robe and magical tools. The spirits themselves must have summoned me home, using the soul of the drum as their instrument.

But like it or not, I was here, in my own tent, the vision swirling around my head. Stepan would run in at any moment, fresh from his play. He couldn't find me so unsettled. How would I explain to a child what had happened?

I thrust my distress to the back of my mind, determined to put one foot in front of the other until I completed the many tasks of the day. Sometime—tonight?—when the tent was quiet and no one could see me weep: then I would face what I'd seen in trance, wherever that realization led me.

I took several deep breaths, blinked back my tears, and brushed the moisture from my cheeks. Moving as quietly as possible, I walked to the far side of the tent and ladled portions of the stew I'd prepared yesterday into an iron pot.

I hung the pot over the hearth fire and sat beside it, stirring. I took care not to disturb Mansur. Indeed, I went out of my way not to disturb him, because I had no idea what to say to him when he awoke—or how to conceal that I had fallen in love with him even though he had said nothing of the sort to me. Instead I waited for Stepan to return and tried to shut out thoughts about my vision and what the spirits had forced me to see.

It didn't work. The memories poured into my brain faster than I could push them away. The spirits wanted me to hear their message, and as on that long-ago day when they selected me to serve them as shaman, their determination overwhelmed my paltry attempts at resistance.

I'd asked them what Mansur felt for me, and they'd answered me in their own obscure fashion. He did love me, passionately, as I loved him. But would our fate bring us together or keep us apart? The way he vanished when Suzukei shrieked warned me to expect the worst.

I couldn't bear it. Those evenings of shared talk, the days spent laughing together with Stepan, the nights when we slept in separate beds but close enough to hear each other breathe, the mornings when we awoke to my son's delighted calls, the glances exchanged over my endless repetitions of "Ivan and the Gray Wolf," and the times we'd flown side by side in other realms—all these things had created a bond I couldn't break. What had I done to myself and Stepan by falling in love with Mansur? Who called me his angel but in the end might walk away and not look back.

Because that was my curse: to lose everyone I loved.

The days that followed stretched my self-control to its limits. The warriors did not return, and Mansur remained in my tent. I took pleasure in that, but I wanted so much more from him than he offered, and I didn't know what to do about that—especially with a child so often nearby.

It wasn't that Mansur expressed *no* interest in me. We talked and we flirted. I often caught him watching me. Whenever I did, I was tempted to ask him what he was thinking, but each time the words caught in my throat before I could say them aloud. The vision of losing him haunted me. What good would it do to challenge him? He was here, for the moment. I should enjoy each day while it lasted.

I buried my fear and my grief in a flurry of tasks both domestic and spiritual. I began preparations for the move that must soon follow the return of Ogodai Khan and his men: drying meat, making cheese, packing unneeded goods to leave as few tasks as possible for the last day. I showed Mansur how to make and use the tools he would need if he did decide to become a storyteller—including the most important of these, his own drum. I listened as he regaled Stepan, a ready audience and mimic, with epic tales learned from other storytellers. And I watched Mansur teach my son how to handle a sword, hold a bow, improve his seat on the pony Daniil had lent us, and care for his mount at the end of each ride. Mansur's patience seemed endless, his humor contagious, and Stepan greeted each lesson with delight. His "Mansur, Mansur, look!" resounded through the tent almost as often as "Mama!"

I saw Mansur lose his temper only once, and not in response to any misdeed by Stepan. It was a clear day a week or so after Ogodai and his warriors set out, cool but sunny. A crisp breeze blew snatches of dried grass past our faces. Mansur and I were walking side by side along the central pathway, Stepan leaping and calling his mismatched numbers, when we ran into Anfim Fadeyev coming in the other direction. His face clouded over at the sight of us, but he smiled at Stepan and tipped his head in my direction before fixing his eyes on Mansur with a stare I could not consider friendly.

"So he's the reason you turned down my proposal," Anfim said. "Do you really prefer your little man?"

"What nonsense is this?" I took a step forward. "My son always comes first! Besides, you know very well why I turned you down: because you want me to give up being a shaman."

Only when Mansur gripped my arm did I realize I'd misunderstood. I didn't think of Mansur as short—he was a good three fingers' width taller than me—but I saw now that Anfim wasn't talking about my son. He'd seen the three of us walking together as if we were a family, and he didn't like the thought that I'd picked someone else over him. In short, he was jealous—wrong, or at least half-wrong, but jealous. Whether he cared about me or his reputation didn't matter. He was looking for trouble.

I glanced at Mansur in time to see his mouth compress and his eyes flash. "Behind me, Stepan. This instant," he said.

My son ducked behind Mansur's back without a word. I couldn't tell whether he understood what Anfim had said, but the snap in Mansur's voice got through just fine.

Anfim sneered. "What are you going to do, little man?"

I winced. *Really* looking for trouble. I was willing to bet he'd found it, too. Shorter than Russians or not, Tatars were deadly in combat, and Mansur looked ready to rip Anfim apart with his bare hands.

He let go of my arm, and I went to stand next to Stepan. I could call down the heavens if need be, and I would if I had to, but I doubted Mansur would appreciate an attempt to rescue him, especially from a woman. I'd wait and see.

Indeed, despite the crutch, which he still needed to move with ease, Mansur limped forward faster than I would have believed possible and gripped Anfim by the throat. While he struggled and turned red, Mansur pinned one of Anfim's feet to the ground with the crutch. In Russian he snarled, "Apologize. To her, not to me."

To me? He's defending me?

I could hardly believe my ears. While Stepan and I stared wide-eyed, Mansur released Anfim's neck, unsheathed the dagger no warrior left his tent without, and held the tip to the Russian's ribs. "She doesn't want you, and she said so. That's the end of it. Her reasons and her actions don't concern you. So leave her and her son alone from now on. Do I make myself clear?"

His cheeks scarlet, Anfim glowered at Mansur. Stepan grabbed for my right hand, which lay on his shoulder. I could guess that the men's anger scared him. My throat dry with shock, I pulled him in front of me, patted his head to reassure him, and waited.

Mansur tightened his grip on the hilt and pressed the tip harder against Anfim's coat. I saw it cut through the fine turquoise wool. "Well?" he asked, his tone almost conversational, but I heard that hard warrior edge beneath the surface calm. "Do I withdraw or slam this home, *little man?*"

Anfim's mouth opened and closed. As he gasped like a fish pulled from the river, Mansur pushed the dagger tip through another layer of clothing. Anfim's turquoise wool coat acquired a long slash, and the linen shirt beneath it parted as well. I caught a glimpse of pale pink skin.

"Damn you," Anfim choked out, right at the point when I saw Mansur's grip tighten for the third time. "I apologize. I spoke out of turn."

"I spoke out of turn, Honored Shaman." Mansur stressed the last two words, in the same way I might correct Stepan, and left the dagger in place.

Anfim turned redder still, until I wondered if he would fall dead of an apoplexy before he could yield. Indeed, I saw him bite his tongue as if he could hardly bear to let the words escape his lips.

At last he yielded. "I spoke out of turn, Honored Shaman," he said, spitting out each word as if it burned him. Whatever drove him—jealousy or fear or something else altogether—thank the saints I'd had the sense to reject his proposal. Imagine putting my life and Stepan's into the hands of such a madman!

Mansur withdrew the dagger, sheathed it, and lifted the crutch pinning Anfim's foot to the ground. "Better." He placed the crutch under his right arm and held out his left hand. "Let's go to the corral, Stepan. I have something to show you."

I released my son and resumed my place at Mansur's right side, where I could help him if we encountered a muddy patch or other obstacle likely to topple the crutch.

Leaving Anfim muttering curses behind us, the three of us headed for the corral.

Once we'd put the distance of half a dozen tents between us and the Russian, Mansur released Stepan to run and turned to face me. His eyes sparkled with amusement, and a smile curved his mouth. "I've wanted to do that ever since I came to that day in the tent and heard him ranting at you. By the Prophet (on whom be peace), did you see his face?" He started to laugh. I glanced behind him, not wanting to start another confrontation, but Anfim had left.

Mansur put his arm around my waist, and I leaned against him, speaking quietly even though I thought Stepan, who had eyes only for the horses, wouldn't hear us. "*Batyram*," I said, and this time I wasn't flirting. I meant it. When had a man last stood up for me in that way? Any warrior in the horde would defend a shaman, but what Mansur had done was different. He'd defended *me*. My right to choose and have that choice respected, without question. He must love me. So why did he maintain such a distance between us? Did he not understand that I wanted him too? "Thank you. I'm glad you were here. That was good for Stepan to see."

His eyes still twinkled. "He's a brave boy, but not quite old enough to protect his mother. I'm glad I was here too. I doubt that Russian will trouble you from now on, but if he does, *fereshtem*, tell me. I'll gut him and make him eat the pieces."

"I think he may have figured that out," I said. Even though I didn't need Mansur to defend me, I was glad he wanted to—and I suspected Anfim understood the danger posed by Mansur more readily than he could grasp the risks of enraging me, despite my demonstration that day in the tent. "After what you just did, I doubt he'll approach me again." Gathering every scrap of my courage, I raised my heels enough to brush my lips across Mansur's cheek. "But if he does misbehave, I promise to let you know."

His arm tightened around me, and he pulled me close, lighting a flame of desire that seared my whole body. His mouth was a finger's breadth from mine when Stepan let out a shriek that must have reached half the camp. "Mama, Mansur, my pony is gone!"

My heels hit the ground again, and I swore under my breath. *So close!*

"Gone?" I asked.

In the same breath, Mansur called, "Be right there, Stepan!" To me he added, "Until later." I nodded, but he was already limping toward the corral. Sending a silent protest to the heavens, I ran to catch up with him.

Chapter Fifteen

LATER, HOWEVER, WAS DELAYED BY THE NEED TO SEARCH for Stepan's borrowed pony. Mansur helped while we circled the corral, but a long walk would put too much strain on his wounded leg. So I encouraged him to wait for us at home while Stepan and I checked the outer limits of the camp. I hoped the wretched beast hadn't run off into the steppe, because then I'd have to plead with Guzel or Timur to hunt it down. But fortune favored us, and we discovered the pony happily grazing behind the farthest tent. Stepan scolded it in Tatar as we walked it back to the corral, although the real question seemed to me to be how it had slipped its rope in the first place. I decided to request another lesson from Mansur on how to tie a good knot. In the meantime, I took care of the matter myself, promising my son that he'd have a chance to ride and tend to the pony tomorrow.

As we came within sight of our tent, I recalled with longing the sensation of my lips against Mansur's cheek. I would see him again at the midday meal. After that, I could send Stepan off to play. *Later*, he'd said ...

The thrumming that had twice hauled me out of a deep sleep slammed into these blissful thoughts like a boulder rolling down a mountain. The earth shook once more. The only difference was that this time the whole camp was awake. Not two hours had passed since Mansur's run-in with Anfim.

I grabbed Stepan's hand, and we dashed back to the corral. When we reached it, I hoisted him onto the rails. Then, maddened by impatience and fear, I raised my skirts to mid-calf and clambered up beside him.

My shoulders dropped. I let go a huge sigh of relief and jumped off the fence. I lifted Stepan down even as he clung to the top rail.

I gave him a little push. "Run and tell Mansur not to worry," I said. "You saw the winged horses, scarlet and black. The khan's troops will be here in the blink of an eye, and Alexei Sultan's men with them."

Stepan ran. Struggling to catch my breath, I walked as fast as I could down the path. My joyous anticipation had fled. However relieved I felt to see our own warriors returning, the arrival of Alexei's men forced me to confront the truth I'd fought so hard this last week to keep hidden.

Mansur's comrades were on their way, with or without their lord. The man I loved would soon depart with them, and our days as a pretend family would end. I'd known this moment would arrive—braced myself for it, even—but now it was here.

How will I manage without him?

Warriors packed the camp and spread out across the steppe. Round tents clustered like patches of mushrooms as far as the horizon. At night they would appear lit from within, like the dwellings in Erlik Khan's kingdom: gold-flecked stars against an indigo sky. The noise would deafen a dog: cheers and laughter, the joyous shrieks of reuniting families, the clang of armor and weaponry falling to earth, male voices raised in complaint and in song.

And the horses! Ogodai's five beys had fielded three thousand warriors in addition to the khan's personal fighting force of a thousand, drawn from here and nearby camps. Each of them traveled with two to four mounts, and the force sent by Alexei Sultan matched ours in size. The sight of the massive herds grazing in the open grasslands sent Stepan and his friends into a state close to ecstasy. If any child in the camp slept tonight, I would be amazed. The excitement alone would keep them awake until dawn.

More was to come. The khan ordered a feast to take place on the morrow to celebrate his warriors' great victory against the raiders, with bonfires for luck and games to entertain the crowd. As shaman, I would have a part early in the ceremony, thanking the spirits for their blessings and gift of good fortune after Haji Rahman led the introductory prayers. Even before then, Nasan and I expected to have our hands full dealing with the injured. The casualties had been lighter than expected, most likely because the combined forces had far outnumbered Sheikh-Mamai's "renegade" troops, and any warrior with a minor wound had received treatment right after the battle. Still, we had a good thirty or forty patients to examine as soon as the initial excitement of reunion abated.

While waiting for that moment to arrive, I took refuge in my own tent with Mansur after agreeing that Stepan could run about with his friends Borya and Irek, so long as he didn't pester the returning warriors or chase the horses.

"Did Alexei Sultan come with his men?" Mansur asked as I passed him a flask of koumiss. "If so, I should pay my respects."

I dropped into place opposite him and sipped from the cup I carried before placing it on the floor. Chill and crisp against my tongue, the apple juice helped restore my calm after the tumult outside. "Not yet," I said. "According to Nasan, he sent a message to expect him soon—before we leave to follow the flocks, he hopes—but warning he might be delayed if the Crimean forces retreat slowly."

"Before you leave to follow the flocks? Won't that be as soon as the celebrations end? We're halfway through September. If my lord intended to arrive before then, he'd be here already." Mansur tipped back his head and squirted koumiss into his mouth from the flask.

"If he's delayed, he'll come after us. He may not catch up before we reach our destination, but he knows where we're headed." I hesitated, not sure whether I wanted to hear Mansur's response to the next piece of information I'd learned from Nasan, then gave myself a mental shake and went on. "Your lord has ordered one part of his forces to escort us as far as the winter grazing lands, to prevent any more trouble. So we have every reason to believe that he *will* join us. He promised to visit his son, remember?"

Mansur gazed at the fire, not speaking, the familiar frown creasing his brow. His expression told me he recognized that I'd told him this news for a reason, but not whether he'd choose to stay with us for a while longer. I wished I could see into his thoughts.

Not two hours had passed since he'd threatened Anfim in defense of me. Since I kissed his cheek and he pulled me close. Since his whispered *Later*. So I knew he did care for me. He must.

But the warriors' return changed everything. He could request an assignment to the escort or leave with the larger group that would soon ride back to Kolomna. Which option would he pick?

"Will you ask to join the escort?" I asked, not sure what his answer would tell me yet eager to keep the conversation going.

Mansur put down the flask and gazed at me. His mouth curved, but he studied me as if I were a book he sought to master. "Would you like that, *fereshtem*?" he said after a long pause.

I'd wondered about *his* choice, but this was mine. If I said yes, he would know I wanted him to stay with me. Did I dare show him how much he meant to me? Right now, at this moment when he hovered on the brink of leaving, when he might already have decided to go?

I must. Saying no was unthinkable—a lie in every sense. "Yes," I said. "I understand that you have to work things out with your family and your lord, but I've loved having you with me. If you leave, I'll miss you. Stepan will miss you. And I fear that once you're away from us, you'll forget that we exist."

He reached for my hand. "I'll never forget you, my shaman, whatever fate holds in store for me. I love you more than you know. It's been a month I couldn't have imagined, and I promise I'll return or die trying."

He wrapped his arms around me, and I nestled against him. He spoke words I'd longed to hear, and I welcomed them.

Even so, a thought nagged at me as I melted into his kiss. He loved me, but ...? What more could I need to hear?

As he pulled away far enough to caress my cheek, I realized what he hadn't said. "And your gift? Will you

241

follow the road the spirits have laid out for you?" My voice shook, with desire but also with fear. Surely he understood what a refusal would mean for him. Had I not explained the costs a dozen times?

But Mansur was a Muslim. He didn't believe in the spirits' power. He'd told me that as often as I'd tried to convince him otherwise.

"I can't overturn my life on the word of a peri." His firm tone confirmed my worst fears. "I've searched my soul, and I still can't decide whether storytelling is the right course for me. I do want to spend more time with you, to see where that takes us. But I'm in service. I go where I'm sent. Before I can make promises, I have to talk with Alexei Sultan. Confer with my mother, my brothers and sister. Do what I can to provide for them. Once I'm sure of my path, I'll come back to you. If I can. I don't know if Ogodai Khan needs a storyteller, but he can probably find a use for a seasoned warrior." He brushed his lips across my fingers, then kissed me hard once more. I was still lost in a warm, tingling, passionate heaven when he released me and struggled to standing.

While I watched—blinking, dismayed—he positioned the crutch under his right arm and tipped his head in my direction, the closest he could manage to a bow. "The men are back," he said. "I should stay with them. I don't trust my self-control around you, and I can't risk getting you with child when I'm not here to look after you. You've had to live with the results of men's carelessness long enough."

Without waiting for an answer, he limped from the tent.

I stared at the closed door. Tears stung my cheeks. It could have been worse. Mansur said he loved me. He kissed me—and *how* he'd kissed me, as if he'd been starving for weeks and couldn't get enough. My insides still quivered at the memory. He wanted to settle things with his lord and his family so we could be together. He didn't want to leave me alone to raise another child, as Stenka had done—not deliberately, of course, but that my previous man hadn't intended to die didn't make the results of his untimely passing easier to bear.

I was being unreasonable. Mansur had shared his doubts with me from the beginning, from that first conversation after the spiritual journey we took together. Nothing had changed. He was still weighing his choices. He had obligations he'd taken on before he met me. He might yet find a way to satisfy the spirits' demands.

Besides, I'd known him for no more than a month. How could I feel so certain that I loved him, never mind expect him to upend his life to stay with me? He'd promised to come back, if he could. You'd think I was no older than Stepan, the way I was carrying on.

It was because of my vision, the shriek that sounded like Suzukei warning me that the spirits would keep him from me. If he didn't do what they wanted, or because of something in me—the curse that caused me to lose everyone I loved? I didn't know.

Foolish, perhaps, but I couldn't shake the belief that if I let Mansur out of my sight, I would never lay eyes on him again.

And oh, how was I going to explain his absence to Stepan?

I threw the nearest object across the tent. It happened to be the pouch containing Borya's chessmen, and it hit the side of the chest where I kept my shaman's gear with a satisfying series of plunks. I smacked the pillow where

Mansur's head had lain for the last month or so, but that did nothing to relieve my anguish.

After a while, I dried my useless tears and stood. I knew the course I should take: before Stepan returned, I should ask my spirit guardians for advice. Yet stubbornly, I refused. I didn't think I'd like what I heard from them. Whether they wanted me to learn that I shouldn't endanger others with my love or that I could have Mansur only if he agreed to their demands, I didn't know. But I understood one thing. Unless something changed—and fast—I faced an uncertain future.

Enough moping. I had tasks to perform. Injured men required my care. Mansur must follow his own path and live by the consequences of his choices. When he went away, I would grieve. If he returned, I would rejoice. If he didn't, I would miss him. But I would always know that for a short time he loved me, and that would have to do.

I washed my face in water left in the jug from last night and donned my shaman's costume. Should I wear my headdress, even though I didn't usually don it for a simple healing ceremony? It would hide the tracks of my tears from curious eyes.

I picked up my magic mirror and, standing directly in the light streaming through the smoke hole, examined my cheeks from every angle. No, I could manage without the headdress. I took a deep breath, straightened my robe, checked that I'd filled my bag with the tools I would need for my healing rituals, and headed for Nasan's tent.

The spirits helped me despite my avoidance of the trance. I ran into neither Mansur nor Anfim on the way.

Nasan was not in her tent. Nor did I find Guzel and her son at home, although Timur's absence surprised me less, as I assumed he'd joined his uncle and perhaps his father's men, many of whom he must know even if he hadn't met Mansur until the day of the raid. I ignored the distress that flowed through me at that beloved name and asked Kiraz, whom I caught scurrying toward Nasan's home, if she'd seen her mistress or Guzel.

"There." Kiraz pointed at the meeting tent. I thanked her and quickened my pace. Of course, Ogodai and Nasan would put the injured there. My conversation with Mansur had addled my brain.

But when I entered the tent, I realized it looked the same as it had before its conversion into a makeshift hospital—except for the massive crush of people, that is. When the beys arrived in response to Ogodai's summons for war, he must have ordered it restored to its normal state so they could sit and plan. But if the patients were waiting elsewhere, what brought Nasan and Guzel here?

Amid the crowd, I saw Mansur surrounded by comrades—talking and laughing, trading stories and koumiss. I averted my head and moved on before he had a chance to notice me.

Timur, as I'd half-expected, stood with his uncle and Ruslan. As I watched them, Daniil arrived, trailed by a servant carrying a pottery jug and cups on a wooden tray. Several men I didn't know joined them, with more back slapping and toasting. But still no sign of Nasan and Guzel. I needed to get to the women's side of the tent, which wasn't easy given the number of warriors blocking my path.

Diligent shoving and the ability to slip through spaces too narrow for men in armor—of whom I saw more than a few in addition to quilted jackets, finery, and bandaged limbs—brought me at last to the far side of the circle. There I spotted Guzel standing with Nasan and two familiar faces I'd thought I might never see again.

"Firuza! Dina!" I ran to them, my mixed emotions forgotten, and hugged first one, then the other. "Are you all right? How did you get here?" Tears ran down my cheeks once more, this time for joy. They hugged me back, crying as hard as I was. Guzel and Nasan hugged us too, and after a bit they pulled us aside to sit as a group and handed around cloths to dry our faces.

"Tell me what happened," I said when I could talk. "Tell me everything. I tried to find you with the spirits' help, and they sent me such confusing pictures that I didn't dare tell the khan that you might be captured or escaped or dead, but I didn't know which. He was frantic as it was, and Ruslan as well."

"Yes," Nasan said. "She's right. Tell us everything. They just arrived, Grusha, so we don't know either. But we want to."

"We absolutely do," Guzel agreed. "We're so glad to see you safe that we can't find the words, so begin at the beginning, with how you were captured, and tell us the whole."

"It was the weirdest combination of good and bad luck you can imagine," Firuza said. "We'd been riding on either side of Nasan, and when she took the hit from the arrow, we both turned toward her, intending to help. Instead, two of the raiders grabbed our reins and hauled us onto their horses. They raced off, dragging Kubelek and Moon Shadow behind them. When we tried to fight them, they threw our reins to another pair of raiders and knocked us out."

Dina picked up the story as the rest of us gasped. "We woke up in a nomadic tent, under guard but not, *mashallah*, bound. Once we were sure neither of us had more hurts than a bruise to the chin and some roughing up, I got as close to one side of the door as possible and listened. Firuza did the same on the other side. We'd guessed there must be guards, and there were, but they didn't seem too concerned about us."

"We couldn't see them," Firuza went on. "But we could hear them, and after a while we felt pretty certain there were only two. Then a third man came with food. We scuttled back to the center of the tent, near the fire, and pretended to be helpless females."

"The armor must have made that hard to believe," Nasan put in.

Dina shook her head. "Men can be so dense," she said. "Not all of them, of course. Our husbands wouldn't fall for a trick like that. But if you make your eyes big and scared and act like you don't know how you ended up in armor in the first place, the silly ones accept you at face value. We were plenty scared, but we hoped that if we could convince them we were harmless, we might have a chance to grab their weapons and stab them if they tried to rape us."

"As soon as the third man dropped the food and left," Firuza said, "we ran to the door and heard him tell the guards to stop anyone else from entering because their leader had ordered them to keep us apart as a gift for their bey. I'd thought of telling them we were the wives of a khan and a sultan, then demanding they release or ransom us, but when the third man named the bey as Sheikh-Mamai, I knew that would never work."

"Because he hates Ogodai," Guzel interjected. I could see her working the story out as she spoke. "Ruslan too, I suppose, since Ruslan played a big part in Sheikh-Mamai's defeat by our horde."

"Exactly." Dina clenched her hands into fists. "He'd have violated us, thrown us in his harem, and made sure our husbands heard every detail. So we decided we had nothing to lose by trying to escape. The worst they could do was kill us."

"I saw that in my vision," I said. "I didn't hear what was said, but the spirits sent pictures of the two of you in the tent and riding through the night. I couldn't figure out how they went together. There was a third one too, but go on. You decided to escape."

Firuza took over. "We went to the back of the tent and undid the ties holding the frame together. Not so much that it would collapse or that the man with the food, if he came back, would notice, but enough that with a bit more work we could push through one section of the frame. And Dina picked apart two of the panels—again, to loosen the stitching to a point where we could rip the seam on the felt and wriggle through."

"So that's what you did?" Nasan asked. "And you managed it without drawing the guards' attention or collapsing the tent? That's amazing!"

"We were lucky." Dina dipped her head at me. "Maybe the shaman's spirits helped us."

"I think they did," I said. "But I do wish they'd told me what they had in mind. I wouldn't have worried myself half-sick!"

"But you're only partway through the story," Guzel reminded them. "Firuza, how did you get away?"

"As Dina said, we were lucky. As soon as full dark settled in the first night, we slipped through the hole we'd made, tied the frame roughly back together, and ran. We kept the tent from falling in by having Dina hold the frame while I crawled and me holding it for her."

"We raced for the corral, expecting to grab the first two horses we saw," Dina told us. "We'd ride bareback as far and as fast as we could, then hide while we figured out where to go for help. That was the plan."

"But when I saw you," I put in, "you had Kubelek and Moon Shadow. They even had their saddles and bridles."

"Yes, that's another place where luck was on our side," Firuza explained. "We saw our own horses, still in their gear, so we grabbed them. They came straight to us; we didn't even need to whistle. We mounted and rode like devils away from the camp, let the mares have their heads. We went for what seemed like hours, until the horses tired. Not just the horses, either: we were both exhausted. We were looking for a safe place to rest, with water and grass, when armed men came out of nowhere. Before we had time to do so much as shout, never mind ride away, we were surrounded—"

"What!" Nasan, Guzel, and I said with one voice.

"Surrounded by warriors," Dina said. "We thought our escape had been in vain, that we'd ridden in circles. I was ready to die, right there on the spot. I went for my knife, but the raiders had taken it. I can't remember ever feeling more terrified."

Sympathy for their plight shocked me into silence.

"Me too," Firuza said. "I would have sold my soul for a dagger or a sword—to use on these new captors, preferably, but on myself if need be. Then the leader rode up, and we saw the winged-horse standard behind him. I swear, I almost fell off Kubelek. I have never in my life been so glad to set eyes on someone—not even my beloved husband this afternoon—as I was to see Alexei's face at that moment."

"Was that the third picture you saw, Grusha?" Dina asked. I heard nothing more than idle curiosity in her words, as if the world of the spirits remained unreal, despite her earlier comment and their intervention in support of Mergen and the other children of the horde. And despite my vision of what had happened to her and Firuza, most of which had in fact taken place.

I remembered Mansur then, asking me if the third vision couldn't convey a meaning instead of an inescapable truth. Another wave of sadness rose in my throat, but I pushed it down.

Tears won't change anything. Whatever happens, I can get through it.

"In a way." I struggled to keep my sense of having lost something precious out of my voice. "I saw you under the banner of Alexei Sultan, spread over you as if it were a bed covering. The two of you lay side by side, eyes closed, but I couldn't tell whether you were sleeping or something more dire. That's why I didn't share the vision with the khan."

I told only Mansur, and he listened with respect and reassured me that the vision might not mean my friend's deaths. Would I ever enjoy the comfort of his wisdom, his affection, again?

Stop it. Stop whining. Only children and weaklings rail at fate.

I did force myself to stop. But the sorrow remained.

Chapter Sixteen

"I DON'T KNOW WHEN I'LL RETURN. I HAVE TO FIND ALEXEI Sultan, talk with my brothers, stop in Kolomna to visit my mother, then travel on to Moscow to check on my sister. It will take me several months at least." Mansur kept his tone reassuring, but I heard a certain frustration he couldn't conceal. He'd repeated the same words a dozen times or more since the day he'd moved into the men's tent.

"I'll join you in the east," Mansur went on. "Assuming that's possible. If all goes well, you can expect me by the shortest day, or soon thereafter. If not, I'll try to send a message."

"The shortest day," I repeated. Christmas, although I hadn't observed Christmas in six years. Unlike other holidays, though, its timing was easy to identify even when living by a different calendar. "We settle south of Kazan, so it's closer to Moscow than this camp, and you can travel by road to a point beyond Kasimov. I don't know exactly where the turnoff is, but Alexei Sultan and his captains do. Once you reach that path through the woods, the rest is easy. The inhabitants aren't hostile, for the most part. Just follow the river until you get to the grasslands, then look for our herds. The camp lies between the Sura River and the Volga, in a region sheltered by the mountains. I'll expect you then."

"If it's possible," he reminded me. "If not, I'll show up eventually. You needn't despair if I haven't arrived by the new year. I'll get there as soon as I can."

"I understand." I gave him a quick kiss. We'd already said our farewells in my tent. "I trust you. May the spirits bless you on your journey." I still feared I might never see him again, but clutching at him would not help. He must follow his own path—and the one set out for him by the spirits—like everyone else. With luck, *my* path would bring him back to me.

Mansur nodded and mounted his horse. I dipped my ladle in the cup I held and tossed the contents in the air—three, four, five times—opening the milk road of good fortune for him, then watched as he rode off, head high.

I hoped he might glance back, although I'd lived in the horde long enough to know that Tatars never did look behind them when they left because they considered it bad luck. And indeed, Mansur did not, although I saw him lean sideways in the saddle and clasp Stepan's shoulder as he reached the end of the path where the boys played.

Stepan, his face intent, said something I couldn't hear. He gripped Mansur's hand in both of his, until Mansur pulled away and tousled Stepan's curls before riding off with his fellow warriors. Stepan ignored his friends, watching the horses. But as soon as the group passed the outermost tents, my son came running. "Mansur's really going? I want him to stay with us."

"He serves Alexei Sultan," I said. My voice wobbled, but I refused to give in to the grief that tugged me as I watched the man I loved ride off into the distance. "He's gone home. He has a mother and brothers and sister in Russia. He needs to take care of them, too."

"He doesn't love us anymore?" Stepan's face crumpled as he pressed a sleeve against his wet cheek. "He's gone and we'll never see him again?"

"He says he'll come back if he can," I told my son. "After he makes sure that they're safe. But he doesn't know when that will be, and neither do I."

By the shortest day, he'd told me. If possible. But *would* it be possible? There was the curse on me to consider and the risk that he might yet fall foul of the spirits because he decided not to respect their wishes and their power. There were dangers on such a long journey, even for someone who traveled with a force as large as Alexei Sultan's troops. Mansur might discover that his family still needed him, or love for them could, in the end, overwhelm his feelings for me. He had, after all, known them his whole life and me not much more than a month.

So many things could go wrong. And in any case, the time from here to the shortest day was too long an absence for my son to grasp. Such assurances would have no meaning for Stepan. They barely had meaning for me.

Hugging my child tight, I stopped pretending I was in control and wept.

Mansur's outline was still visible against the sky when I released Stepan, dried my tears, and started back toward my tent. About halfway there, I noticed Anfim Fadeyev standing next to a saddled steppe pony. All around him, Tatar warriors in full armor were mounted and setting off in the same direction as Mansur or milling around the corral preparing their horses and supplies for the journey. Those still readying their animals and goods, judging from their dragon-boat banners, were the couriers returning to Kasimov, who would travel with Alexei's men for protection during the first part of their journey. Soon only the escort and Ogodai's personal troops would remain in the camp. As I'd predicted, the beys and their thousands of men and horses had left for home right after the celebration ended.

Since most of Alexei's men had already ridden out—Mansur occupied a position in the middle—I guessed that Ogodai had released Anfim to return home with the group heading for Kasimov. Curious, I walked toward him. Which Anfim would I find: the one who'd been attracted to me, even jealous of a man he saw as a rival, or the one who feared my power? I'd liked him at times, disliked him at others, but on the whole I wished him well. And he had no reason for jealousy today: he was leaving, and Mansur had already gone.

When I asked, Anfim confirmed that he planned to ride with the couriers as far as Kasimov, then join a group heading for Moscow.

"Your family will be relieved," I said. "I hope you have a successful journey, and that you find them healthy and happy when you get there."

Having said my farewells, I moved toward the central pathway, but the sound of his voice brought me to a halt. "It's not too late. You can come with me, if you like. I'll marry you."

I stopped and stared at him. "You still want to marry me? Why?"

He shrugged. "Why not? You're attractive, healthy, not too old to bear sons. You listen well, and you're a decent mother. You seem like a good woman, even if that Tatar doesn't have the sense to appreciate you. Other than the sorcery, I have no complaints. Give it up, and I'd be happy to marry you."

I didn't know where to start. Did he honestly believe that I'd meekly surrender my ties to the spirits because he asked me? After all I'd said?

Yet Mansur had left, and I could only hope that he would one day find his way back to me. For the briefest of moments I was tempted to grasp at the straw Anfim held out. He must experience some desire for me, given the persistence he showed in pursuing me and his jealousy of Mansur. And Anfim himself was not unattractive, although I doubted I could ever desire him as I did his rival. At times, when he'd displayed intelligence and humor despite the stress of his captivity, I'd felt drawn to him. Most of the time, he'd been nice to my son, who needed a father more with each week that passed. Although Stepan disliked him, my son might change his mind as they got to know each other better.

Common sense returned. I heard Suzukei's warning shriek in my mind and realized I'd again come close to denying my own gift. And here I claimed I couldn't understand Mansur's reluctance to accept his!

"I can't," I told Anfim. "I was chosen by the spirits long before I met you. Long before I realized it, even. When I was a child in Kostroma. It would never work. You need a different wife, and I need a different husband. I told you that before."

"As you wish." He sounded sympathetic—pitying, almost. "But think. I would take care of you. I would raise your son right. And unlike your little man, I'd never ride off and leave you."

I stared at him, stunned. They were the very words I'd yearned to hear from a man for so long. And they left me unmoved.

What happened to me? When did I change?

In that moment I felt sorry for him. Glad I'd refused his proposal, but still sorry for him, that he grasped so little of the rich other realms in which I lived.

"The answer's still no," I said. "Your kind of marriage wouldn't suit me. I'll raise my son here in the horde, among people who value what we do. We have nothing more to say to each other."

I didn't wait for his reply. I left him standing in the pathway, and I did not look back.

He was Russian, but he wasn't Russia. I might choose one day to visit the land of my birth, but the longing I'd felt for so many years, the sense that I needed the village and my relatives to complete me—that had vanished as I grew into my own power. As I accepted my place here on the steppe. As I flew with my snowy owl, wingtip to wingtip into other realms.

My owl companion had left, and I grieved his departure. But in his presence I had learned to appreciate my own strength, and that gift would stay with me forever.

I held out until evening, but with Stepan fed, washed, and fast asleep after yet another retelling of "Ivan and the Gray Wolf" and round of lullabies, I sat alone on my pile of felts, staring at the place beside the fire that Mansur had occupied for that one magic month. There were no coverings there now; I'd put them away the morning after he moved out of my tent. But in my mind I envisioned him as he'd looked that first night, his eyes wide and dark as he said my name.

Fereshtem—I might never hear that word again. Mansur and I had been friends for a while, he'd helped me with Stepan, he'd told me he loved me—and he'd left. He might return, and he might not. But he'd given me a set of precious memories to cherish.

I wrapped the coverlets around me and lay back on my bed. Above me, through the circle of the smoke hole, the stars twinkled, scattered across their dark background like wildflowers across an indigo steppe. I opened my hands, palms up, curled to hold the wisdom of the spirits if they chose to send it.

I couldn't avoid the trance state forever. I was a shaman, after all.

This time the wings that lift me through the smoke hole belong to neither an angel nor an owl but to a pure white stallion with a mane the texture of silk. I ride effortlessly, as I never have in life, soaring above the steppe on a journey unlike any I have undertaken before.

I don't know where my spirit steed is heading. We pass over Alexei Sultan's men, camped for the night, and my mount dips to salute his embroidered comrades on the banners as we go by. We seem to be heading north, because I recognize some of the landmarks from my soul retrieval journeys. Are we heading for Erlik Khan's underworld kingdom then? How can that be when I, whose intent determines the direction in which we fly, have not expressed a wish to visit there?

Indeed, we don't dive into the opening when we reach it but fly on. I see no eagle, no snowy owl. I sense no other spirit of any kind except myself and my mount, riding through the night sky.

The winged horse sweeps in a curve to my left—west, if we were heading north before. Below me I see the endless Russian woods, broken by the occasional clearing. We descend, and as we come close enough to identify plants by the light of the full moon, I see a cluster of puffballs mixed with Death Caps here, a clutch of fly agaric there, scraggly untended rye and wheat, a group of three huts on the brink of falling down, a barn already half-collapsed.

In some manner I can't describe, the horse vanishes from beneath me, and I am standing in the clearing. As I walk toward the largest of the huts, a strange sense of familiarity mixed with discomfort assails me. This is my home. The home I thought I saw on the day when I retrieved Stepan's soul, only to discover that hut was different. This is in truth the home of my childhood, which I haven't visited in fourteen years. It appears completely deserted.

I enter the largest hut. No one is inside, but the house looks as if the owners just stepped out: iron pots on the plank table; a moldy loaf on a wooden board, dull knife lying next to it; ladles and other kitchen tools hanging from pegs on the wall; bed coverings laid out on the flat-topped clay stove; a ragged winter coat thrown half-on, half-off the bench that lines the longest wall. But the stove gives off no heat, and the only signs of life come from mice scurrying past the acorn bread—even they won't touch it—and insects circling the empty but unwashed bowls piled on the table.

Puzzled, I visit the second hut, then the third—which, as I recall the moment I see the wooden coops on the other side of the door, houses animals. Chickens, mostly, but also the occasional family of ducks, the pig sacrificed each autumn to feed the family throughout the winter, and the shoats that will grow into its replacement. Only there are no chickens and no eggs in the third hut, no pig or shoats. The bedding in the second hut supports no sleepers. The tumble-down barn contains neither the horse that pulls the shallow-bladed plow nor the cow housed there in the rare years when my parents can afford one.

And that's when I see the dug-up patch behind the barn. The dirt mounds with crude wooden crosses at their heads— unmarked, because no one here can read or write. Four graves. I sense who lies in them without being told: one each for my mother and father, my two brothers at their feet.

I may never learn exactly when or how they died. But I do know why they didn't come to find me. And that if my father hadn't left me with the Kolychevs that day, I would be lying at their side.

The thrum of beating wings signals my spirit mount's return. Because I have learned what the powers above sought to teach me.

What separated me from Mansur during that last trance was my fear, not his intent. I am not cursed. I am not alone. I have my son and the spirits, the horde and my pride.

Together, whatever comes to pass, we will thrive.

As I'd expected, the horde broke camp the next day. Two weeks later, we caught up with the flocks and herds, and ten days or so after that, we reached the winter grazing lands.

The shortest day came and went. Mansur didn't return. Nor did he send the promised message. However often I begged my spirit helpers for news, they refused to show me where he was or what was happening to him. The blank scenes and swirling fog I'd seen during that first journey I'd taken in pursuit of his third soul obscured every attempt, as if my own fears that he'd come to harm or written me off as no more than a passing fancy made it impossible for me to pierce the veil that separated us.

As the snows eased and the fresh shoots of the new grass turned the dry steppe to green, I stopped expecting either him or the snowy owl who once accompanied my spirit journeys. The memory of those few magic moments when we embraced—first during my trance, then in reality—continued to tug at me. Hard as I tried, I couldn't forget what he'd meant to me.

Lambs, kids, calves, and foals were born, staggered on shaky legs, learned to frolic and to run, grew strong enough on their mothers' milk that the herders could imagine them surviving the long journey west. As the days lengthened, the strengthening sun melted the snows that lay between us and our summer grazing lands. Yet still there was no sign of Mansur. Couriers arrived from Kolomna with some regularity, but none of them carried news of his whereabouts, other than to say he'd left months ago on an errand for Alexei Sultan. When I asked whether they had any reason to believe he still lived, they shrugged their shoulders and looked helpless.

The moment came when the khan announced that we should prepare to move the next morning. By then, I was ready to leave. I understood, thanks to the vision where the spirits had revealed the fate of my relatives, that nothing flawed in me caused those I loved to walk away without regret. I mourned my family, who had died of starvation or disease—probably before I completed my first year of Lady Natalya's training. I accepted that my parents' decision to sell me, as much as it had hurt me at the time, proved that they *had* loved me, just as my father had said. They'd saved me when they couldn't save themselves, and what more can a parent do for a child than that?

After months of raging and moaning and refusing to face facts, I grew resigned to the idea that, for whatever reason, I wouldn't see Mansur again in this life. Surely he must still be alive, or word of his death would have reached his lord and—through Alexei, who hadn't kept his promise to visit Timur but sent messages at regular intervals—wended its way to us.

But there were other obstacles that Mansur might have encountered. The spirits could have sent him another injury because he'd rejected their call to serve. He might have had second thoughts about asking Alexei for permission to leave. Perhaps pleasant memories of our month together had already paled next to the obligations of a lifetime. Without guidance from my helpers, I couldn't tell. I should forget him. There were other men in the world.

And yet on this afternoon of the khan's order, as I anticipated returning to the same river and the same hills where I'd been happy for such a short while, I shivered. Had my wounded heart truly healed?

I thrust the thought away. It could do me no good to cling to a love already lost. No spell would restore Mansur to me. Whether he'd meant to keep his promise or not, so far he'd failed. It was time to move on.

By evening, I'd finished packing and filled the cart I would drive the next day with Stepan at my side and a horse borrowed from Nasan and Daniil in the shafts. I stood in the middle of my tent, turning in a slow circle as I checked to ensure that everything except the covers we needed for the night and food to keep us going during the first stage of the long journey was on the cart. I heard Stepan laughing and playing with the other boys outside, where I'd told him he could spend these last few moments before bed.

I should go and collect him, as it was getting late, but as I always did before leaving a place, I had set aside some time to thank the spirits of air, water, earth, and fire for their hospitality during our stay. I fed them with koumiss spritzed in the air and chunks of fatty meat thrown into the hearth fire. I burned the herbs they loved and walked the sacred circle, asking them at each cardinal point for blessings on the journey and a safe return to their guardianship in the spring.

It seemed impossible that six months would go by before I saw these lands again. Stepan would be seven by the time the fall migration ended. Another year closer to manhood and still fatherless—I should do something about that this summer. Let my memories of Mansur go and find someone else.

A yell from Stepan spun me around. It sounded like joy, almost a cheer, and I dropped my smudge stick in the fire as I ran for the door. Before I could reach it, it opened, and Mansur walked in.

I stopped mid-step, staring. He was the last person I expected to see. "Where have you been?" I stammered. "I thought you'd forgotten us." And just like that, I was furious with him. Relieved to see him in one piece, but furious. "I was worried sick about you! How could you stay away for so long?"

He crossed the short distance between us and took my hands in his. "Hush, *fereshtem*. I know I told you to expect me by the shortest day, and that passed ages ago. But when you hear my story, you'll understand. At least wait till you do before you rip up at me."

Tempted to drag my hands from his, I stopped. Angry as I was, I found his grip comforting. I settled for glaring at him. "So tell me. The spirits refused to show me a thing. I've been imagining you dead on the road, locked in the arms of a new bride, or stuck in some jail in Kolomna because Alexei Sultan refused to release you from service. And that's just the beginning."

He laughed, and it was all I could do not to smack him. "That's even worse than what did happen."

His clasp tightened as I instinctively pulled back. "Hush," he said again. "Let me get it out. I had one setback after another from the moment I left your camp. I kept falling behind on the trail, because of my wretched leg. I lost sight of Alexei's men altogether for days at a time, and when I did catch up, I discovered Alexei himself had moved farther south than I'd expected. There was no hope of talking to him, or even reaching him, then. I had to wait weeks in the rear for my brothers to return from the foray they were on, then wasted more time searching for my mother in Kolomna before I found a neighbor who confirmed that she'd gone to visit my sister in Moscow. By then, the shortest day had come and gone, and I was still less than halfway through my list of tasks."

Befuddled, I shook my head. "And what about your gift?" He wouldn't have searched for his mother unless he intended to accept the spirits' call, would he?

No, what was I thinking? Of course he would. He'd left her in Kolomna in July, before he rode here as a courier. She must have been as frantic about why he hadn't returned as I was. "Did you ever see Alexei Sultan? Did you ask him to release you?"

He lowered his eyes then and gave me a rueful smile. "Yes, I saw him. And no, I didn't ask him to release me. It's only two years since he took me on, when he didn't have to. I couldn't ask him to let me go after such a short time."

Horror pinned my feet to the floor and widened my eyes as I stared at him, my anger forgotten. "You're rejecting the spirits? They'll kill you!"

"Let me finish." He caressed my palms, which he still held, with his thumb. "I talked with my brothers, I saw my sister, I tracked down my mother—"

His mother again! That was when I remembered that he'd mentioned bringing her to live in the horde. "Is your mother here?"

"No. She decided she'd rather stay in Moscow with my sister, but that caused another delay, because we had to go back to Kolomna, pack up her things, and get her moved and settled." He released one hand long enough to caress my cheek. "Are you ever going to let me tell you the rest, *fereshtem*? I'm sorry I upset you. I truly did intend to return, but there was no point in leaving things undone. I'd have to go back and finish them, and then you'd be worried all over again."

He had a point. "Tell me the rest, then." I heard the grudging note in my voice, but I thought he'd earned it, after what he'd put me through.

"At last, I settled my mother and went back to Kolomna for the third time. Alexei Sultan had finished with the Crimeans by then and returned to the fortress. I didn't ask him to release me from service, but I did ask for permission to marry. I can't do that, either, without his consent, you know."

"Marry?" That was an option I hadn't considered. My head spun as if I were burning juniper.

"If we wish." His eyes twinkled, as if my surprise amused him. "It would be better to have that sense of permanence, don't you think? For Stepan, especially."

Now I knew he was teasing me. I made a face at him that my son might have envied. This was what I'd missed, the many months he was away—the gentle humor, the affection on his face and in his voice, the sense that he understood me in a way no one else did. "For Stepan," I said. "You want to marry me because it will be good for Stepan?"

"Isn't it always about Stepan where you're concerned?" Laughing, he flicked my cheek with his finger. "But yes, I would like it too, and who knows? You might enjoy it yourself. And it paves the way for me to transfer here one day. Alexei Sultan has already agreed in part to such a move. He received word that he might be summoned to Moscow soon, so he chose me to lead the group he sent to collect Prince Timur. The other men will return with the prince, while I stay and fight for your khan. It will give us a chance to work out what we mean to each other, and it doesn't matter whether I become a storyteller or not."

I opened my mouth to remind him again that it *did* matter, if he wanted to survive his next battle. But my brain roiled with the reality of his offer. He wanted to marry me? To stay with me for the rest of our lives? And something about his expression told me he wasn't finished.

"You led the group," I said. "But when did you start? Why not send a message before you left Kolomna, so we'd know to expect you? What got in your way?" In a flash, I saw the answer: this was what the spirits had refused to tell me. But it was his story, not mine, so I kept quiet.

"Everything you can think of." He laughed again and tapped my nose. This time I didn't glare at him; I was starting to predict where this would end. "Except the unwanted bride—didn't I tell you I loved you about a thousand times before I left?"

I blushed and didn't reply, and he went on. "So not that, but everything else. My injury flared up; the horses slipped on the ice and stumbled over stones; one warrior after another fell ill; we went round in circles, as if the road itself kept twisting; the weather shifted from snow to rain and back again. You'd have thought the route from Kolomna to Kazan wilder than the deserts rumored to exist in the east or the treeless ice plains of the far north."

When I still didn't answer, he gave me that rueful grin again. "I know. You warned me, and I was slow to understand. At last, after the journey stretched to four times its usual length and we couldn't reach the turnoff whatever we did, I remembered how you'd taught me to contact the spirits. That night I reached out to them, and the peri—I swear, the very same one—told me that I was wandering in a wilderness of my own making. Only if I would accept the burden placed on me would she and her kind allow me to return to you. I saw you, in the distance, your owl self clear against a distant sky, that eagle you called your teacher at your side. You didn't look at me, and I didn't know whether that was because you didn't see me or because you'd lost patience with me. What I did know was that I wanted you, and if being with you meant becoming a storyteller, then that's what I must do. I haven't quite figured out how to make it happen, but I'll find a way."

While that assurance rang in my ears, he released my hands and wrapped both arms around my waist. I pressed my cheek against his shoulder. "I'm so glad," I said in a choked voice. "I missed you so much. I couldn't find you, even in trance. I haven't seen you in the other worlds since the day you flew beside me to beg the spirits to save the horde. My helpers wouldn't show me what was happening to you. That was the worst part about your being gone."

"Dear heart," he said. "I hurt you. I'm sorry. But here's the good news: after I stopped fighting my destiny, the obstacles disappeared. Like magic. The skies cleared, the men and horses healed, and I found my way to you. If I hadn't experienced it myself, I wouldn't have believed the spirits had such power."

He was here. He was really here, and he intended to stay. To marry me, if that's what we both wanted. He hadn't died, he hadn't suffered another wound, he hadn't even had second thoughts. He'd striven to return to me despite every barrier the spirits had thrown in his path. And from the sounds of it, they'd thrown more than a few—enough to discourage most men.

Joy filled my throat, and no words could escape. Cursing myself for behaving like a complete idiot, I wept into the soft tunic that covered his mail shirt.

He wiped my tears with his thumb. "Alexei Sultan's troops are right behind me," he said in a soft, chiding tone. "They'll be here by morning, but they decided to camp by the river overnight. I couldn't wait to see you, so I rode ahead as soon as I realized your horde was still here. I know I was gone for far too long, but I always intended to keep my promise. Why are you crying?"

He'd ridden ahead. Alone. He wanted to see me so much that he couldn't wait for our reunion.

My cheeks grew hot, and I struggled to speak past the tears, which continued to fall. Tears of relief and happiness as much as grief, but there was grief too, a relic of the past.

"Everyone I care about leaves," I said. "My parents, my brothers, Suzukei, the men I've loved. My family died—I saw it in trance—but I still miss them. Stepan is too small, but one day soon he'll leave me as well. He has to, if he's to become a man. I couldn't bear to lose you as well. If I counted on seeing you again only to have you disappoint me in the end, that truly would have broken my heart."

I took a long, sobbing breath as Mansur tightened his hold on my waist. "You can't lose me, sweetheart," he said. "I'll have to leave you sometimes—it's the way of the warrior. But I'll be with you in spirit. My angel, my owl, my woman with wings. You look after everyone except yourself. I love you. What do you think about this marriage thing? Will you say yes?"

I clung to him, sure I was dreaming. The wild ride from sorrow to joy robbed me of speech.

"Well?" he asked when I didn't respond right away. "Did I move too fast? Did I misunderstand?" His grip loosened, and he took a step away from me.

I raised my head then and put both hands on his shoulders, letting my happiness light my face. "You didn't misunderstand. I would love to marry you. I'm so glad you came back I can't think straight."

"Then won't you kiss me, *fereshtem*? I've been waiting for months." When I nodded, he took me in his arms and kissed me as if he, too, had thought he might never see me again. I pressed myself against him, giving into my yearning, my desire for him—my life's companion, my snowy owl.

"Mama!" A tug on my skirt interrupted us. I pulled back enough to see my son, hands on his hips, glaring at Mansur. "You're not supposed to kiss my mama," Stepan said. "Only papas can kiss mamas."

I opened my mouth to reply, but Mansur placed a finger on my lips. When I nodded again to show I understood, he released me and knelt in front of my son so their heads were at the same height. "You're right," he told Stepan. "But I just asked your mama if I could be your papa. She said I could, but now I'm asking you. I'd like to be your papa. Would you mind?"

Stepan's chin dropped, and his eyes grew as round as those of my owl spirit. "You'll stay with us from now on? In our tent with Mama and me? Will you teach me to shoot and give me a pony of my own? Will you tell me stories?"

"I will," Mansur told him. "That's what papas do. And lots of other things too. What do you say?"

My son broke into a wild dance, hopping around the tent laughing and clapping his hands. "I have a papa!" he shrieked. He ran to hug Mansur, then raced to the door of the tent, calling, "Borya, Irek, come and see. I have a papa. A *good* papa like yours!"

"I think that means yes," I said to Mansur, who rose to his feet, chuckling and shaking his head at my son's enthusiasm.

"It would seem so." He returned to my side and put his arm around my waist once more, only to have Stepan skid to a stop in front of us.

"It's time to sleep," I told my son. "Get into bed, and I'll tell you a story." I looked at Mansur. "We can talk after I have him tucked in."

"Will *you* tell me a story?" Stepan caught Mansur's sleeve and pulled on it. "Since you're going to be my papa?"

"I would love to." Mansur took Stepan's hand and led him to his bed. He sat my son down, helped him remove his shoes and his outer layers, washed his hands and face with a damp cloth, watched while he rinsed his mouth, then sat next to him. "How about 'Ivan and the Gray Wolf'? I have a feeling you might like that one."

Stepan snuggled into Mansur's hold as if he belonged there. "You know it's my favorite."

"Very well." Mansur's voice hummed with amusement. "If you're sure. Once upon a time, a tsar had three sons ..."

I went to the barrel that held our food for the migration and pried off the top. Mansur must be hungry after his long journey, although he'd neither demanded a meal nor complained of my failure to offer him one. I arranged dried meat, cheese, and bread on a wooden board, said a blessing over them, then set it aside for him to eat when he finished the story. A warm glow of contentment surrounded me as I sat on my own bed and watched the two of them.

I had the husband of my heart. I had my son. And after a decade and a half in exile, I'd found my way home. Which, it turned out, was right where I'd lived for the last six years.

Historical Note

INFORMATION ON CENTRAL ASIAN SHAMANISM, AND Eurasian shamanism more generally, as practiced in the sixteenth century is lamentably scarce. Although the oldest religion, attested in one form or another throughout the world, shamanism has typically been passed directly from one practitioner to another. In some ways eternal, in others flexible, its rituals have always responded readily to changing circumstances, and despite the inroads made by more centrally organized faiths, shamanism continues to exist openly in many places and more covertly under the umbrella of the great world religions.

Eurasian shamanism, however, faced particular challenges in the last century. The atheistic Soviet Union aggressively opposed religious expression, especially during its first thirty years of existence. Shamans could operate under cover at best, and lines of knowledge transmission were broken. Since the collapse of the Soviet Union, there have been energetic attempts to revive the ancient traditions, but how closely the current understanding of shamanist practices resembles that of the sixteenth century is impossible to determine. As a result, most of Grusha's shamanic trances are entirely my invention.

Still, we are not entirely wandering in the wilderness here. We do know that the Tatars of Central Asia continued to practice many of the ancient rituals after their conversion to Islam in the fourteenth century; that they regarded women as particularly powerful shamans because they tended the hearth fire, which connected the realms above and below to the middle world of earth; and that they saw storytellers (an occupation that seems perfect for both Mansur and Stepan, for different reasons) as also chosen by the spirits, just like shamans. Some shamans did use psychedelic mushrooms, including fly agaric, to aid them in achieving the trance state, although many others attained that state through rhythmic sound and motion, with a little help from juniper and other mildly hallucinogenic herbs.

One area that may surprise some readers is my depiction of shamanism's relationship with Christianity and Islam. Although a lack of written sources makes it difficult to research how any of these three religions were practiced in the Tatar lands five centuries ago, we know that into the eighteenth century, when a religious reform movement began in Saudi Arabia and gradually spread through the Muslim world, Central Asia and the Volga region included a large animist population as well as Christian converts and inhabitants whose ancestors had embraced Islam anywhere from four hundred to eight hundred years before. The result was a complex, overlapping combination of Sunni and Sufi Muslim, animist, and Christian customs overseen more or less equally by imam, shaman, and priest. For more on this culture and how it evolved over the course of the nineteenth century, see Agnès Nilüfer Kefeli, *Becoming Muslim in Imperial Russia: Conversion, Apostasy, and Literacy*; and Razia Sultanova, *From Shamanism to Sufism: Women, Islam, and Culture in Central Asia*. For an earlier period, Devin DeWeese's magisterial *Islamization and Native Religion in the Golden Horde: Baba Tükles and Conversion to Islam in Historical and Epic Tradition* remains unsurpassed.

In addition to a healthy dose of imagination, my descriptions of Grusha's rituals and costume come from dipping into the following sources: Julian Baldick, *Animal and Shaman: Ancient Religions of Central Asia*; Nora K. Chadwick and Victor Zhimunsky, *Oral Epics of Central Asia*; and Kira Van Deusen, *Singing Story, Healing Drum: Shamans and Storytellers of Turkic Siberia*, among others. I also consulted the works of several modern shamans, including Michael Harner, *The Way of the Shaman*; Sarangerel, *Riding Windhorses: A Journey into the Heart of Mongolian Shamanism*; and Katie Weatherup, *Practical Shamanism: A Guide for Walking in Both Worlds*. Special thanks to fellow Five Directions Press member Gabrielle Mathieu for recommending Richard Evans Schultes, Albert Hoffmann, and Christian Rätsch, *Plants of the Gods: Their Sacred Healing and Hallucinogenic Powers*, where I had a great time hunting for fungi that might affect Suzukei and discovered that Siberian shamans used fly agaric to attain trance states as well as the existence of psychedelic mottlegills (we call their non-hallucinogenic cousins Portobello and Cremini).

One area where I disagree with some of the modern practitioners is the idea that traditional shamans never identify themselves as such because it would appear to challenge the gods through a lack of humility. Certainly in other regions of the world and for individual shamans that statement could well be true. But in the traditional societies of Eurasia the shaman held a prestigious social position because she provided a crucial lifeline for those who lacked her ability to connect with the ancestors, spirits, and ancient gods who had enormous influence over the destinies of both the living and the dead. There is no evidence that Eurasian shamans, through modesty or for any other reason, refused to accept the role assigned to them before that admission became politically dangerous in the 1920s and 1930s.

Anfim's predicament—capture and imprisonment with the alternatives of ransom or slavery—was far from uncommon in the sixteenth century, although the Crimean princes' decision to attack this particular group of envoys is fictional (the massive raid launched against the Russians, however, is not). The campaign also suggests a direct slap at the power of Sahib-Girei, the Crimean khan, which although possible in general historical terms would be unlikely under the specific conditions prevailing in the summer of 1542. Hence my assumption that the "renegades" were in fact nothing of the sort.

The Crimean Tatars, in particular, because they operated as vassals of the Ottoman Empire, made a large portion of their income supplying the Turkish slave markets, and most of those captives came from Muscovy and Poland-Lithuania, especially the region of Ruthenia (modern-day Ukraine and Belarus). Exact numbers are difficult to determine for the early sixteenth century, but one estimate for 1600–1650 runs between 150,000 and 200,000 Russians alone. The high numbers drove prices down, and as a result the Crimeans often preferred to ransom higher-status and wealthier prisoners, to the point where Ivan IV "the Terrible" established a special tax to ransom government servitors in 1551. Anfim is luckier than most in attracting the attention of Ogodai, who has relatives in Russian service and is generally well disposed toward Moscow even though he prefers to operate independently as khan. For more information, including the estimate of numbers given above, see Brian Davies, *Warfare, State, and Society on the Black Sea Steppe, 1500–1700*.

Acknowledgments

IN ADDITION TO THE SCHOLARS MENTIONED IN THE Historical Note, I tip my hat here to my invaluable writers' group, which will soon enter its twelfth year, and to the members of Five Directions Press for their encouragement and support. *Song of the Shaman* has benefited immeasurably from their comments—especially those of Ariadne Apostolou, Courtney J. Hall, and Gabrielle Mathieu. I would like to express particular gratitude to Ann Kleimola for the many wonderful queries, suggestions, and corrections she has supplied for my Russian historical novels—first the Legends series and now this new one. And thanks, too, to Terry Gamble, whom I met through New Books in Historical Fiction while working on *Song of the Siren*. Not only is she a wonderful writer, but she has shown a level of support for both that book and this one that warms my heart.

To my husband and son—and, of course, the cats, who purred encouragingly at all the right moments—words cannot express my gratitude. Alas, this is the last novel to receive the personal supervision of my older cat, who passed away at the grand age of almost eighteen before I completed the final draft, but our younger cat is carrying on the fine tradition he established.

The Author

AS A CHILD, C. P. LESLEY THOUGHT EVERYONE MADE UP stories while falling asleep. It never occurred to her that anyone would pay her for them, and for a long time, she was right—no one would. But after years of producing horrible prose, reading books about novel writing, and pestering hapless fellow-writers and friends to read her drafts, some of the advice stuck, and she finished *The Not Exactly Scarlet Pimpernel*, then *The Golden Lynx* and its sequels: *The Winged Horse*, *The Swan Princess*, *The Vermilion Bird*, and *The Shattered Drum*. Five Directions Press published *Song of the Siren*, the first in her Songs of Steppe & Forest series, in 2019.

She is currently working on *Song of the Sisters*, which explores the choices facing Darya Sheremeteva—whose father once intended her to wed Daniil Kolychev—as she strives to construct the life she wants despite opposition from her family.

When not thinking up new ways to torture her characters, Lesley edits other people's manuscripts, reads voraciously, maintains her website, and practices classical ballet—an interest reflected in *Desert Flower* and *Kingdom of the Shades* (Tarkei Chronicles 1–2). She also hosts New Books in Historical Fiction, a podcast channel in the New Books Network. You can find out more about her and her books at www.cplesley.com.

BOOKS BY C. P. LESLEY

The Not Exactly Scarlet Pimpernel

Songs of Steppe & Forest
Song of the Siren
Song of the Shaman

Legends of the Five Directions
The Golden Lynx (1: West)
The Winged Horse (2: East)
The Swan Princess (3: North)
The Vermilion Bird (4: South)
The Shattered Drum (5: Center)

Tarkei Chronicles
Desert Flower
Kingdom of the Shades

FORTHCOMING FROM FIVE DIRECTIONS PRESS

Song of the Sisters

SONGS OF STEPPE & FOREST 3

Moscow, July 1543

"OH, DARYA, YOU *HAVE* TO SEE THIS. A STRUTTING PEACOCK just entered our yard!" Solomonida stood on tiptoe, leaning forward until I worried she might tumble right through the unshuttered window in her eagerness. The late morning sunlight glinted off her jeweled headdress and found an answering glow in the wisps of blonde braid that had worked their way out from under the edge as she sewed.

"Peacock?" I stared at her and sighed. It wasn't fair. My older sister was lovely, even at thirty-one—something of a peahen herself, in truth. Not just beautiful, either, but vivid and charming—outgoing, outspoken, eager to interact with life beyond our courtyard gates. Next to her I felt like the quiet mouse she teasingly called me. "How could a peacock get into our yard?"

"See for yourself." She beckoned to me.

Sorely tempted, I glanced at the altar cloth I was embroidering. I'd set myself the task of stitching the golden edge of the Blessed Virgin Mother's halo before I left for church, and I wasn't even halfway through. "I'll never finish this if I stop every time a bird flies into the yard, Solomonida."

I rubbed the pure white rose I'd embroidered yesterday between my thumb and forefinger, imagining the flower's aroma—the scent of holiness. The thread, soft against my skin, reminded me of the real petals I'd stroked this morning on my journey through the courtyard. The sky-blue satin behind the flowers caressed my fingertips; the thread set aside for the halo glittered with the light of Heaven, its sensation harder, more metallic, than the thread used for the flowers because of the flecks of real gold that clung to the yellow strands. I liked nothing better than to watch my needle threading in and out, connecting one delicate chain stitch to the next, directing my thoughts and dreams along a clear, simple path.

Although I'd never seen a peacock outside of a book. And a peacock on every corner would make the altar cloth quite unique. Why waste the chance to find out what a real one looked like?

"Don't be silly," Solomonida said. "That altar cloth won't get up and walk off by itself. It will be there when you get back to it. Do hurry, or you'll miss him."

Temptation won, not for the first time. I dropped the altar cloth on a nearby table and ran to join her. When I saw what had attracted Solomonida's attention, thoughts of embroidery vanished from my mind as I too gave way to giggles. The young nobleman crossing our courtyard— the toes of his scarlet leather boots turned up; his brocade robe stitched with gold lions as long as my forearm, the full skirts held in place by a tasseled silk sash of a rich, bright blue; his high collar framing a face topped with reddish hair and a green hat; his long cane (obviously for show) tucked under one arm; his shoulders thrown back and his chest thrust forward—did indeed resemble nothing so much as a strutting peacock.

I whispered an apology to the powers above for my irreverence, but bright little bubbles of amusement continued to burst inside me.

"Who is he?" I asked. "I don't recall seeing him before."

A statement that meant nothing. How many noblemen had I met in the last seven years? I'd spent most of that time nursing Papa, rarely leaving his side and expecting every week to be his last, but he'd clung to life like a limpet until losing his final battle this spring.

Caring for him had turned me into a hermit, to the point where I often wondered if I shouldn't forsake the world altogether and adopt the rough wool habit and simple prayer rope of a holy sister. As Matryona, who'd cared for me since babyhood, never failed to remind me, no man wanted a bride of twenty-five.

Although Papa promised to take care of us, didn't he? To find me a husband who would help Solomonida and me manage the estate. "You should be married, not stuck here wasting your youth nursing an old man. I have a plan. Trust me." I heard every word as if he'd said it yesterday, although I'd seen little evidence that anything had come of his vaunted plan. His promise had been the last thing he said to me before crumpling over, gasping for breath, and I'd clung to it ever since. There hadn't been one moment between then and his death when I could safely question him, still less find out the name of the bridegroom he'd had in mind for me or whether he'd had a chance to complete his plans.

I stared at the peacock, striding across the courtyard as if he owned the place.

Could Papa have picked this man, whoever he is?

No, that was impossible. Papa wouldn't have given me to such a pompous ass.

"I don't know." Solomonida shook her head, and a few more blonde strands slipped free of their pearl-strewn bounds. "The peacock's a strange one, in more ways than I can count."

"You don't think it could be the man Papa chose for me, do you?" I put my fears into words. "The one who was supposed to help us with the estate?"

She turned toward me, my own shock mirrored on her face. "Oh, surely not!"

Again on tiptoe, she turned back to stare at the courtyard, as if assessing this dreadful possibility. I took a deep breath, seeking to calm myself. Through the open windows the scents of summer wafted, some pleasant—sage, thyme, lilies, ripening fruit, dried grass, the roses I'd buried my face in this morning—and some not, such as horse dung and refuse from the Moscow streets. On the whole, though, the pleasant smells conquered the unpleasant ones. The breeze from the river must be blowing in the right direction today.

The peacock continued to strut toward the main building, where we were. He seemed oblivious to the servants who clustered in groups of five or six—staring at him, giggling and pointing, muttering behind their hands. Some of the girls regarded him through eyes round with awe. The men, without exception, looked as if they hadn't seen such a good show since the last time traveling minstrels set up in the market square, surrounded by jugglers and dancing bears. I had to admit, in this case I agreed with the men. Anyone but a nobleman, and they would have demanded to know his business when he first strolled through the open gates, but they seemed to see this visitor as more entertainment than threat.

"What I don't understand," Solomonida went on, "is why this young man, whoever he is, is prancing through our courtyard without a care in the world. Does he not know we're here?"

She redirected her finger toward a second man, less ostentatious than the first, with a light brown beard and hair and a handsome, clever face. He trailed the peacock by a considerable distance and to my critical eye looked as though he sought to avoid any connection between the swaggering nobleman and himself. If so, his ploy seemed to be working. The servants, their gaze fixed firmly on the peacock, had no attention to spare for anyone else. "And who's that?" Solomonida asked, still pointing at the second man. "Are they together, do you think?"

"One the master, the other his servant, perhaps." I too stood on tiptoe, trying to make sense of this strange sight. The shutter I gripped for support felt smooth under my hand. Beeswax and oil coated the pads of my fingers and thumb, and when I sniffed them, they gave off a whiff of lavender. "Although even the not-peacock looks a bit well-off for a servant."

A leather sack swung from the second man's left shoulder. A cream-colored furl of paper peeped out of the opening, together with a set of quills. "Oh, look, I'd guess he's a clerk or bailiff or something like that. For the peacock, I suppose. But why would a stranger bring a clerk here?"

Solomonida wrinkled her perfect nose. "We'll find out soon. They're heading this way. They'll be on the second floor before we know it. Let's go down and greet them, shall we?"

"I suppose we may as well." Wondering what I would find, I followed my sister down the stairs.

So much for my unfulfilled task. The Virgin Mother's halo would have to wait for its golden rim.

http://www.fivedirectionspress.com/song-of-the-sisters

ALSO FROM FIVE DIRECTIONS PRESS

Song of the Siren

SONGS OF STEPPE & FOREST I

Wawel Castle, Poland, December 1541

"LADY JULIANA WILL LIVE," A MALE VOICE SAID. "NOT AS SHE did before, of course. I doubt the young king will have much use for her now, despite her charms. It's too bad about the scarring. She was a beautiful woman." The cool, dispassionate tone contradicted any hint of concern implied by his words.

Was? She *was* a beautiful woman? I lay flat on my back, too weak and dispirited to demand that he explain what he meant. I tried to force my eyelids open, but I hadn't the strength even for that. Trapped in a nightmare world, I huddled, shivering, waiting for the ogre to appear at the door. I pushed and twisted, but my arms weighed heavy as granite on the bed and my feet stuck to the floor.

The doctor's callous verdict echoed in my head. Too bad about the scarring? She *was* a beautiful woman?

Tragedy bared its teeth, sucked me into its vortex. Without my face I was nothing. I had no purpose, no means of survival, no self. I existed to mirror the desires of men, to fulfill their passions while expressing none of my own. My beauty was the only currency I possessed. If I could not use it to draw men to me, I would starve. What point, then, in living?

Tears slid from the corners of my eyes, wetting the linen beneath my head. I lacked the power to wipe them away. "Oh, look," another voice said. My maidservant, Hanna. "She's crying. Do you think she heard you, Doctor?" A soft cloth touched my cheeks.

"Perhaps." The doctor still sounded indifferent, as if discussing my case at some society of physicians. If I had the energy, I would slap him. "I see no sign that she's awake, but I've had other patients report things I said under similar conditions. Smallpox causes extreme exhaustion. She may be able to hear but not respond. Just in case, you should talk to her, reassure her, like this."

Garlic-inflected breath passed my nose, and I guessed he had bent closer to examine me. "You will recover, Lady Juliana," he said, and this time I heard actual kindness in his voice. "The worst is over."

But I knew he was wrong. The worst lurked somewhere down the road of a bleak future, waiting to pounce when I was least prepared to resist.

http://www.fivedirectionspress.com/song-of-the-siren

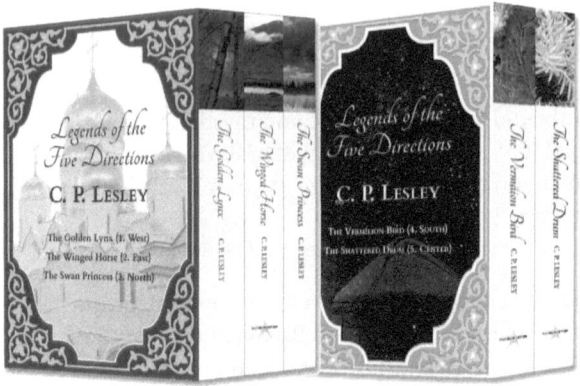

WHO IS THE GOLDEN LYNX?

This question drives the first book in Legends of the Five Directions, a series that will sweep you to the distant world of sixteenth-century Russia, amid the descendants of Genghis Khan and courts that could teach the Borgias a thing or two about political ambition, assassination, and chicanery. Follow Nasan and her kinsfolk as they struggle for power, honor, identity, and love across the steppe and through the vast forests of the Russian North.

"A 'ripping good yarn,' as adventure stories have always been. Enter the exotic, cut-throat world of sixteenth-century Muscovy in the company of a Tatar princess whose skills would have made her equally a heroine on the American frontier. The Kremlin court of the not-yet-Terrible toddler Ivan and his mother-regent Elena Glinskaya, boyar intrigue, arranged political marriages, spirit animals and ancestors pointing the way to restoring balance and order in the universe—what more could a reader want except further adventures, which are heralded by the advent of another animal messenger?"

—Ann M. Kleimola, professor emerita of history

Find out more at http://www.fivedirectionspress.com/boxsets.